# WHITE SKY

# WHITE SKY

### Volume I
### of
### In the Shadow
### of the She-Wolf

## Lara Campbell McGehee

ALNIM
BOOKS

This is a work of fiction. Any resemblance to actual events, locales, or persons, living or dead, is purely coincidental.

GLEN LYON PRESS

ALNIM BOOKS
is a division of Glen Lyon Press, LLC
Flagstaff, Arizona
Visit our website at *www.glenlyonpress.com*

WHITE SKY
Volume I of
IN THE SHADOW OF THE SHE-WOLF

Front Cover Photograph: Aleksey Solodov/Dreamstime.com

ISBN: 978-1-942-46100-5

*For Heather,
for the countless hours of hard work and
for always believing in the potential of the 'NFH'!*

# CONTENTS

the she-wolf Perdita
has come back
to sleep beside me
. . . . . . . . . . . . . .
we are racing over the dark auroras
you and I with no shadow
with no shadow
in the same place
. . . . . . . . . . . . . .

we have run
these hours together
again
there is blood
on the paw under my fingers
. . . . . . . . . . . . . .

in her tracks
our tracks
but vanishing like a shadow


From "The Paw" - W.S. Merwin

# PART ONE

# THE SHONAN'S MISSION

I

THE WHITE TUNDRA passing beneath the cruiser stretched as far as Omalda could see. Endless, silent, empty. Occasional patches of mottled brown or grayish-green made the surface appear rippled, like water. She imagined herself in the belly of an enormous seabird that searched for fish swimming beneath strange white waves. Although the speed they traveled was relatively slow, the surreal landscape swept below them rapidly. And yet how great a distance it would be, Omalda thought, if one were walking across it.

"Glad I'm not down there," Aldas said, echoing her thoughts.

She glanced over and saw he was looking through his binoculars, searching the tundra for less fanciful things than the silvery glint of a school of herring gliding through the snow. When he twisted in his seat to follow something in the white world beyond the curve of the window, he bumped her with his elbow.

"I'm sorry, did I . . ." he began, turning back to her.

She gave his arm a playful shove. "It's all right," she assured him. Pulling against her safety harness, she leaned over to look out the window on his side, her shoulder pressing against the solid muscle of his upper arm. "See anything interesting yet?"

"No . . . but I thought I saw something moving, and then I lost it."

Omalda settled back into her seat. Once more she loosened the harness; it was definitely not intended for women in the later stages of pregnancy because the 'X' made by the two shoulder straps was too low to accommodate her large midsection. If her husband were here he'd probably say this was yet another sign she had no business doing this.

What a stupid thing to think of now! she admonished herself. Before leaving for the port this morning, she'd made an effort to act as if she'd forgiven him, but in truth her anger hadn't faded.

Yesterday afternoon she'd been studying the weather map when he spoke from the doorway behind her. "I told you—the storms are coming. It's too late in the season, Malda. On top of everything else. It'll have to wait till spring."

Wincing at his tone of voice, Omalda had kept her eyes on the screen. A neon blue wave showed at the very top, illuminating the edge of the front that would bring the grip of winter back to this harsh land, where summers were all too brief. But there was still enough time to complete the mission in Kruvak and get out before the first of the winter storms struck—the data confirmed a safe window of at least four or five days.

"We won't be on Bakraga next spring!" she snapped. How could a man so passionate about his own ambitions refuse to understand what this meant to her? The treaty was the culmination of her assignment here, the culmination of everything she'd been working on for so long. And he could hardly pretend he didn't know when he'd been hearing her gripe about every minute detail of the process for nearly a year.

The pattern of bright colors on the screen—cold blues and greens contrasting with warm yellows and reds—looked like an abstract painting manipulated by some invisible artist; as Omalda watched, the borders of the waves and splotches

4

shifted almost imperceptibly. Thinking of patterns, changing and unchanging, reminded her yet again of how long the coming snows would hold dominion in Kruvak. Just imagining what it would be like to live in a such a place made her feel gloomy and cold.

"Besides," she added, "that's ten long months away! And the prospect of facing another winter like last year's should just give them more incentive to consider our proposal—meeting with them now should actually be an advantage."

Her hopes were high that the Torvik people would accept the treaty. She'd fought hard to ensure the final version was mostly for their benefit; they had much to gain, very little to lose. But she knew it was important that she and her team didn't overstay their welcome. Added to the weather issue, this meant they would have only a short time to make their intentions clear and win the Torviks' trust. Then, no matter what the outcome, they would be gone.

"Those people have been coping with winter on this planet for two hundred years!" her husband retorted. "And they were completely on their own before the New Contact teams made it out here. Besides, it was their choice to live like that."

"They lived in the forest in winter—not way up there on that frozen wasteland!" She swiveled her chair around to face him. "Don't you understand, hon? There is *nothing* up there! That village is completely exposed, so it's even colder. There's very little for the reindeer to eat, and what there is ends up under a meter of snow. They've lost nearly half of those poor animals in the time they've been up there. Are we all supposed to forget that little detail? Pretend we didn't know about it until it's too late? And they've never 'coped with winter' with as few resources as they have now. This is why I keep telling those idiots in the Post Council this is practically a death sentence— we might as well have banished them to an ice floe in the middle of the sea!"

"All right, all right. You're the big expert. Obviously I'm

just the great Shonan's naive little spouse, tagging along for the ride."

She bristled—and wondered if he realized how childishly envious he sounded. "You could have stayed home, you know!"

His scowl deepened. "I thought you wanted me to come. And what's the point of being married if you live apart for an entire year?"

"Oh, I don't know. Tala and Melos seem perfectly happy."

"Yeah—'seem'. You think she tells you everything? He told me that when they got together over the holiday he didn't think his daughter recognized him."

Omalda rolled her eyes. "She's seven months old! What does he expect? She's going to squeal, 'Hada, you're home!' and jump out of her crib and throw her arms around his neck?"

He sighed loudly and mirrored her gesture. "I may not be an expert on babies either, but I think you can tell if they recognize you even when they can't talk yet."

"Oh, never mind that! Will you just stop this, please? You know I'm going no matter what you say."

But he wasn't about to give in. She would have been very surprised if he had. "Come on, Malda. Think—what good's it going to do at this point? Even if you get the treaty signed, how are they going to get the herds and all the people south in time?"

"With help! We'll appropriate some of Niomco's monstrous freighters—they can get through any weather this planet can dish out. It's not going to cause those greedy pigs financial ruin if they close a couple of the mines for a few days. And the reindeer would be migrating south right now if they were turned loose. By Zennix! Even if some of the people have to travel in the middle of a snowstorm, it'll be a hundred light years better than sitting up there dying! Besides, they'll have a future to look forward to—as rightful citizens of their own miserable rock. At least they'll have a reason to keep going."

When he shook his head a piece of his thick black hair

flopped onto his forehead and he shoved it back with obvious irritation; he was in need of a haircut, and she wondered if he'd put it off out of rebellious spite because she'd commented on it two weeks ago. "You know, there's a reason you're one of the youngest Shonans in history," he said with a mocking smile. "It's because most people our age are too foolishly idealistic for the job. And no offense, my dear girl, but you're no exception. Council must have been out of their minds."

Omalda glowered at him. "And you're just jealous, my dear boy. You really are."

It wasn't the first time she'd made that accusation, and as usual he denied it vehemently. "I'm not. Not one iota. Because I know I wouldn't be ready for this. But neither are you. You can't do this. You can't go." He set his wide mouth in a firm line, reminding Omalda of a pouting child.

"So you no longer believe this is the right thing to do? Is that what you're saying?"

He flared up just as she knew he would. "Don't be ridiculous! I don't mean that at all—and you know it. I only mean you're not the one to do it." He bit his lip and added in a low mutter, "Especially not in your present condition."

She clenched her jaw so hard it sent a stab of pain up the side of her face. The baby kicked suddenly, as if protesting her loud words and the anger he could surely feel. Placing one hand on her belly, Omalda made a silent apology and forced herself to breathe slowly.

She'd specifically warned her husband, more than once, not to make the mistake of referring to her 'condition'. Of course he'd done it now in deliberate retaliation, and she wanted to punch him. She'd always hated that expression. It was one of those silly archaic things that had survived largely in a joking context, and she didn't think it was funny at all. It infuriated her that sexism seemed to be on that list of monsters that kept rearing their ugly heads even though people had been trying to stamp them out for hundreds of years—the odious list that included everything from racial prejudice to war.

There was one philosophy—which had recently regained popularity—that these issues could never be eradicated because they were too deeply rooted in human biology. Omalda despised that idea too; if humans were intelligent enough to see that these things were wrong, they were intelligent enough to stop doing them. No one would ever convince her otherwise.

"All right, let's talk about my condition," she said coolly. "What's it going to say to these Torviks when I show up to talk to them like this? Have you thought about that?"

He looked away. "No, I haven't. You tell me."

"If we were coming to threaten them, if we had some underhanded motive in this, would we send a pregnant woman to talk to them? Or if we didn't trust them at all—if we thought they were crazed barbarians and this would probably come to violence? Of course not. So despite your feelings about it, I think my 'condition' may actually be one of our assets, rather than a handicap for me. I've been thinking about this for some time, and the more I think about it the more certain I am. This is exactly the right time to do this."

"Smooth. So now you're the perfect harbinger of peace: a messenger from the powers that be who's a living symbol of motherhood and love. I see." He was very good at sarcasm, usually delivered in a perfectly matter-of-fact voice. He added, "Do you think they'll respect that, Malda? Do you think it will matter to them?"

"What do you think these people are? Have they ever done anything violent that could *not* be attributed—directly or indirectly—to self-defense, and defense of their land? Have they?"

Again he stared at her with his mouth set in a stubborn line. Then he shrugged. "Some of it has been . . . well, questionable. But perhaps you're right. Like I said, you're the expert here. You've been poring over their history for the past umpteen months. I haven't. What do I know?"

"Well, I think they'd have to be very brutal, heartless people not to respect this." She gestured toward her stomach. "And I've learned nothing about them that would suggest that." She turned her eyes back to the waves of radiant color on the monitor. "Look, I'm not arguing about this any more. Everything's arranged. This time tomorrow, I'm in Kruvak."

At that thought she remembered to check the clock in the corner of the screen. She saw with relief that she was supposed to be at a meeting in a few minutes. "I have to go now or I'll be late. I'm going over everything with Hav and Aldas one last time, and making sure everything's been packed. You never know what'll get forgotten when you have an entire blundering delegation of people assigned to do a job!" She laughed, aware that he knew quite well it was a pretense. She was trying to show him that everything was fine, that he hadn't upset her. But she could never fool him.

"I think it would have been easier if we'd done all the packing ourselves, rather than doing all the silly memos and authos. It reminds me why I hadn't wanted to be in government." In a last stab at getting back at him, she added, "And don't you laugh yet. If more of the old red giants keep dropping dead, you'll be a Shonan yourself in a year—just watch. When they call you up I'll just sit there and wait for you to tell them you think you're too young and you're not ready. You wouldn't dream of it, and you know it."

He chuckled and reminded her that chances were good he'd be working at the Astro Institute and would be unavailable for the position before they could choose him. She felt deflated. With him, it was nearly impossible to get in the last word. All he had to do at the end of a discussion was to murmur a couple of condescending words, such as, "Well, maybe," and the person who'd been on the other end of the argument would be left feeling foolish.

Now, as she put her face close to the window and watched the white landscape rolling beneath them, Omalda reminded herself that at least he'd had the decency to help her up from the chair before he left the room. And this morning she'd felt downright sorry for him; he'd made a big effort to be his old self—warm, witty, and supportive—although she could see it was a struggle. She was sorrier still that they'd fallen into a pattern of quarreling so often, but thinking of that only brought back her annoyance with him for provoking yesterday's confrontation.

Rebuking herself again for dwelling on the subject, she sighed and folded her hands on her stomach—in its current shape it provided them with a convenient resting place. She'd discovered this simple action was calming, perhaps because it brought up a mental image of herself looking like the statue of a smiling fat man in her grandmother's house, which was supposed to bring good luck if you rubbed its belly. She'd loved to do so when she was a young child; the stone was cool and smooth, and the little man looked both amusing and kind.

She'd also been fascinated by her grandmother's stories about the statue. Ancient and priceless, it was created on the Motherworld in a far distant past, and the superstition about its powers as a luck charm was as old as the statue itself, passed down from lip to ear. The Capitol Museum had tried to buy the statue from Omalda's great-grandfather for an inordinate sum, but he wouldn't let it go. So it had stayed in the middle of a low glass table in the Coradzhi family home, where it surveyed the sitting room and could easily be reached by small hands who wanted their own piece of ancient luck, for some small and present reason.

It wouldn't be long, she reminded herself, before she would see that statue again. First, this mission would finally be over, then the baby would come (and what a relief to have her body to herself again!), and then, not long after that, her assignment on Bakraga would end. They'd go home to Laishani and she'd take her first real leave of absence.

I'll sit around and do as little as possible, she mused, while

Hama and Hada play doting grandparents—and Nali, too—and my silly husband will get to read and fool with his star scopes to his heart's content. And maybe, just maybe, we'll stop fighting all the time, because there won't be anything to fight about.

She smiled sadly at that thought. No doubt it was true that if two people were going to fight they'd always find some excuse to do so. But since they'd rarely quarreled before all of this—before she'd been assigned to the Contact Post on Bakraga, and then, even here, before her pregnancy—at least she had reason to hope it was only their present circumstances that kept bringing them into conflict. Foolish, perhaps—but she could always hope.

Unfastening her safety harness, she leaned sideways to pull her large white satchel from the space beneath her seat. She rummaged in the outside pocket for a container of lip moisturizer. Perhaps because her body was accustomed to the semi-tropical climate of Laishani and refused to adapt to the cold dryness of this world, it seemed her lips had been dry and chapped throughout the entire planetary year they'd been on Bakraga. As she tucked the canister back inside the pocket, she took a moment to rearrange the contents of the satchel. Packing it was one of the last things she'd done, quickly tossing in the things that would be handy to have ready access to, and a few items she thought she might need that hadn't already been meticulously packed.

Pulling out her pocketbook, she flipped open the cover out of habit, her fingers reaching toward the gray screen, and for half a moment she considered checking for weather updates. But the signal was ground-based and it would be poor up here, if she could even get it at all. In any case, there wasn't much on the infobase of a small colony like Bakraga aside from weather and news—just the usual array of business and personal sites for Port Addar, where most of the population lived, and Niomco's forum for its employees. And for once it wasn't as if

11

she needed to check her schedule for the afternoon. That felt a bit odd—but oddly freeing.

With no reason to rouse the dormant screen, she found herself looking instead at her husband's picture, which graced the inside of the cover. She frowned at it for a moment. It was an older photo she'd put there shortly after they became engaged, but he hadn't changed much since then.

Although he had the air of a self-satisfied intellectual, he was rather boyish—and unquestionably good-looking. His face was wide with strong cheekbones, a rounded aquiline nose, and deep-set eyes. In this photograph, the folds of laugh lines narrowed those eyes, and the wide mouth displayed the big smile that had hooked her. But the photo could only hint at his presence, and couldn't convey the glow on his face when he talked of any of the many things he was passionate about.

Looking at the picture also reminded Omalda that she didn't find him attractive when he was brooding. Unfortunately, he was almost as good at being stubborn as she was, and when he was sulking he even seemed cool and distant, like the kind of self-absorbed man no one could get close to. Thankfully, that was far from the truth. And it was some comfort just to see the oh-so-familiar smile; though it had been appearing less often lately, it was still his hallmark.

She sighed, put everything back into the satchel, and stowed it back under the seat. As she straightened up and refastened her harness, she saw that Haveron—who sat across from her—was watching, his brow furrowed with concern.

"Everything all right, Shonan?"

"Oh, I was just thinking about something that happened yesterday . . . Torturing myself, I suppose." She smiled wryly. "All I'll say is this: be glad you're a bachelor, Hav. That about sums it up."

The big man rubbed his jaw thoughtfully. "He really didn't want you to do this, did he?"

"No, he didn't. So yesterday he was trying every last

desperate argument he could come up with to talk me out of it." She gave a faint laugh, knowing her disaffected air was now so false anyone could see through it.

"Well, it's only natural he should be feeling very protective," Haveron said.

Omalda grinned. "As you two are as well—and don't deny it. And I told him that a couple of days ago when he tried suggesting that he come along. I assured him I've got plenty of protection—I don't need a chaperone, too."

"Aw, you should have let him come, Shonan," Aldas teased. "We'd have had fun with Big J along—get the scientific angle on the socio-political scene in Kruvak, and nobody'd give us trouble 'cause they'd be too busy trying to figure out how to answer all his rhetorical questions!"

She gave Aldas a mock glare. She was grateful that these two men were so easy to confide in—not only in matters regarding her position, but also at times like this. It was a relief to be candid without having to worry about losing their respect. She didn't know Treimon, the pilot of the cruiser, as well as she knew the other two, but she'd found him to be good-natured, if rather unexpressive; he appreciated Aldas's antics and Hav's puns in his own understated way. More importantly, Omalda had learned she could have confidence in his professionalism and discretion, which was mandatory for every member of a Shonan's staff.

So she continued, speaking loudly to be sure Treimon could also hear. "I made the mistake a few days ago of reminding him I'd be carrying my 'Z's—what's the point of being entitled to them if you don't wear them when you're carrying out your duties as a Shonan, right? Of course I was just trying to give him some reassurance about my safety.

"But it led to a double catch; when I tell him that of course I'll wear the belt under my coat so the Torviks won't see them, since their purpose would be obvious even to the younger people who've never seen a Zendi, that sets him up to point out that they won't do me much good if I can't reach them if I need them quickly. So then I have to assure him that I *won't* need them, which makes me the fool for mentioning them in the first place!" She sighed and shook her head. "You see, that's what it's like arguing with that man."

"Yeah, but I don't know anyone else with the mind to keep up with yours, Shonan," Aldas said. "And please don't take offense, but I've known him longer than you; he may annoy people by saying exactly what he thinks, but you can count on his heart always being in the right place." He grinned. "Of course, I gave up on arguing with him a long time ago, since I figured out he was always right!"

Omalda looked sideways at Aldas with a catty smile. "Not *always*," she reminded him in a slow, emphatic voice, knowing he hadn't intended what he'd just implied.

He caught on, widening his eyes and laughing sheepishly. "Let me clarify that. He was always right when he was arguing with *me*."

"If you say so," she murmured with feigned coolness.

Across from her, Haveron's dark eyes sparkled with amusement. She flashed him a playful grin, then turned her gaze back to the window. She was just in time to see something starkly different in the white landscape ahead: a black line—far too straight to be natural—marching across the tundra to the east and west, as if it continued infinitely in both directions.

"There's the border," Aldas said.

Omalda nodded but didn't answer. Her heart quickened as she watched the line come closer and closer, finally revealing that it was a tall fence of black wire, every strand barbed with razor sharp points and the top crowned with twisted spirals of the cruel metal. She watched until it passed beneath them, and once again there was nothing to see but the far-reaching expanse of snow-covered ground. She let her breath out slowly. They were officially in Kruvak now.

When she looked up, Haveron was staring out at the

tundra as well, black brows pulled together and a frown on his lean face.

"All right, it's your turn to tell me what's on your mind, Hav. You've been quiet all day. Are you nervous?"

"Sorry, Shonan." He offered a faint smile. "To tell the truth, I'm not worried about the Torviks. What's bothering me is the thought of dealing with the opposition again when we get back. I know this isn't the time to think about it, but I guess until last week's session I hadn't seen what a mean streak some of those old apes have when you cross 'em. I've seen some tense moments in High Council, and I suppose it's only natural that emotions run a little hotter at a Post session where things are more informal. Still, that scene was pretty jagged. I thought Peltras and that Niomco rep were going to come to blows." With a wry chuckle he added, "And no need to mention names, but certain super-heated politicians who probably drain weight off a lot of cards were far from diplomatic. If looks could kill, you'd be long gone, Shonan."

Omalda laughed and rolled her eyes. "I know. But you're right—you're not to think about it now. Or ever. It's my problem, Hav, and not yours. I won't let my aides get dragged into that. Dealing with undiplomatic behavior is, alas, part of diplomacy, and that's my job. But speaking of last week's session, I'm sure you noticed that the one fellow—that foreman from the East Mine—was entirely on our side. That was a plus I hadn't dared to hope for."

"Yeah, I did," Haveron said. "I think he realizes the Torvik miners will be a lot more amenable—and it'll be easier to get good workers—if they know something's finally going to come back to their own people. That man struck me as having something of a brain—at least a good dose of common sense. Which is a lot more than I can say for most of the others." He sighed, shaking his head.

"I know," Omalda agreed, glancing past his shoulder to look out the forward window.

The aud-com had crackled, then emitted a few words. Treimon answered, rattling off their coordinates in the quiet, almost deadpan voice he used on the com; though the words were spoken rapidly, he sounded as if he could have done it in his sleep.

Omalda added, "Good thing I had a couple of mentors pound it into me: it gets nasty sometimes, just ignore it. Never take it personally, never let it past your scans. It's all part of the routine."

Haveron grinned at her with undisguised fondness. "You're right, as usual, Shonan. And you do handle it very well. I must tell you I was impressed. Still, you know, I was just unnerved by the level—"

"Look—look there!" Aldas interrupted, gesturing with his free hand as he stared through the binoculars. "Wolves, Shonan. I think they're wolves."

"Where?" Omalda grabbed his arm, turning again to look out the window beside him and tugging at the sleeve of his uniform with childlike eagerness. "Where do I look?"

"Just to the right of that dark area, below that bit of a rise. They're in a line. See them now?"

From her research Omalda knew the patches of gray and brown on the white landscape were moss and earth uncovered by the autumn winds and the pale sun. She sought the place Aldas described, and then—all alone in the middle of the strange, stark world—there was a single file of tiny gray figures moving across the tundra. "I see them, I see them!" she proclaimed, still gripping Aldas's sleeve. She could just make out their shapes: long bodies with heads and tails carried low as they trotted head to tail in the tracks of the leader.

"Here," he said, passing her the binoculars.

She snatched them and strained even harder against the harness that held her as she searched for the landmarks that would guide her to the spot. She adjusted the focus, bringing the two vivid circles of grayish white that leapt out bright in front of her together into one image. Moving down, she found the rise and the hazy sky above the horizon. Down a little more . . . and there.

"Got them," she whispered. The one in front was a lighter color than the others, and it was carrying its tail up so she could see the heavy silver brush. She could see the sable patterns in their thick coats and see their shoulders moving as they trotted, see the triangular ears on the tops of their long heads. There were six of them, in varying shades of gray—ranging from the leader, who was almost white, to one in the middle who was a dark iron color.

As she studied the animals in wonder, she vaguely heard the three men talking. Aldas directed Haveron and Treimon where to look, and both soon voiced their success at spotting them. But as close as the wolves appeared through the lenses, Omalda wished she could see them better—that she could see their faces as well. Just as she had that thought, one of the wolves—whose acute hearing may have picked up the sound of the cruiser—turned its head to look over its shoulder.

Her binoculars were focused right on its face as it turned. The haunting green-gold eyes in a gray and silver mask seemed to look directly at her, as if they knew she was there, knew she was watching. A shiver ran through her, a heady mixture of uneasiness and joy. "They're beautiful," she whispered, more to herself than to her companions.

When Aldas spoke, his voice sounded too loud and close to her ear. "Yeah, but I wouldn't want to be down there alone and meet up with that bunch, Shonan."

As Omalda reluctantly returned the binoculars, she saw that Aldas was grinning.

"Rather look at them from this distance—nice and safe," he added.

The pilot glanced back. "I don't know—they couldn't be much worse than a Post Council session. Eh, Hav?"

It was Haveron's turn to grin ruefully, shaking his head

and running a big hand through his short black hair. "You're right, Trei; I think I might prefer to take my chances with these four-legged predators."

Omalda was silent as the men chuckled. She was still staring at the line of tiny gray figures, rapidly disappearing into the vast landscape as the cruiser left them behind.

"So what happened with that paragraph in the treaty about the housing? I never heard the final decision on that," Treimon said. "Did it stay in?"

Pulled out of her reverie, Omalda looked up toward the pilot's seat, addressing the back of his head. "Yeah, it stayed. I'd say that ninety percent of the treaty is still just as we wrote it, which is rather amazing, considering . . ."

"There's someone down there," Treimon said, with a touch of surprise in his normally unexpressive voice. "I'm sorry, Shonan," he added quickly.

"Where?" Omalda demanded, oblivious to the fact that he'd interrupted her. "A person, you mean?"

"Yeah—a person. Up ahead, off to the right. I don't think you folks can see him yet. He's just standing there . . . not moving. We're going to fly right past him."

Again Omalda strained against the seat harness, trying to peer up and over the silver epaulet on Treimon's right shoulder to see out the front of the cruiser. She could only make out the moving white surface of the tundra, below the swathe of hazy blue that spanned the upper half of the windshield.

"One person by himself?" Aldas asked. "I wonder what he's doing out here."

"Maybe he's hunting," Haveron suggested.

"Might be. Looks like there's a rifle in a sling on his back," the pilot said, deadpan again.

"As long as he's not pointing it at us!" Aldas said, and Haveron gave a dry chuckle.

"No, there's nothing in his hands. He's raising one arm. Wonder if he's . . ."

A booming roar shuddered and echoed in Omalda's skull, reverberating like thunder through her entire frame, as if she'd been struck a blow from inside her body. The sensation of lurching sideways and starting to drop was also her own, as if the bottom had fallen out of the cruiser but she alone was dropping through the hole. A tilting panorama painted in blue and white flashed beyond the glass framed by the cream-colored interior of the vehicle. A tremendous weight pressed across her chest and shoulders, so great it was almost pain.

The pressure—along with all feeling of weight—ceased for the briefest moment, then slammed through her with doubled force. A dull thud was followed by an ear-splitting, metallic wrenching and scraping. When she became aware that everything had stopped moving and the only sounds were a low creaking and a slow hiss, it seemed that some time had passed, but she had no sense of how long it had been.

After that there was a period of silence—though again she didn't know how long it lasted—before she heard a soft, rhythmic crunching. Silence again. Then a burst of loud staccato blows, rattling against something very close, something that seemed to be above her. A low voice, also loud and very close, gasped out a half-cry, half-groan. Something told her to be still—to make no move, no sound. The harsh rattles stopped, then started again, dwindling in frequency before ceasing a second and final time.

Omalda heard someone speaking, but the sound was eerie and faint—and growing fainter, as if it were moving away. She couldn't understand the words, and she wondered why. Her mind seemed to follow the path of each thought very slowly, as if she floated in a half dream, aware yet not connected to anything she perceived. Perhaps that was the reason . . . the reason she didn't comprehend what she heard. Or maybe it was the fault of the words themselves. There was anger in them—that she understood. But there was no meaning.

## II

OMALDA WOKE into stillness. She heard a soft moan, and wondered if she'd been awakened by the same sound. For a moment she also wondered if she'd made the noise herself; her shoulder hurt, and her head felt thick and heavy. She was aware of a strong burnt odor, and the images she saw were dim.

In the unfamiliar scene before her was a large figure in a pale uniform, slumped against an angled surface. Blinking, she realized she was looking at a slanted, twisted seat. The human form was held against it by the dark lines crisscrossing his chest. His head was hanging, his chin touching his shoulder and his face in shadow.

Slowly Omalda lifted her head. She could see a wide rectangle of bluish light above. The air had grown very cold, and perhaps that had roused her as well.

She tried to sit up, but found she was pinned by her seat harness and a heavy weight against her left side. Her right arm was trapped underneath her, and she had a feeling she didn't want to try to move it. The left was held against her body by whatever lay against her.

With an awkward effort, Omalda managed to pull her left arm free. As she reached out, her fingers met a surface that was flat, smooth, and cold. Turning her head as well as she could, she glimpsed her outstretched hand, just visible in the light coming from overhead, and saw the window frame below it. The window. But the direction it was facing was down, she was sure—and the glass was dark and blank. She could feel the firm seat behind her, and was becoming more and more aware of the pressure from her harness. It seemed to be pulling against her with a will of its own, determined not to let her go.

Struck with claustrophobia, she started to struggle like a panicked animal before she regained control of herself and stopped, aware of the senselessness of the action. For a moment she lay still, her breath coming in great gasps. She felt a strong flutter in her abdomen as the baby kicked, roused by her movements and her rapid heartbeat. She fumbled with her free hand for the buckle on the harness. Trembling violently, her fingers found the release; the pressure eased.

Pushing at the weight against her left side, she fought her way up into a sitting position, and pulled the straps of the harness away from her body. The movement caused a stab of pain in her shoulder, and there was an uncomfortable pressure from the large weight that was now lying fully against her left leg. When she touched the heavy form, she felt cloth over something firm, and as she tried harder to push it off her leg, the voice that wasn't her own moaned again, and her hand brushed hair on the top of a head.

Leaning forward, with her belly pressing against the surface beneath her, she slowly drew her left leg out from under Aldas's shoulder. She could see that he was also suspended by his harness, and now that she was no longer under him his upper body was tilted head downward. One of his legs was trailing but the other appeared to be held against the side of the cruiser.

Omalda felt vague relief as the sensation pricked back into her numb left leg, and she found it seemed to be all right. It was her right side that posed the problem. She could move her right hand, although it tingled, but moving that arm sent a new burst of pain through her shoulder.

She reached out to touch Aldas's chest, feeling for the harness. "Aldas?" she whispered, surprised to find that almost no sound came out. She tried again, but it came out only a little louder, and it sounded unfamiliar, as if she spoke with someone else's voice.

Finding the buckle, she had even more difficulty getting the release to move than she had on her own harness, since almost all of his weight was against it. When it finally opened, she cringed as he slid away from the seat, his head and shoulders dropping to the surface beside her, his left leg still caught. But she was relieved when he groaned and stretched out one hand, groping.

Omalda clasped his hand, and was comforted when she felt the warmth of his palm and the strength of his grip. Then she got up onto her knees to carefully feel his trapped leg. The foot was caught under something with a hard edge, and as she felt her way along it she found that the surface buckled outward, with sharp points jutting from the contorted metal. She tried to turn his foot, then pulled on it cautiously.

Aldas gave a short grunt of pain; from the sound she knew his jaw was clenched.

"Sorry, hon," she murmured. "We've got to get you loose."

But her mind still seemed to be working slowly. Her head ached, and when she let go of his leg, she sat motionless for a moment, staring ahead, before a possible solution came to her. Turning to face the slanted seat behind them, she groped under it and found her satchel and, still wedged behind it, the rough-textured heavy brown case. She dragged it out and fumbled to open it.

With her good hand, Omalda lifted out one of the two objects inside the case. It felt even heavier than usual. Wincing, she brought her right arm up to rest the familiar shape in the palms of both hands. The faint light above her reflected off its ornate surface. She cradled the weight of it in her left arm and used her right hand to open the small panel in the barrel. Her numb fingers felt odd and clumsy as she dialed down the adjustment to the most focused level of the Burn phase. Then she returned to Aldas, carrying the cold weapon clasped against her chest.

She was forced to use both hands since she wouldn't have enough control with only her left, and she needed to try to cut the bent edge close to Aldas's leg. It was very difficult to raise her right arm high enough, and she clenched her teeth against the burning pain in her shoulder, trying to shut it out of her mind. Picking a line centimeters from his trouser leg, she squeezed the trigger. The intense white beam appeared, as bright as a stream of sparks. She blinked, and smelled the sharp ozone scent as the metal began to melt.

When her arms begin to tremble, she paused. Bringing the Zendi down, she let it rest on her knees. After the glare of the burning white light, it was even harder to see in the dark space, but she saw that she'd succeeded in making a cut nearly a decimeter long. Just a little more, she thought.

After two more excruciatingly slow cuts, Omalda let out her breath and sat with her eyes closed, waiting for the metal to cool. The heavy weapon on her knees was warm, too. When she raised both hands again, now empty, she slid her fingers under the edge of the cut section. Pulling at the metal flap, she tried to twist it up, gasping aloud at the pain in her shoulder. The baby chose that moment to execute another strong kick, as if in complaint—as if he were linked to the pain she experienced. She tried to slow her breathing, and whispered soothingly, "It's all right, baby Tally."

But she'd raised the piece of the panel a handbreadth, and now she pulled again at Aldas's leg. He stifled a yell, but his foot came free. Jerking the leg from her grasp, he rolled over and sat up. She waited silently beside him, listening to his trembling gasps. He sat hunched over with his head bowed, holding his leg below the knee.

Omalda looked at the window above them. The glass was blurred and there was a blue shadow, like a glaze, spread over part of it, and on the other side were bubbles with dark centers. Along the back edge was a narrow band of white, and it took her a moment to see that the edge of the window was out of the frame—what she was looking at was the sliver of light coming through the gap, unimpeded by the damaged surface of the glass.

When Aldas groaned again, the sound made Omalda aware that she could hear something else—a sound that had been building so insidiously it had been easy to ignore: a soft whistling that intermittently changed from one pitch to another. Extending her hand up toward the crack in the window, she felt the draft of frigid air.

She laid her hand on Aldas's arm momentarily. Then she twisted her heavy body around in the small space and crawled to the other figure, which still rested just as it had when she'd opened her eyes. As she moved, she felt the surface under her shift, and there was a low metallic creak.

Reaching out to touch the closest leg, she found the knee under the thick material. "Hav?" she said softly. "Can you hear me?"

There was no response. Slowly and carefully, she felt over his body. But she couldn't tell if he were breathing—at first she was sure she felt movement in his abdomen, then was unable to find it again. From what she could see of the side of his face, his eyes appeared closed. She pushed aside the impulse to shake him, even gently, knowing she might worsen his injuries.

His uniform felt wet, and her fingers found holes in the material on his chest and shoulder. She stretched out her hand into the thin ray of light coming through the crack at the edge of the window, almost out of her reach. The tips of her fingers showed smears of red.

She searched yet again for signs of breathing, then tried in vain to find a pulse on his neck. Some part of her knew that she should stop—there was no need for her to do anything, for nothing she could do would help him now—but another part of her refused to believe he wouldn't be comforted by her touch, and she stroked his shoulder softly.

At the sound of movement behind her, accompanied by another groan, she turned away and crawled back to Aldas. He was leaning over with one arm bracing him up, and both legs extended to the side. Breathing quickly, he stared straight ahead of him, seeming to see nothing. Softly she told him to stay still and rest.

A purpose had formed in her mind. Out. They had to get out. Holding onto the edge of the slanted seat with her left hand, she got her feet under her. Very slowly she managed to stand, reaching up, toward the light, toward the wind. Her hand met the window frame and grabbed onto it.

She had to keep her knees bent, as she was too tall to stand up straight in what had been the width of the cruiser, but she now saw that there was also a narrow crack at the edge of the door, behind the window frame. Putting her fingers into the crack, she felt the cold wind moving past them as it forced its way into the ship's interior.

When she tried the door, it started to move, then stopped, unyielding. Most likely the frame was so bent it would be impossible to slide it any farther. It had opened just far enough that she could have squeezed through if she hadn't been pregnant, but the men wouldn't be able to get through in any case. Shaking and gasping with exertion and frustration, Omalda turned back to the displaced window.

Again she tried to use both hands equally, her jaw set in stubborn refusal to acknowledge the pain, but she could scarcely feel the fingers of her right hand. The thick window glass protested, creaking, then gave way, coming the rest of the way out of the frame with a soft pop. A clump of grainy white powder showered down into the cruiser, brushing her face and hands with its icy fingers.

When Omalda put her head through into the light, she winced both at the stinging brightness that made her squint, and the sharp bite of the air. She found that when she pulled her head and shoulders through, she could stand, leaning sideways, her belly below the opening, her chest and arms outside. She craned her head to look around, still half-blinded by the dazzling glare.

At first it was hard to tell what part of the cruiser she was looking at; it appeared oddly distorted. Slowly she identified the side flares, and the lights running along the ribs up to the nose, which was half-buried in the crusty white surface of the tundra. The snow that formed cresting waves around the wreckage was marred with pieces of scattered debris. Much of the exposed white shell of the ship was frosted with a spray of snow, frozen into crystalline beads that made the surface appear rough and glittery. Behind her, the rear of the vehicle was clear of ice, and rose above the surface of the tundra.

Beyond the downed cruiser, the empty landscape stretched in all directions. The sound of the wind being diverted around the white metal shape was like the strains of some ghostly music playing far away. With little comprehension, Omalda's mind registered that there was a single set of footprints leading away from the cruiser, and one person had clearly come and gone in the same path.

It would take some effort to pull herself all the way up and through, but it would be easy to get down, since the window and the side of the cruiser were slanted, sloping toward the ground. She leaned the other way now, to maneuver her cumbersome figure back through the opening, and ducked down inside the dark interior. Pausing for her eyes to readjust, she moved carefully around Aldas's legs, seeing that he was still sitting up, but slouched against the upended seat.

"Aldas?" she murmured, relieved that her voice sounded more normal now. "Are you awake?" She reached for the hand she could see, and again felt a wave of relief when that hand closed on hers with a powerful grip, though he didn't speak.

When he let go, she reached up and patted his shoulder. "Just take it easy and rest," she told him again.

On her hands and knees, Omalda crawled over to Haveron's still form. There had been a space next to his seat through which the passengers could reach the cockpit, but although he was still held by his harness, he was partly blocking that space, and the only way she could get past was to clamber over the seat, climbing over Hav at the same time. When she brushed his arm, which hung limply across his chest, she reached back and touched it gently, and had to assure herself that she hadn't hurt him.

Going toward the front of the ship meant going down because the side panel that was now the floor sloped toward the nose of the cruiser. Though it was a short distance, her progress was impeded by objects she couldn't identify in the faint light, and by the uneven surface she crawled over. But she'd scarcely gotten clear of the back of Haveron's seat when she could go no farther. The sides of the vehicle seemed closer together, perhaps because they had buckled inward, but also because twisted debris filled what remained of the space. All she could recognize was the torn and partly burned back of a seat, and the smoky odor was stronger here.

Tentatively probing the wreckage in front of her, she brushed a piece of metal that was hot to the touch, and jerked her hand away. Then, in a fragment of light coming through the only unobstructed part of the front window, she saw something that made her draw a quick breath.

Protruding from under the scorched seat was a man's hand, spread flat with the palm down. Her first impulse was to try to dig the debris away quickly, but it was clearly impossible. She stretched out so she could reach into the low space and extend her trembling fingers to touch the hand. It was cool, and the fingers felt stiff as she closed her own over them.

Lying on her side, she moved her grip back until she

reached the wrist. For a while she lay still with her eyes closed, holding onto the lifeless hand and feeling the strong tendons in the wrist and the place alongside them where there should have been a rhythmic force. She heard only her own breathing and the soft whistling of the wind outside.

Finally she gave the pilot's hand a tender squeeze and let go. She crawled backwards, again struggling to move over the jumbled surface. She tried to keep her right arm close to her body; each time she extended it, the throbbing in her shoulder intensified.

When she got back to Aldas, he had moved over a little and was directly under the patch of light coming through the broken-out window, sitting with his head bowed again.

She nudged his arm and murmured, "Aldas, do you think you can stand up? We can get out—the glass was popped away from the window frame and I pried it out the rest of the way. Can't open the door."

He lifted his head and looked at her, as if only now seeing her. Omalda stood again, pulling herself up by grabbing the edge of the bent window frame. Then she twisted around to hold a hand out for Aldas.

Though he cried out, making her shiver in sympathy, he was able to rise and stand next to her, balancing on one leg and steadying himself by gripping both her arm and the edge of the window. She looked at their dark hands on the white border of the window frame, vivid in the bright light. For a long moment they stood there, squinting at the bleak panorama of the white tundra.

Then Omalda steeled herself to make the attempt to climb out the opening. As she struggled and pulled, gasping aloud at the lances of fire burning through her right shoulder, Aldas managed to help, pushing her with his free hand and leaning against the frame so she could brace against him. And then she was outside, sitting on the sloping flank of the cruiser, aware of how cold that surface was beneath her legs.

After Aldas joined her, moving stoically as he pulled himself through the window and only wincing when his injured leg bumped the edge of the frame, they sat on the ship and again stared silently at the impossible scene around them.

When Aldas turned to Omalda, his expression showed more comprehension than before. "The com . . ." he said, his voice slightly breathless.

Omalda swallowed and shook her head slowly. "No. Can't get to it. It's buried. We can't even get Trei out. There's no way we could reach it, even if it still works. They'll have to . . ." She trailed off, not wanting to follow the progression of the images that arose when she thought of what would happen when someone came. Came to get Trei out, and to take Hav . . .

She shook her head again, then regretted it, because it made the headache she'd been trying to disregard grow stronger. The weight of her own words settling in her mind further increased the feeling of pressure closing in around her skull. They couldn't use the aud-com, and they had no other means of communication—no way to report what had happened, no way to call for assistance.

Even in Port Addar most of the pocketbooks didn't work both ways; one could look at the infobase, but couldn't upload data or send messages. There was no sense in climbing back inside the ship to retrieve hers from the white satchel. And she'd taken off her P.I. band, leaving it on the dresser in their quarters, a week after coming to Bakraga. On this remote world, where there were only a few weather satellites in orbit, the only P.I. feature that still functioned was the clock.

There were time displays in almost every room Omalda passed through, and it seemed appropriate to simplify here. Having a bare wrist even gave her a sense of lightness and freedom—an echo of early childhood memories, perhaps—and it served as a very small but welcome offset to the pressure and responsibility draped about her like some absurdly heavy garment.

Omalda thought of her very first P.I.. A gift on her fifth birthday, it had sported a flower-shaped display and a pink striped band, and its call tone was the tune of an insipid nursery rhyme—much to the annoyance of most adults within earshot when it went off. But how grown-up and sophisticated she had felt wearing it! She smiled sadly at the recollection, and for a moment she closed her eyes against the white glare and pressed her left hand against her forehead.

Almost everyone else she knew on Bakraga continued to wear their P.I.'s—only a few weeks ago someone in the Post Council had commented that he'd feel naked without it, evoking sympathetic laughter all around. Many regularly complained about feeling literally out of the link without the immediate communication and data access everyone took for granted at home. Omalda's husband had used this as one of his many arguments against her mission—with only such tenuous means of communication as the aud-com on the cruiser, any venture was inherently more dangerous. On Bakraga, the ship coms used primitive radio waves and were even subject to interference caused by the weather or the planet's sun. It was a far cry from the way it was at home.

As partners often did, Omalda and her husband had set a location link between their P.I.'s just before they were married. But Omalda had actually been glad—especially after they'd begun to argue so much—that here on this strange, cold world he didn't always know exactly where she was. Now was the first time she wished that he did. Though it still seemed surreal, it was sinking in slowly: what it really meant to have no means of making contact—not only with him, but with anyone at all. She felt suspended, as if she dangled from a thin rope over a dark abyss.

She opened her eyes and looked over the shape of the wrecked ship they sat upon. Her mind seemed to be groping for something it couldn't quite reach. Biting her lip, she turned her gaze back to the barren landscape. Though it appeared to have no identifying features, she saw now that there were a few low rises, and a suggestion that the ground sloped slightly upward, in the direction of the line of footprints.

Finally Aldas spoke, his voice sounding husky and strained. "We'll have to get back in, Shonan. To stay warm. We'll have to wait here. Stay with the ship."

She saw then that there was a crimson stain on the left side of his chest, seeping through the gold cloth of his uniform. He'd folded his arms across his chest and was holding one hand near the middle of the stained area.

Omalda nodded. Her claustrophobic urge to be free of the wreckage was valid in one sense—it was good to know they weren't trapped inside of it, and were both able to stand up and move. But Aldas was right, of course. They needed to stay inside the ship, out of the bitter wind, and wait. They also needed to find all of the coats and blankets—something she hadn't thought of until then.

The baby was restless now, and his movements added to the pressure she'd been ignoring since she awoke. After Aldas turned around, grimacing as he swung his legs back through the window, and slowly eased himself inside, she slid down the side of the cruiser to land heavily in the ice-encrusted snow. Leaning against the ship, she fumbled up under the long jacket of her uniform to unfasten her pants, and then squatted down, awkwardly trying to hold her clothing out of the way. It had occurred to her that even if she could crawl back to the toilet inside the ship, that fixture—like everything else inside the vehicle—would be in a horizontal position.

Getting back up was none too easy. Steadying herself with her left hand only, she managed to find toeholds on the ribs and lights on the side of the ship; the beads of ice that roughened the metal surface also provided a bit of traction. Then she got hold of the window frame, found another precarious foothold, and heaved herself up until she could straddle the edge of the window.

Inside, Omalda squeezed past the back of the seat to reach the small cargo area behind it. Most of the cargo was in the much larger storage space that was accessed from a separate door on the outside. She didn't fancy the idea of climbing along the icy body of the foundered cruiser and trying to see if the cargo door could be opened. Luckily, she found she could get into one of the lockers in this inside compartment, and pulled out two insulated jackets and her own sleeved cloak, which had been a recent present from her mother. To her frustration, she found that the lockers on the right side of the ship, where she felt certain blankets had been stored, were bent and jammed. It was a small relief to find one blanket that had been folded into the space under the seat.

Aldas was shivering when she pulled the blanket over him, though she'd already helped him into one of the jackets. There was no room for them to lie comfortably side by side, so Omalda settled for helping Aldas move into a space where he could lie down, and sitting close beside him. She pulled one corner of the blanket around her, in hopes that the cloth barrier would help to keep the heat of their bodies together.

The baby inside her seemed to have gone back to sleep, and Omalda dozed, always conscious of the whistle of the tundra wind coming through the cracks in the broken ship. Her mind replayed a sensation of falling, sometimes causing her to shudder and reach her left hand out to steady herself, bringing her back to momentary wakefulness, only to doze off and then feel her body dropping again, lurching downward with a vividness that was hard to disbelieve.

Some time later she was walking, struggling over rough, snow-covered ground with patches of gray earth showing beside the trail she was on, which was only a line of footprints. She bent down and studied the prints—large, oval pawprints, with the marks of clawed toes at their tips. Then she stood slowly, clasping her arms around her belly, and walked on, following the tracks.

A wolf trotted ahead of her, lean shoulders moving under dark gray fur, its head low, its ears folded flat against its head, the thick brush of its tail centimeters from her face. For she was a wolf too, following close behind, keeping her head down, but sure of some purpose.

The traveling became easier; she was almost floating, she moved so lightly and quickly. Now there was no one in front of her, but she knew still that she was a wolf, and the pads of her feet carried her swiftly over the surface of the tundra. The tracks she followed were now faint, as if the one who'd made them had also traveled as lightly as she did, scarcely making an imprint on the frozen snow.

The dream faded and she became aware that something was wrong, but fought the sensation away as she turned and struggled to find a more comfortable position. The baby was moving a lot. Her husband had gotten out of bed, and he'd been gone for a while, because the place where he'd been lying was cold. She wished he would hurry back, because she was getting cold, so cold, and it made her shoulder hurt. She thought she should get up and go find him. He was probably out on the deck, looking at galaxies again. She couldn't remember what that newly-named galaxy was called—the one honoring the man at the Institute with the silly-sounding clan name. Why could she not think of it? She would get up, and find him, and ask him. Getting up and walking often quieted the baby as well.

Again and again Omalda told herself she would get up—she fully intended to—but then she would find that she still hadn't done it, and she was alone in the cold bed, and her shoulder hurt, and the mattress felt too hard. Then she thought her husband must have come back, because she could hear him breathing, close to her left ear. But it wasn't right somehow. The sound was rhythmic, but it was too loud, too strained. With it came a nameless anxiety and a sense of foreboding whose source she couldn't identify.

Then she was awake, seeing the dim interior of the wrecked ship and feeling the draft coming from overhead, and knew where she was. Aldas was breathing with difficulty—each breath a slow, labored effort with a soft groan accompanying it. She took hold of his shoulder and squeezed it gently.

He opened his eyes and sat up, but his expression was vacant, and she could get no response from him beyond an incoherent mumble.

A sinking fear crept through her. She crawled sideways to get under the window opening. Then she stood slowly, to put her hands on the edge and look out at the desolate landscape, wincing at the glare. The strength of the wind had increased, and judging by the position of the small, pale sun, it was late afternoon.

Omalda looked down at the line of footprints, recalling her dream in a muddled haze. She was surprised and puzzled to see that these tracks were made by human feet, and not by the paws of a wolf like the ones she'd been following. But that made no sense. Of course they were human tracks; she'd heard a voice, and Trei had seen . . . Was it this person, that Trei had seen? Her head ached. She squeezed her eyes closed and dropped back out of the wind, pushing back the loose strands of long black hair that had been blown across her face.

She'd found a box of snack foods that had fortunately been in the locker with the jackets and her cloak—most of the food was in the main cargo compartment—and there were canteens under the seats, where they could be reached during the flight. Now she sat with one of the canteens, a canister of dried fruit and nuts, and a package of nutrition bars between her outstretched legs. Chewing slowly, she stared into the gloomy interior of the wreckage in front of her. It was an effort; she didn't feel hungry, but the baby's restlessness was a reminder that she had to eat, especially for his sake. She eased her tingling right hand onto her belly and murmured, "I'll take care of us, Tally. Everything'll be all right."

The throbbing ache in her shoulder seemed to be moving up to her neck and head, and her jaw felt stiff as she ate. She shifted over to sit beside Aldas, and she got him to drink a little, but he wouldn't eat, and didn't speak. He appeared to breathe more easily when he was sitting upright, so she carefully moved his legs to prop him up, hoping he would stay in that position even if he slept.

Shortly she fell asleep herself, curled up against Aldas with her knees drawn up against her belly; she had spread her cloak as well as the blanket over both of them. When she woke again, aware of being extremely cold, the wind had quieted down and she opened her eyes to complete darkness. She shut them again to close it out, and pressed even closer to Aldas, feeling the hard muscles in his shoulder and upper arm against her own, and listening to his slow, heavy breaths.

Later she dreamed—something about wolves again. But the dream wouldn't stay in one place long enough for her to grasp it, but shifted around her, as if taunting her, leaving her only with fleeting images: a silver wolf trotting in the tracks of a man's boots, and the face of a wolf whose gold eyes looked into hers—intelligent, almost human eyes holding a knowledge that should have been her own, but of what she couldn't recall.

III

THE WIND moving around the wrecked cruiser was loud again when Omalda fought her way out of a deep but troubled sleep, and in the sound she seemed to hear jeering, hissing laughter. She woke with a feeling of anger, knowing that in a nightmare she'd argued with someone—someone who must have laughed. Unable to recall any details from the dream, she was left only with the ringing echo of the emotion. She struggled quickly to her feet and stood, trembling, hunched over with her right arm across her belly, looking down at Aldas. The light coming through the opening over her head was pale and grayish instead of sharp and white.

Morning. How long had it been now? she thought, staring at Aldas's inert figure and listening to his breathing, which sounded rougher and more labored although he was still propped up against the tilted seat, his head lolled sideways. It had been late morning, she figured, when the cruiser went down. There must have been concern when too much time passed since their last contact on the aud-com. A report of their landing—of their arrival in Kruvak—would have been expected. And that arrival should have been less than half an hour away, Omalda realized, from when they'd last communicated with the C.P. port.

How long would it be before they came looking? She felt

she ought to know the answer to that question. The weather-tracking satellites circling Bakraga didn't have the instruments to detect something as small as a cruiser in this desolate place. Unless someone scanned for it from an orbiter, no one would know what had happened until they sent another ship to search. For now all they could know was that something must be wrong, since there'd been no communication from the Shonan and her team for far too long.

The baby began to move, and each small kick seemed an assault on her crowded bladder. "Give it a rest for a sec, will you, Tally?" Omalda pleaded to the baby as she concentrated on the task of heaving herself up and out of the window again, this time without any aid; she wasn't about to ask Aldas to get up and try to help her. Again she slid down the icy surface of the ship, her boots breaking the crust of the snow with a loud crunch when she landed. It seemed to take even longer to climb back up this time, and she tried to think of nothing but the physical effort.

Once she was back inside, she lowered herself down beside Aldas, taking his hand. When she touched his face, he opened his eyes and blinked at her.

"Ay," she murmured. "How do you feel?"

He blinked again, shook his head slowly, and licked his lips, moving his mouth as if he were going to speak, but then started to cough. He choked and spat, and when he took away the hand he'd put to his mouth, Omalda could see the dark froth in his palm.

"Your lung's bleeding," she whispered, not really speaking to him. She put her good arm around him and patted his shoulder. "Hang on," she said, close to his ear. "Don't leave me, you hear? Someone will come soon. Someone will come and take care of us. You'll be all right."

But as she sat in the cold wreckage beside him, conscious of the effort that went into each breath he took, watching the patch of light from outside grow stronger and hearing the wind grow louder still, she doubted her own words. How soon? Would it be soon enough?

She encouraged Aldas to drink some water, helping him to hold the canteen. His hands were shaking, and despite her efforts some water sloshed down his chin, dripping onto the front of his jacket. As she put the cap back on, she found that her own hands were trembling as well. She was startled at how upset she was that she hadn't kept him from spilling the water, but the last thing she wanted was to make him colder. And there was something distant about his eyes—as if there were a haze over them—that was part of the reason she felt gripped by a sense of alarm.

Claustrophobia threatened as she sat in the dark space, and again she got to her feet and pulled herself up, putting her head through the opening to look outside. The bitter wind was like ice pressed against her face. As she looked out across the tundra in the direction of the line of footprints, she chewed her lip and frowned. It couldn't be that far, she reasoned. If someone had come out here on foot, and the cruiser had been very close to landing—she was sure of that now, as she thought back on it—the village of Kruvak couldn't be far from this place.

Omalda thought then of the person who'd made these prints. She didn't know what he'd actually done here, nor how he'd been connected to the crash, though she was sure he had been connected in some way. But even if this one person, whose actions seemed to have been hostile, had come from Kruvak, it was hardly proof that the people there were all hostile. She still knew nothing about how they would react when . . . How they *would* have reacted yesterday if her delegation had gotten there and . . . But that didn't matter now. All that mattered was getting help for Aldas. And quickly.

So she would hike to the village, following the tracks, and get help from the Torviks. Someone among them would come to her aid. Other than her shoulder injury and the fact that she probably had a slight concussion—which would explain why she'd been so drowsy yesterday and why her brain seemed fuzzy—she was fine. There was nothing wrong with her legs, and she hadn't let pregnancy alter her exercise routine enough to affect her fitness. Judging by how much the baby inside her had been moving in the past day and night, he was fine as well. Resolved now, she ducked back inside the cruiser.

After checking that every closure on the jacket she wore was securely fastened, she put her long burgundy cloak on over the jacket and wrapped it around herself, using a spare strap as a belt. Under her jacket, she'd already buckled on her Shonan's belt, a wide band of silver and gold to which the Zendi guns were attached; she had to wear it low on her hips now to get it on.

As she snugged up her hood, tucking in loose strands of her hair, she had an impulse; reaching up underneath the layers of clothing to the Shonan's belt, she unfastened one of the Zendis. She secured it to the strap on the outside of the cloak, causing the makeshift belt to twist and hang quite crooked. Just in case, she told herself, to avoid giving weight to the idea of danger posed by the villagers themselves. She might run into a wolf or something.

She'd taken one of the canteens and tucked a small package of food into an outer pocket of the jacket. Now she pulled the cloak tight around her again, and shuffled awkwardly over to Aldas, putting a hand on his shoulder and bending over to kiss his forehead. He opened his eyes and looked at her.

"I'm going to get help," she told him. "The village can't be far from here."

He mumbled something, struggling between breaths to force the sound out, but all she caught were the last two words: ". . . with you."

"What?" Omalda said, tightening her fingers on his shoulder.

He answered by lurching forward and trying to rise. He

managed to get onto one knee, his injured leg stretched out to the side. He repeated, more loudly but still not very clearly, "I'm goin' with you."

"But Aldas, your leg . . . and—"

He shook his head.

Omalda knew he'd slow her down a great deal, and common sense said that walking would aggravate the bleeding in his chest, but part of her also wondered whether getting up and moving might actually keep him going. It was all too easy to imagine leaving him and coming back to find what she feared. If he were with her . . . Aware that it was probably foolish, she relented.

After retrieving a small tool box from the inside cargo space, Omalda made a makeshift splint by unscrewing a bar that had been a handhold on the interior wall of the ship and using adhesive tape to bind it to Aldas's leg. The task was made more awkward by the clumsiness of her right hand, in spite of how hard she tried to ignore the pain and tingling in her arm and force that hand to do its share. Before attaching the split, she pulled on the heel of his boot to straighten his leg as much as she dared. He scarcely reacted, still staring ahead of him blankly. Once the splint was in place, she checked all the fastenings on his jacket as she'd done with her own, pulling everything snug, and helped him wrap the blanket they'd been using around him like a cloak.

It was a relief when they were finally out of the cruiser and Aldas was standing beside her, though he was breathing heavily as he braced himself against the glittering flank of the vehicle. Taking his hand, Omalda stepped onto the trail of footprints left in the crust of the snow. Aldas was able to put some weight on the bad leg, but it was very slow going.

Omalda's existence became an agonizing pattern, like a strange dance in which she walked with slow, heavy steps, her left arm stretched awkwardly behind her to hold Aldas's hand, as if she were pulling him along. The only sound was the

unsteady crunch of their footsteps, and their breathing—
Aldas's loud and rough, her own strong but fast, with a slight
wheeze due to the coldness of the air. The icy wind played over
them, brushing her face with its cruel touch. She would close
her eyes now and then, walking blind—though the intense
white glare still showed through her lids—then open them
again to see that they still followed the trail of footprints.

Time dragged, and the weak sun moved across the hazy
sky. When Omalda finally paused, squinting at a dark line on
the horizon, Aldas staggered to a stop behind her, wavered,
and then went down on his knees. As Omalda turned back to
him, he sank to the ground.

Kneeling next to him, she coaxed him to try to stand. He
was slumped on his side, staring through her. His fight for
breath was painful to listen to, and punctuated by weak fits of
coughing. She could see a smudge of blood on the blanket, but
couldn't tell whether it had come from what was already on his
stained clothing or if the wound had also bled a lot more.

The wind had grown even stronger, occasionally tossing a
spray of fine powdery snow into her face, stinging her eyes. She
turned to look again at what she'd seen on the horizon ahead—
a line of varied, squarish shapes that showed stark against the
tundra. Buildings. She was sure of it—they could be nothing
else. And there was no question that the tracks they were
following pointed to those shapes in the distance.

"I can just see the village, Aldas—we're almost there.
Come on, you have to get up. It's just a little farther. Come on,
get up."

She didn't dare to leave him now, lying exposed in the
wind. She hovered over him, coaxing, pleading, pulling at his
hands and arms. She persisted for some time, until it finally
began to sink in that she wasn't going to get him up; there was
no way for her to physically lift him up, and he was no longer
making any effort, or even any response. So she squatted
beside him, holding his hands, silent, not knowing what to do

next, waiting, but not knowing what she waited for. She looked repeatedly over her shoulder at the shapes on the horizon. In this clear, dry air they might be farther than she'd first thought, she realized, but they couldn't be too far. And someone would help her.

The rhythm of Aldas's ragged breathing became erratic, broken by pauses followed by long gasps, and Omalda tried once again to pull him up, to at least make him sit. Rocking back on her heels, she used her weight to pull on both of his hands, ignoring a searing stab of pain in her right shoulder, and feeling the salty sting of tears in her eyes as she begged him again to get up.

When a long pause in the struggle was followed by a breath that sounded different from the others, then by another pause that lengthened into silence, shock came over her like an icy shadow spreading through her body. In spite of everything, some part of her hadn't let her believe in the possibility of this moment and was entirely unprepared for it.

She blinked through the tears, staring at Aldas's motionless form, his gloved hands still clasped firmly in her own. "Aldas?" she whispered. The wind pulled the sound away, scattering it into motes of nothingness. The silence was large and heavy, creating a void in her mind where the sound of his breathing had been. Since some time last night, that sound had formed the rhythm of her consciousness.

After a while Omalda became aware that she was growing very cold. She didn't know if it had only been minutes, or if an hour or more had passed since they'd stopped walking. Her whole body now ached with strain and weariness, and her face burned where the tears had run and the wind had dried them.

She wrapped the blanket Aldas wore around him, covering his face. Slowly she got to her feet, bracing her legs as she raised herself upright. Then she tugged the burgundy cloak closer around her, trying futilely to tighten the makeshift belt that was stretched down on the left side by the weapon hanging at her hip. As she smoothed down the cloak, she numbly studied the swirling black trim on the bell sleeves and the plush surface of the wine-colored cloth. Tiny beads of ice clung to it where it had brushed the ground. She thought she hadn't really looked at the cloak before this, for she didn't remember having seen the trim on the sleeves, nor having noticed the texture of the material.

A soft ripple ran through her belly as the baby stirred. Omalda took a deep, shaky breath and stood for a moment with her eyes closed. When she opened them again, she glanced only once at the shape under the cream and gold-patterned blanket—it looked very large on the empty white ground. Then she turned toward the village, stepping back onto the path marked only by a single pair of footprints, going and coming.

Omalda didn't look back again, but pressed on, covering ground more quickly now, alone. Her legs were tired, and her head ached again, though perhaps that was just from squinting against the wind and the glare of the landscape. But she was able to tell herself with certainty that she was all right. She'd gotten almost used to the dull throb in her right shoulder and the numbness in that arm, and had pushed it into a small corner of her mind, where it was just an awareness, not a pressing concern.

Soon she could distinguish the buildings from one another. Most were low and square, some appeared rounded, all were in shades of brown or gray. The trail still led directly toward them, and her progress was sure—despite the weight she carried, her strides were even and her legs had ceased to tremble, her breathing was calm and steady. To spare her eyes and face from the punishment of the wind, she walked with her head bowed, only lifting it periodically to survey her goal. You'll make it, she told herself. You're almost there.

IV

A TORVIK TALE
How the Old She-wolf Chased her Shadow
and Caught It at the Edge of the Earth

ONE SPRING the Old She-wolf's husband died, and the youngest of her children went away to see the world for himself. The She-wolf's other children had left home a long time ago, and lived in other villages a long way from there. Then the other people that had lived in the wolf's village were leaving too. Fox and Weasel and Hare gathered their belongings and went away. They were old too, and they all said the winter had been too long. Even Tern—who always used to go away before winter and come back at the thaw—he didn't come back that spring. Everyone was leaving, except the Old She-wolf, who was the leader of the village. Because she was so wise, all the others used to listen to what she had to say. Now there was no one to listen to her. But she would not go with the others and leave that village.

Now the Old She-wolf's shadow saw that everyone was leaving, and it decided to go too. It was tired of following the She-wolf everywhere and only doing the things that she did. So after the others had gone, the She-wolf's shadow left the village, and went out on the tundra by itself.

When the She-wolf saw that her shadow had left, she was angry. She knew it was a bad thing for people's shadows to go wandering around by themselves. So she had to leave the village too, to go after her shadow and bring it back. But the shadow saw the She-wolf coming, and it didn't want to be caught. So it ran fast across the tundra. The She-wolf was much heavier than her shadow, and she could not run so fast. Even when she was young, she could not have run as fast as that shadow was running.

But the She-wolf just kept following that shadow. And when she could no longer see it, she had to track it. This was hard, because the shadow didn't leave much scent at all. But because it was her own shadow, the She-wolf could tell where it had been.

The shadow tried to trick the She-wolf by going in circles and crossing back and forth over its own path. But she always found the shadow's trail again. She hunted the shadow for many, many days. She grew very weary, for she was old and did not have the strength she used to have, and it was a long journey.

The She-wolf followed her shadow across rivers and mountains and glaciers, until she was so weak she could barely move. But finally the shadow came to the edge of the earth, where the sea begins. When the She-wolf got there, she saw her shadow down on the rocks of the beach. The shadow was busy hunting seals, so it did not see the She-wolf.

So the She-wolf lay down on the rocks by the sea, and lay very still, resting. One of the seals climbed up onto the rocks right beside her. Because she was lying so still, the seal thought she was a gray rock and paid no attention to her. The seal came so close that the She-wolf opened her mouth and caught him without having to move at all.

Then the She-wolf ate the fat and the meat, and saved the skin. She saw that her shadow was still hunting farther up the beach. It hadn't caught anything yet, because the seals kept jumping into the sea, and the shadow was afraid to go into the water. Now the She-wolf climbed into the skin, and lay back down on the rocks. She was looking out of the mouth, and she could see her shadow coming closer.

When the shadow saw the big fat seal just lying there on the rocks, not very close to the water, it grew very excited. It ran up to that seal without thinking that it might be a trick. The shadow opened its mouth wide and leaped up to grab the seal. But when it opened its mouth so wide, the She-wolf jumped out of the seal's skin and jumped right down inside the shadow.

The She-wolf started biting and scratching the shadow's insides. The shadow howled in pain and rage and jumped and rolled all about. But it was only a shadow, and now that the She-wolf had caught it, she was stronger, and it could not get her out. Then the shadow knew that its little game was over. So it turned itself inside out and went back to its proper place, behind the She-wolf.

Now the She-wolf did not have to hunt any more, so she lay down on the rocks there, looking out at the sea. And she is still there, lying on those rocks at the edge of the earth, with her shadow beside her where it belongs.

And that is how it happened.

# PART TWO

## EMPTY WALLS

I

PERHAPS JEM had the dream only because he'd seen the wolves that morning. But if he'd told Enkara, or one of the other old people, they might have said it was a sign. Like the wolf in the story, he'd gone seeking something, and had come to the edge of the world he knew as solid, to find a different world he couldn't fathom—a world whose border was inhabited by shadows. And they were shadows of himself.

When he awoke, he realized his dreaming mind had faithfully played out a story he knew well. It was one Enkara often told when people crowded into the big, smoky room at the Women's House to trade tales and songs—the story about the old mother wolf hunting for her shadow. Some of the images in the dream were hazy, as if in a white fog, but most were vivid and clear, as if he'd actually followed the wolf, seen the gray seals among the rocks on the beach, seen the shadow itself.

That morning Jem had left the Birthing House on his regular errand to the poultry keepers for their ration of eggs. He was always glad to be outside, and away from Nadka and the other midwives who mocked him. The sharp edges of their words cut into him, and were harder to keep out than the physical blows—harder to keep away from that deep-inside place within him, in spite of the layers of protection he'd constructed to guard it, adding to them year after year like layers of sod added to the walls of an old house.

Yet Jem could sometimes look at himself and those around him as if he stood outside of it all, watching. Some days he could see that it was funny that the other women were so afraid of Enkara's disapproval. Most of the women who scolded him at every opportunity—or, like Nadka, struck him at the least provocation—rarely dared to criticize him in front of Enkara. And Nadka, who spoke badly of him even when Enkara could hear, had never let the old woman see her hit him. Enkara said they were cowards, whose hearts were shriveled and empty from years of bitterness, and Jem was easy for them to target—not only because of his differences and what he represented, but simply because he was young.

But Enkara could stop their abuse with nothing more than a hard look or a silent gesture. And that was amusing because Enkara, who was one of the oldest of the midwives, was also one of the smallest women in that house, and she didn't look strong. But Jem knew that in truth she was larger than the others. On the inside, where it really counted, she was bigger than all the rest of them put together.

In the dim light of the acrid-smelling poultry house, old Goplak peered at Jem through watery blue eyes. His round face was etched with deep wrinkles and an unchanging scowl, reminding Jem of a full moon streaked with clouds. The old man nodded, but didn't speak. He knew Jem well—or at least, knew the sight of him well—and didn't have to ask what he needed. Stoop-shouldered, he shuffled off between the rows of hutches. A woman and another man sat hunched close to the yellow flame rising from one of the oil lamps, staring into the gloom.

Jem fidgeted, his back against the rough-hewn stone wall beside the door. Feathers rustled, and the snowy kiruna hens clucked softly. Jem's nose wrinkled at the smell. The floor was littered with grit and droppings that crunched under his boots.

Though the building that housed them always seemed a sad and dreary place, Jem liked the birds; he enjoyed watching them out in the small fenced area behind the house, or when they were allowed a little freedom to scratch and peck in the snow beyond that enclosure, under the questionable protection of movable wicker pens. The kiruna were resilient little characters who could keep warm by burrowing under the snow, and Jem thought they looked as if they wore feathery boots. When their sleek plumage changed from glistening white to a speckled brown that matched the earth in the summer thaw, they transformed slowly, wearing attractive patterns that were partly each color. They never looked ragged and unkempt the way foxes and hares—and the reindeer—did when they shed their changing fur.

The kiruna were kept mostly for eggs and feathers, and although the old hens and some of the young cocks were eaten, their meat was roasted only during festivals; usually it was boiled into a broth, to make it go farther. Jem had only tasted roast kiruna once. Like almost everything edible, the eggs were also rationed carefully. And in spite of the poultry keepers' valiant efforts, they couldn't always protect the birds themselves.

"Curse that geatki!" Goplak's shrill voice came from the far side of the hutches, a thin and brittle sound made thinner by the oppressiveness of the low-ceilinged space. "And curse the Ancestors for bringing the beasts!"

The other poultry keepers only glanced in his direction. The woman gave a shrug and a sigh, stretching her hands out over the lamp and rubbing them together.

The old man tottered back, muttering to himself. "Two pullets gone and not an egg in the hutch. It was that big one again, sure as winter. Won't go near the traps—too clever! What good are the beasts if we can't catch them? Too clever . . . Nice pelt it would be too—big pelt." He nodded at the other man. "Get up. Fix that hutch. And find the hole."

The man got up very slowly, then faded into the shadowy stench.

Old Goplak took Jem's little egg crate and filled it. In spite of the thievery of foxes and ermines, and the occasional wolverine—the beast called geatki in one of the old tongues—it seemed there were always just enough eggs. Jem was thankful he'd never had to go to one of the other poultry houses. This one was nearest to the Birthing House, and, more importantly, Jem was used to the silent treatment he received from the sullen old man, and that made it tolerable.

Though Jem had never seen a wolverine alive, he knew the geatki was a giant weasel with wonderful dark fur that never turned white. Enkara had put wolverine fur around the hood and bottom hem of his old winter parka, which he'd been sorry to outgrow. The one he wore now was plainer, made entirely of reindeer skin. Jem also knew that the wolverines were not common in Kruvak—most of them lived in the forest, far to the south. But a few had come up onto the tundra and lurked around the village, especially around the poultry houses. They could make their dens under the squat stone buildings, and the foxes and ordinary little weasels took advantage of the holes they dug—even though they were also prey to the wolverines themselves.

The wolves, of course, could do real damage in the poultry houses. If a wolf managed to get inside, it could easily break into a hutch and make off with a flapping kiruna in its jaws. The last time Jem had come here there'd been a fresh wolf pelt hanging outside the door, telling how the story had ended for one unfortunate thief.

Jem took the handle of the egg crate, thanked the old man, and saw how the rheumy blue eyes flickered over him with cold distaste. He'd grown so much lately he was now taller than Goplak. He stepped outside and paused, pulling up his hood and gulping in the sharp air that made his chest tighten. As he turned away from the stoop of the poultry house, he stopped short.

At the corner of the building, scarcely two meters away, was a large wolf. It stood with its head lowered, the coarse silver hair on its shoulders raised, amber eyes staring up at Jem. Its muzzle was scarred and white and its mottled gray coat patchy. But the greatest evidence of age—and wisdom—was in the haunting eyes.

Jem froze. The wolf gazed at him steadily. For a long moment they stood, looking at each other. Jem swallowed. He couldn't look away, but he wasn't afraid. He'd never been this close to a wolf before, and in those intense gold eyes he saw neither ferocity nor fear. But even more important to Jem was the realization that there was no judgment in that gaze. There was just a quiet regard, as if the old beast and the tall boy were equals—as if some understanding flowed silently between them. No human ever looked at Jem like that any more—not even Enkara.

The feeling of alarm ebbed quickly. Jem felt warm and energized—almost exhilarated. His heart was still beating fast, but in a different way. He didn't want to bring this spell to an end, so he kept still, staring into the strange and beautiful eyes of the grizzled predator standing before him. They were kindred spirits in a way, Jem thought wryly—they were both always hungry and always unwelcome. But that thought summoned a vision of someone approaching and shooting the old wolf while it was distracted, and Jem couldn't risk that. He wouldn't give anyone the chance to intrude on this moment, to shatter this eerie magic.

He swallowed again, his eyes still bound to the wolf's, and said a silent farewell. He began to back away. The wolf watched him, motionless. Even if the animal weren't afraid of him, Jem thought, it would be too cautious to follow, and he could just walk away as if the old wolf weren't there. So he turned around. But he had to glance back to be sure.

Jem gasped and felt the egg crate slip from his grasp,

heard the thump as it hit the well-trod snow. Where there had been one wolf, there were now two.

They stood side by side. The second one was smaller, but also showed the white muzzle and shabby coat of old age—surely the first one's mate, and the female of the pair. Jem wasn't surprised when she, too, only looked quietly at him, her yellow-gold eyes seeming to draw him in. There was a maternal softness in her face that made her gaze even more compelling, and Jem felt his stomach tighten.

He felt as if he'd been transported to another time and place, or as if time had stopped. He was acutely conscious of the sound of his own breathing, and of the steam released with each breath, rising into the brittle stillness of the morning air. There was nothing unusual about wolves prowling around the poultry houses, but they usually came into the inner village only at night. Jem felt a shiver run through him—a mixture of thrill and uneasiness.

It was the wolves themselves who broke the spell. Before he moved again, they both turned away. Then they vanished behind the gray stone wall, like shadows retreating from the white glare of the sun.

Jem exhaled, and then looked down at the egg crate in the snow. Four of the beautiful brown-splotched eggs were broken. He swore aloud.

For a while he stood in the narrow street and brooded, growing cold. There was no sense in going back in and asking for more. He could walk to the next poultry house and say he just needed four eggs—and face new stares and ridicule. Or return to the midwives with the broken eggs—and probably get beaten. He debated, stomped around, and threw a well-packed snowball against the wall of the squat stone building. To his satisfaction, a white clump stuck to the stone.

Then he looked sullenly in the direction the wolves had gone. They would soon be out of the settlement and on the lonely tundra beyond the reindeer pens. At that moment he envied them. Although the wolves that lived in Kruvak had once followed the migrating herds across vast distances, but now spent much of their time prowling around the outskirts of the village, they had far more freedom than he did.

But it was easy to feel sympathy for the reindeer, who were often confined in the corrals—in part to keep them from trying to follow their old migration routes and leaving behind the banished people who depended upon them, in part to make it easier for the herdsmen to guard and protect them. Still, like the kiruna, the reindeer weren't much safer in the pens, for they couldn't run far, and it wasn't difficult for the wolves to get through the old corral fencing and make a kill, especially when there were young calves.

Some of the villagers were quick to argue that most of the wolves subsisted on voles and hares, and to talk of how the Ancestors had viewed them with much respect and admiration. And if meat that wasn't stored well out of reach became a wolf's meal, many agreed that the fault rested with the person who'd been careless. Yet it was inevitable that the wolves that targeted reindeer calves and kiruna hens sullied their reputation, even though the animals could hardly be blamed for taking advantage of any opportunity that presented itself— just as the people themselves did. And because the wolves were wise and wary, usually no more was seen of them than dark shapes moving through the haze of dawn or dusk, or perhaps the silver brush of a tail disappearing out the far end of an alley. Their tracks were plentiful though, and sometimes they would leave a trail of blood and feathers telling of a successful raid on a poultry house.

Thinking of the poultry houses reminded Jem that he'd rarely gone into the other two, and the more he thought about it, the more he dreaded the prospect of how the people there might treat him. At the Birthing House there was Enkara. That was the only remotely happy thought that came to him. So he went back with the broken eggs.

He went in the side door next to the meat-drying shed, which led down into the little pantry. He'd scarcely closed the door above him when Nadka stepped into the pantry.

Seeing him, she snapped, "Here, give me those eggs," and reached for the crate. She was a short sturdy woman, well past middle age. Over the patched blue kolte that hung to her knees she wore a white fur jacket decorated with strips of embroidered red and blue cloth, which almost matched the faded ankle wraps worn over her reindeer leggings. She had a hard face and small eyes like shards of blue ice.

As soon as she took the crate she saw the broken eggs. She lunged at Jem and slapped him. He'd started to duck and pull back, but she was quicker. The palm and fingers of her small square hand landed hard on his cheek. He winced and stepped back, brushing the earthen wall behind him.

"Goplak didn't send you off with broken eggs, I'm sure! You incompetent oaf! You can't even do a simple errand. You're good for nothing—nothing! Do you hear me?" She came closer, glaring furiously up into his face—up because he was more than a head taller than her now. That detail didn't seem to intimidate her in the least; she treated him just as she had when he was five years old.

He shook his head, regarding her with a sulky stare. "Nadka, it wasn't my fault. There were these wolves—two of them! They were right outside the door, and I—I ran into them and they . . ."

"I don't care! They didn't eat you up, did they? You're here and you haven't a mark on you, and you bring me broken eggs! That's all I see."

He made a face, knowing he was pushing his luck, but feeling the need to push back against her assault. "How do you know I haven't a mark on me? You haven't looked at me. They could have torn one of my arms off and you wouldn't notice."

Like a piece of driftwood smoking and hissing on the fire that suddenly bursts into a shower of sparks, Nadka exploded.

"Don't you get sassy with me, you demon! I don't care how big you are! I'm not afraid of you and I'll beat you till you bleed!"

Jem rolled his eyes, leaning back until his left shoulder blade was pressed hard against the edge of the narrow wooden steps that led down from the outside door. Chagrined, he told himself he'd asked for this. But that didn't make it any easier to endure.

The sound of Nadka's screeching, however, brought Enkara. She stepped into the dim lamplight of the pantry, a small pale-haired figure with a large red and blue plaid shawl wrapped around her shoulders. But her strong voice—which seemed too big to come from a person her size—was a heavy weight falling upon Nadka's stream of words. "Nadka! What is the matter now?"

Nadka turned toward her, gesturing expansively with her free hand; she held the egg crate in the other. "Broken eggs—he brings back broken eggs!"

"Oh, leave him alone. As if you've never broken an egg, Nadka."

"Four eggs—*four* of them!" Nadka retorted.

Looking at Enkara, Jem took a step away from the wall, visualizing his path of retreat—to the right around Nadka, then to the doorway where Enkara stood. "There was a wolf right outside the door," he told Enkara. "And then there were two of them. And I dropped the crate . . ." He grimaced and gave Enkara a mournful half-smile, sure of her sympathy.

The old woman sighed. "That's all right," she said softly, one thin, wrinkled hand smoothing back a wisp that had come loose from the knot of silver-blonde hair at her neck. "These things happen."

Nadka cut in. "They happen a lot more with him than with other people! Enkara, you can't keep defending him. And he can't stay here forever! He's too old. He should be doing man's work."

"He's only just fifteen."

"That's plenty old enough—especially considering the size of him." Nadka gave Jem a vicious glare before turning back to Enkara. "You should have thought of this in the beginning—that no one would want to have him around, and none of the men would teach him. That's what you're afraid of, isn't it? Well, you can't keep putting it off. He can't stay here!"

Enkara sighed heavily again. "Let's not go through this again, Nadka. He's not your problem."

"He is too my problem!" Nadka's weathered pink face was flushed red with anger. She gestured dramatically at the egg crate. "*This* is my problem. I have to put up with nonsense like this!"

Now that Nadka was facing Enkara, Jem started to sidle away from the doorway, toward the shelf-laden wall to his right.

"He's just a boy. If one of the other children had done this, you wouldn't have been so hard on them—admit it." There was a sharp edge to Enkara's tone; she usually just put a stop to Nadka's abuse of him and ignored her raging lectures, but Jem could tell she was really angry now. "And you're being grossly unfair. It makes no difference that I didn't bear him—he's my son! You know perfectly well he knows nothing about his own people!"

Jem paused to look at Enkara, startled. He'd never actually heard her refer to him as her son. But she'd always been his mother, and it should have been no surprise. Yet somehow the words made a difference. They put an odd weight on him, and he felt an embarrassment verging on shame.

"I'm sorry, Enkara, but you're wrong! Character comes from the blood, too! He is still one of them, in spite of what you've done. You just refuse to see it."

"Because it's not true," Enkara snapped. "He's contrary with you because you torture him. Any child would be. He's not like that with me—or anyone else who's kind to him. That's what *you* refuse to see."

Hearing this talk about himself—as if he weren't there—was a form of torture as well. Jem made his move to dart past Nadka, since her back was still to him, but as he went behind her she turned and grabbed his arm, with amazingly strong fingers gripping down through the thick sleeve of his parka.

"Don't you sneak off, you monster! I'm not finished with you."

"Oh, yes you are," Enkara said, stepping toward them, and Jem, seeing the look on her face, wondered if she were going to slap Nadka. He'd never seen her lift a hand against anyone, but the thought that she might actually hit Nadka was gratifying. The old cow deserved it, he thought, and tried to wrest his arm from her grasp.

Enkara took another step, her eyes saying more than any words could have, and Nadka let Jem go. He bolted for the doorway, tripped and almost fell—stopping himself with a hand on the edge of the door frame—and ran through the big room with Nadka's words, "Clumsy dolt!" echoing in his ears. He climbed the narrow steps in the entryway, shoved open the door, and ran out into the snowy street.

Defiance hot in his blood, Jem ran for some time, only slowing when his throat and chest burned from the cold air and exertion. But his destination was in sight.

The dome-shaped building on the southern edge of the village was unlike any other structure in Kruvak. In shape it was similar to the snow houses many people lived in during winter, but it was made of a strange white substance unaffected by the elements, and it rose out of the ground like a giant egg half buried in the snow, with the roundest part of the shell above the surface. The path that came nearest to it was like most of the streets in the village—a swath of trampled snow formed by the footprints of people and reindeer and the parallel marks of sled runners, and occasionally bordered by the thinner lines of a herdsmen's skis, accompanied by the pawprints of a dog. But where most of the streets ran in straight lines, taking the shortest distance between two points, this one curved to make a wide loop around the dome.

The alien structure was forbidden—taboo. A place of ghosts and lingering evil, a place of grim memories the people wished they could forget. But now that it was winter the reminders were ever present, for at least two moons ago they should have left for the forest a hundred kilometers to the south, where the herds would find shelter and forage beneath the evergreens, and there was wood for fires. And yet because of what had happened years before—because of what the existence of the dome represented—they could not go.

Jem had never seen the forest, but he knew that Kruvak— the name borne by both the village and the windswept plateau it stood upon—was too far north for wintering. At times it seemed that the forlorn buildings in the settlement huddled together as if commiserating about the unrelenting cold. The plateau had once been a place of brief passage during spring and autumn, when there was grazing to be found, between summers spent in the Addak Mountains and winters spent among the trees. Jem knew trees only from drawings and weavings, and from old things made of wood, for there were no trees in Kruvak—only wind-scoured tundra.

Stepping off the trampled route, Jem sank to his knees in the deep snow under the surface crust, and he paused, still breathing hard, and looked at the strange white dome ahead of him. This wouldn't be the first time he'd defied the taboo. But he also had reason to believe that the rule shouldn't apply to him—him alone among all the people in Kruvak. For the dome had been built by the Sanndai.

It was said that the Sanndai had come to Bakraga from the sky, in the same way the Ancestors had when they came to the world long ago and brought the reindeer and all the other animals with them—if one believed the old tales, which not everyone did. But it mattered little where the cruel Outsiders came from, for the story really began when the Sanndai built a settlement at the edge of the forest beneath the Addak Mountains. They'd claimed to be seeking only peaceful trade, but when they found a mineral they valued, they opened immense holes in the ground, and made false deals with the people in exchange for what they took away. Caring only for their greed, they coerced many to work in their mines, and replaced old settlements with their own.

Like all the children of Kruvak who'd never seen the Sanndai, Jem had been taught these stories. The old people, and some of the younger ones who'd worked in the mines but returned to Kruvak, spoke of how the Outsiders were tall in stature and dark in complexion, with hair as black as the feathers on the head of a tern and eyes like the eyes of animals—as dark as a reindeer's. And they told of how those who tried to resist the Sanndai were imprisoned or killed, sometimes tortured.

There were even some who claimed to have seen the invaders make people disappear into thin air—although Enkara and Trevga assured Jem and the other children in their care that such a thing wasn't possible. But they wouldn't deny the alarming tales of the terrible things the Outsiders possessed: gigantic devices to dig open the earth, sky ships like floating sledges that flew at great speed, and sinister weapons that shot bursts of white fire and possessed the uncanny ability to recognize the race of the person who held them—so they only operated in the hands of a Sanndai.

Jem had once heard Neskeb, the old Ongalak, say that the Ancestors had things like these too, but had left them behind because they were unnecessary and often brought evil. He spoke of the sacrifice of the Ancestors as an honorable thing, made to protect Bakraga from harm. For the Ancestors had understood that the world itself—and most of all the animals they brought to it—would provide everything they needed.

But the Sanndai had no respect for the Ancestors' creeds; they defied the people's wishes, and defiled Bakraga. Though some tried hard to fight against them, the Sanndai forced the weary people to flee to Kruvak, banishing them from the rest of their world. And this dome-shaped station—an abandoned outpost of the invaders—now stood as a reminder of all that had happened, like a raised white scar left by a near-fatal wound.

But for Jem there was also another story, one he found even more disturbing than the others. It was the story of when Enkara helped to bring him into the world—and saw the woman who had borne him. A woman who was tall and dark. A woman who had strange features and wore strange clothing. A woman no one knew, who seemed to have come out of nowhere. But Enkara told Jem she must have come north on one of the Sanndai's sky ships, for she couldn't have walked to Kruvak from a settlement far to the south. And from Jem's own features—which the eyes around him wouldn't let him forget— and from Enkara's honest words, he knew he looked the same as his mother. So he was a Sanndai.

If he accepted that statement, Jem could tell himself he had no cause to fear the old station. It had been built by people like himself. His own people. Of course, most of the time he did not—*could* not—think of them as his people. He was repulsed by the appalling stories of the violence and destructiveness of the invaders no less than anyone else. And yet with that repulsion came a perverse fascination with them, and with the one thing left to show that they'd been in Kruvak—the abandoned dome. Whenever he walked to the station and stood in the deep snow banked around its white egg-shell flanks and looked at it, he remembered that they were his people.

Today Jem could faintly see his own footprints leading up to the dome, filled by the brief snowfall that had occurred since his last visit here. He felt proud knowing those tracks could only be his, because no one else would dare to make them in this place. Now he made a fresh set parallel to the old ones, and then walked on around the structure, studying the way the light glanced off the smooth white surface and the shiny metallic frame around the door. The lower half of the door was blocked by a wind drift of snow.

Jem was fairly certain the strange dome had a sunken interior floor, like an ordinary house, because of the position of the door—and because the dome's ceiling would otherwise be rather low for tall people. Studying it now, Jem wondered how far down the bottom of the door actually went. On an impulse, he sat down in the recessed doorway, sheltered by the snow mounded on either side, and began to dig. He worked absently, not caring a great deal how far he got, but vaguely enjoying the physical effort, enjoying seeing the impressions he scraped into the grainy snow. It wasn't as if he had anything better to do.

He'd made a fair amount of progress when his fingers bumped something hard and smooth. Metal glinted in the swept snow. He dug quickly, and to his surprise—and a vague feeling of disappointment—he found that it was only a small piece. He held it up and looked at it, frowning. It was a flat metal bar, just small enough that, with his large mitten on, he could hide it in his closed hand. Curious, he thought, but unimpressive. Jem dropped it into a pocket and resumed his digging.

The weak winter sun, a small white globe burning in the hazy firmament, had moved up to the center of its low arc across the sky by the time Jem had reached his goal. He squinted up at it as he slumped back against the exposed door, squatting on his heels. His arms and shoulders ached, his fingers were sore and cold. The friction of his continual scraping had caused some of the dampness on the surface of his sealskin mitts to seep through to the inside lining. But he'd hit the bottom—a smooth surface like gray stone, and the metal edge at the bottom of the door was clear.

Slowly he stretched one leg out, then the other, so he sat with both legs straight in front of him. Even through his thick reindeer skin trousers he felt the cold, flat surface he'd uncovered underneath him, and he could feel the unnatural smoothness of the door against his back and shoulders. But now he was sitting in front of 'his' doorway, looking out at his own footprints crossing the snowy ground, and beyond to the distant gray form of a small stone building in his line of sight. This was his domain, where he could dare anyone to intrude into his personal space—and know that no one would.

He could be certain no one else had seen this particular view for years, because no one had been in this spot since the day the invaders had fled from this station, turning their backs on the frozen land of Kruvak and everything it held.

Jem had heard people make jokes about the Sanndai leaving Kruvak. They would say, "Of course they left us the bare-ass tundra and this miserable village—why would they want it? Even us crazy Torviks don't want it." And everyone would laugh. When Jem was younger he'd wondered why they laughed—surely it wasn't funny. But now that the view from childhood was dimming behind shadows that grew longer each day, it no longer seemed a strange thing to laugh at.

Jem sat for a while, gazing out at the white world through half-closed eyes. He let the thought of the next step rise slowly in his mind. Now that the entire door was exposed, was there even a remote possibility of getting it open? What were the chances that it wasn't locked or barred in some way?

When Jem got up and faced the door again, he ran one damp mitten along the edge of the metal frame. There was a square silver panel on one side of the door, flush with the frame. That, he reasoned, must be the latch, the handle, the way to opening, even though it was flat and featureless. He pried at it and fiddled with it until, when he was about to lose interest, it moved under his startled fingers, sliding horizontally—not the direction he'd thought it might move. He pushed it back, then sideways again, repeating the action when he saw that the movement was loosening up the plate, causing it to slide farther each time. Underneath the plate was a recessed square in the white surface of the door, with a metal circle in the middle of it. Yet revealing this seemed to bring Jem no closer to opening the door.

Then he noticed that the metal circle under the plate had a rectangular slot in the middle. A keyhole. What else could it be? He pulled off one mitten and poked his finger at the narrow slot in the cold metal. A grin spread across his face, and he put his naked hand into his pocket and pulled out the flat bar of metal he'd found. He was probably being foolish, but maybe, just maybe, it really was a key—the slot was the same width as the bar. It was nothing like all the keys he'd ever seen—brass rods with a loop on one end and a small notched flag on the other. Yet it was possible that the Sanndai—his people, he remembered again—made different kinds of keys.

As he put the bar up to the slot, his cold fingers slipped and he almost dropped it, but he found it to be an exact fit. Pushing the bar into the slot, he tried to turn it. Nothing moved. So perhaps it was a key, but not the key to this door. Perhaps that would have been too lucky.

Leaving the key resting in the slot, Jem put his bulky mitten back on, and turned his gaze to the path made by his own footprints. His stomach had begun reminding him that he'd missed a meal. He hoped Enkara had saved something for him, or that he might get a chance to slip into the pantry and help himself without getting caught by Nadka or Trevga. He made a face at the thought of that; one confrontation with Nadka in a day was enough. But he was getting so hungry it was going past the point of a slight, nagging ache to a hard, tightening pain below his ribs.

These last moons he got even hungrier than ever. Enkara said it was because he was growing so fast, and the food was being used up to make his body larger. He was already as tall as most men in Kruvak. His feet and hands were enormous and clumsy; he was forever reaching too far for something and knocking it over, or stumbling as he had when he'd tripped on the uneven pantry floor this morning. He hated it. He was big enough. Stop growing and taking more than your share! he told his body angrily, as if he were quoting Nadka.

With his mind still on food, Jem turned back and pulled the flat key out of the slot. There was a muted tone, and a tiny flicker of yellow light in the metal circle. Jem swallowed, feeling the abrupt surge of adrenaline in his veins. He didn't know what he'd done to cause it, but something had happened. Quickly he shoved at the door, squeezing his mittened fingers under the edge of the metal plate that had covered the keyhole. Nothing yielded. He cursed with frustration, then laughed at himself—it was hardly worth cursing about.

He was about to give up when he did something different, quite accidentally. With the plate shoved all the way back, he tugged on it, lifting one end away from the surface of the door. There was a soft popping sound. Jem started as the door swung open, falling away from the pressure of his hands.

II

THE INTERIOR was dark. A strange tangy smell Jem couldn't identify came out with the stale air. His heart was pounding in his chest, and he licked his lips. But what did he have to be afraid of? Even if there were also a practical reason for the taboo of this place, Jem knew that reason didn't apply to him.

Setting aside the superstitious fears born of hatred and grief, the taboo might have been justified by the Summer Fever. The Sanndai had brought the disease, and the first epidemic had struck in summer, sixty odd years ago. Although it later became clear that the disease could come in any season, the name hadn't changed. Many people died in each wave of sickness, and whether the invaders had brought the disease upon them by accident or on purpose—it certainly made a formidable weapon—the Sanndai didn't suffer from it themselves. And when the people were banished to Kruvak, the disease came along with them.

The Fever had swept through the Birthing House three times when Jem was a child. He could recall the faces of children he had known who'd tossed and shivered and moaned under their blankets until they grew still and didn't wake again. Jem remembered huddling under his own covers and hearing the keening of the women and older children when a lifeless form was lifted out of a bed and taken away.

After the last epidemic, the bodies of the children and old people who died were burned, along with their furs and clothing. They had burned them because the young Ongalak thought it should be done, on the chance that it would make a difference. But returning bodies to the earth had always been the tradition, and the burning had seemed all wrong—a violation that worsened the grief of those who piled the stones on graves holding only ash and charred bones.

Still, if the disease did linger on anything the Sanndai had brought to this world, it posed no risk to Jem. He'd never had any of the symptoms. When the Fever moved like a cold wind through the people around him, he wasn't affected at all. The last time, when Jem was twelve, he'd felt a hollow sense of guilt at his own wellness. He'd even wished he would become ill. But it had been some consolation to help Enkara and the other midwives, who tended the sick in spite of their own weakness. The small mercy of the disease was that once a person had survived it, the symptoms were mild when it came again.

Listening to the sound of his pulse in his ears, Jem put his mittens up against the surface of the door and pushed it all the way open. Slowly, slowly, holding his breath and wrinkling his nose at the strange smell, he stepped into the interior of the dome. He could see little in the darkness—just vague light-colored shapes—but the space seemed larger than he'd anticipated. The sound of his hesitant footsteps and the whispered scuff of his leather mitt against the wall came back to him in the empty silence.

He began to move along one wall, feeling his way and moving as carefully as his clumsy feet would allow. His groping fingers ran over a raised round bump, and there was an audible click as the slight pressure he exerted pushed it down. In that instant, yellowish-white light was all around Jem, opening up the space and revealing the contents of the room. He flinched, and when he looked up he saw rows of oblong globes in the ceiling. He heard a brief buzzing, like the sound of the biting flies that appeared during the summer moon to torment the poor reindeer in the muddy corrals, making them stamp and shake their heads. The buzz was followed by a sharp click. One of the ovals of light faded. Nothing else happened.

Jem turned slowly. The place had seemed larger in the dark. The soft gray floor gave slightly when he stepped on it, like summer ground or several layers of skins spread on top of each other. He could see that the inner walls—which weren't curved like the exterior, but flat panels joined at wide-angled corners—didn't reach up to the height of the domed ceiling. In those walls were a number of gray doors, some open, some closed, and it appeared there were rooms behind the doors. The central room where Jem stood was a little smaller than the big room at the Women's House.

Most of the objects were gray, white, or tan—pale, lifeless colors—and appeared to be furniture. Jem knew about tables and chairs from a sketch one of the old women had drawn, and Trevga had a small wooden chest with drawers that slid out. So he was able to identify the white chairs encircling a white table with rounded legs, in addition to a couple of long platforms apparently for sleeping on, and a tall gray chest. One of the chairs was lying on its back, and as Jem moved into the room, still holding his breath, he saw a number of things strewn on the floor and the table, and on one of the well-padded beds. There were some dark areas on the gray floor, and not far from the door the spongy surface was stained with a large, irregularly shaped brown mark.

Jem walked from one object to the next, looking closely at everything. His head felt light and hazy. This was a kind of dream, not something that belonged in his life. It was only an interlude—a momentary flight of fancy. Later it would not be real, although it almost seemed to be now.

Some of the things he observed weren't hard to identify: drinking mugs and bowls made out of shiny black and white ceramic—still holding the dry dark residue of something they had contained—and oddly-shaped utensils resting in or beside them. Strange white boots on the floor under the table, and a pair of white gloves with separate fingers—one glove lay on the larger of the two long platforms, the other on the floor nearby.

Many other things he couldn't give a name to, and his eyes passed over them as if he moved through a shifting kaleidoscope of images. On the white table were silver cylinders, longer than his finger but narrower; a sheaf of what looked like brightly colored squares of shiny cloth with strange patterns painted on them; a round black thing like a stone with raised silver circles on it; and a much smaller stack of white cloth-like sheets, all stuck together on one end. That was paper, Jem remembered—for he'd seen old moisture-stained paper when one of the elderly midwives had brought out a small piece of the treasured stuff, to show the children how it held ink better than the skins they learned to draw letters and pictures on.

As his nerves eased, Jem sat, straddling one of the chairs at the table, and toyed with one of the things he'd found—a circular black band of a soft material that stretched and came back to its original shape like a sinew boiled for a long time. Repeatedly stretching the band and watching it spring back, he was unable to imagine what its use had been. Surely all these things had a use.

After a time he got up again, turning to look around at the walls. There were shelves, and a square silver basin set in a waist-high platform with a number of small white doors beneath it. He pulled them open and found shallow spaces that were all empty except for one that held more cups and bowls, and some heavy tan vessels. In one section of the wall there were some horizontal metal panels that looked just like drawers in a chest. Pulling on the silver handles attached to these proved fruitless, and he gave up and went on, looking, touching everything. He'd taken his mittens off and stuffed them into the pockets of his parka.

As Jem continued his survey, the lights overhead remained unchanged, shining their unnatural daylight over the pale room. And in spite of how thin the walls appeared, the air around him didn't seem to be as cold as it was outside. All thoughts of his hungry stomach had fled, and nothing seemed to matter but this discovery. A discovery that would be by far the most important thing that had ever happened in his life—if it weren't only a dream.

Jem stepped through the open doorway of the first of the small gray rooms. There was a chair pushed up against a large table that was next to the wall. On the table was something dark with a recessed, glassy surface that held a dim and shadowy reflection of the room. As he came closer, the dark reflection was altered to include a moving figure that must have been Jem himself. He turned away, not wanting to look closely.

In the second room, there was a narrow white platform in one corner—a bed, neatly covered with white blankets of a weave so close and tight that Jem thought it was some kind of skin or fur, until he felt the material. Pushing both hands down into the mattress, he tried to imagine what it would be like to sleep on such a surface, as soft and dense as a dozen furs piled on top of each other. There was also a chest with drawers, and a rack behind a pair of odd folding doors that pleated like cloth when he pulled them open. Hanging on the rack were several white and gray cloth things—pieces of clothing, he realized, which must have been undergarments, for they were even thinner and softer than his shirt.

Most of the other rooms had the same furniture in them— the white bed and the other things, all just the same. In several there were garments left on the bed, or objects on the chest across from it. One object he recognized as a comb, but made of a green substance he could flex in his hand, another a little figurine—something with large eyes and a funny face, but he couldn't tell what it was supposed to be. Then, on the chest in the last of these nearly identical rooms, there was a very strange thing.

It was a flat metal frame, and under the hard clear surface on one side was a blur of dark and light shapes. When Jem picked it up to study it, tilting it back and forth under the light in the ceiling overhead, it seemed at first to be only a random pattern, but then his eyes began to distinguish vague forms. They looked like shadowy figures under a dappled light. Figures with dark faces capped by dark hair, and big white mouths . . . Smiling mouths. A chill ran down his spine and the cold shiver rippled through him, settling like a weight in his stomach. It was *their* faces. Quickly he put the gold frame down, hiding the images.

Between two of the gray-walled square rooms there was a different kind of door, with a silver handle Jem found he had to twist before he could get it to open. Behind this door everything was stark white, and the room was divided within by a narrow barrier. On one side the walls were made of shiny white stone, on the other there was a larger area with two white basins. On the wall behind the basins was a dark rectangular space, and in one corner of the rectangle a jagged piece of silver reflected a distorted vision of the opposite side of the room. The floor was strewn with shards of the same glinting substance, and Jem could see that the fragments were sharp without having to pick one up. When he felt the crunch of a piece breaking under his boot, he backed away.

As Jem wandered through each space and touched each surface, his mind was adrift, tethered to him by only a thin cord. He was feeling almost nothing, merely recording what he saw. Only the thing in the gold frame that showed images of faces had disturbed him. His emotions couldn't respond to anything else. It was too much to feel now. Later, lying awake in his bed at the Birthing House, the strangeness of it all—the alien forms of the furniture and the nameless objects, even the walls and the floor of the place—would come back to him, chilling him again and moving over his mind like a cold hand stroking his brow.

His survey complete, he sat on the floor, cross-legged, looking around him as if dazed. He tried to remind himself that people just like him had made this place, and all the things in it—all the things he'd looked at and touched. Yet how could people who possessed such strange and impossible things be anything like him? And they were also the same people who'd done all the horrible things he'd heard about.

Jem thought of a crippled madman who'd lived at the Birthing House years ago. The midwives had cared for him until he'd died in one of the Fever epidemics, and the children were told he'd been beaten by the Sanndai because he defied them when they came to send the people away. Jem could remember that man's eyes, and the insane hatred in his stare. He'd often tried to grab and strike Jem, who was only five or six years old at the time. Jem had soon learned to stay away from him, which hadn't been difficult, since the man could scarcely move. Many of his bones had been broken and not healed right. He'd been imprisoned and left to die, then brought out twisted and deformed and sent to Kruvak. Why had the Sanndai kept him alive at all? Only cruelty could explain that.

And a shadow of all the cruelty and treachery loomed over Jem, so large and dark it seemed almost no one could see the real form of the boy who stood under it. For he was still a Sanndai in the sense he could never escape—unless he could leave behind his own body. Although Enkara loved him, and some of the other old people were kind to him, most people didn't like him, regardless of what he did. He'd accepted that a long time ago. He was a Sanndai, and because he was a Sanndai, people didn't like him.

Jem felt the cold weight that had dropped to his stomach at the vision of the alien faces grow heavier and more painful. His head felt strange, and he was dizzy. He had done this—he had found this place, brought himself inside. Yet there was so much here that he couldn't begin to fathom—couldn't even label or adequately describe, if someone had asked him to. It existed in this world, yet it was of another world. A world that was entirely different. He'd been a foolish child to think of this place as his. It belonged to the alien people who had lived here, and who'd fled in such haste that they abandoned possessions, garments, everything. They'd even left food and drink, standing in those bowls and cups on the white table.

Fighting back the tumbling stream of thoughts, for a moment Jem wished he hadn't found this place—hadn't come inside and seen and handled the alien things. He felt as if he were poisoned, contaminated, by his contact with all of it. He wanted to close his eyes to block the images from his mind, fumble his way to the open door, and stagger out into the snow and be sick.

But the part of him that was proud and defiant—the part that had brought him running all the way to the station this morning—knew this was the most important thing he'd done in his life. He'd found a piece that had been missing. Logically it might make no difference—what good could this place do him, after all? And yet it was something that mattered. Something connected to him, even if that connection were shadowy and vague.

As Jem got unsteadily to his feet, it dawned on him why he felt so awful. He was hungry; that was all. It was not because of this place, and what he had found here. He just had to go home and eat. Then he would come back. Maybe tomorrow. And he could face it again. And maybe he would understand more. He would keep coming back to the abandoned station— keep looking, keep exploring, keep discovering this new and alien world.

That night as Jem lay in his corner, hugging his knees to stay warm under the pile of worn furs that didn't cover him as well as they used to, he stayed awake for a long time. With his eyes on the glowing red coals of the smoky fire, he listened to the slow breathing of the women and children sleeping around him, and the faint hiss of wind over the roof of the house. Finally sleep pulled him down, and in that sleep he had the wolf dream.

In the morning he remembered it clearly, in part because the mood of it lingered, and also because it was so complete. It wasn't just images and broken scenes, like so many dreams, but the complete story—the story about the old she-wolf and her shadow. It was as if he'd been placed inside the story, where he had to watch it all, feel it all.

Jem thought he would tell Enkara about it, but during his morning chores he kept thinking about the station, too. As soon as he was free to be by himself, when he might have had a moment alone with Enkara, he put on his parka and went out into the cold day. In the snowy street he broke into a jog and went straight back to the station. Later the dream seemed more distant, and he never told Enkara—or anyone—about it.

III

IN THE MOONS that followed, the station became Jem's sanctuary. He still felt a subtle uneasiness there, among the alien artifacts he couldn't name, feeling the lingering presence of the people who'd abandoned the structure. That tingle of tension and the small burst of adrenaline it gave him helped to make coming there an addiction. But there was also a peace he felt only when he was inside the alien dome, sitting cross-legged on the soft gray floor—a restfulness that came with the knowledge that here, and here alone, he would never be disturbed.

The features of the place, the distinctive smell, and all the strange objects became very familiar to him. He learned to turn the globes in the ceiling on and off as he came and went, pushing the round knob in the panel near the entrance to make the lights appear, pushing it again to make them rapidly fade into darkness. He rarely sat in the chairs, and never lay on the beds—it didn't seem right. Instead he sat on the floor, or lay down on it, sometimes dozing for a while. The mysterious lock relocked itself when closed, and he kept the key in his pocket.

One morning he got in trouble with Nadka again, this time for forgetting to get the eggs altogether. He'd grown careless and forgetful about his chores; his mind had been wandering more and more, as if part of him were always out at the station, and the rest just lost and drifting somewhere far away. This time when Nadka cornered him, Jem surprised himself by calling the shrieking woman an old cow to her face, then managing to yank his arm out of her reach when she lunged for him.

He continued to back away, watching her with sullen apathy and no show of respect or remorse. He scarcely heard what Nadka was saying—he'd heard it all many times before— but he thought he saw something different in her eyes: a flicker of apprehension, perhaps even fear.

Jem turned his back and went straight to the pantry entrance, climbing up quickly and slamming the door closed behind him by letting it drop onto the frame. He half expected it to reopen immediately, but nothing happened. He sauntered off, his large boots crunching loudly over the crisp snow. He didn't run until he was out of sight of the Birthing House.

He stayed at the station for a long time that day, brooding. Sitting on the padded floor, he bowed his head and studied the large dark hands folded in his lap. One of his earliest memories was of sitting cross-legged just like this, but among a group of other small children, listening to Trevga tell a story. Looking at one of his hands planted palm down on the spotted seal skin they sat on, Jem had seen how dark it looked beside the rosy-white hand of the little girl next to him. And the old woman had been speaking of the Sanndai—telling the children that they had come down from the sky. He'd never forgotten that.

Yet it seemed he'd always known he was the only person with dark features in Kruvak—and that was the same as being the only one in the world. That knowledge was a part of the ever-present shadow over him, and sometimes he thought about it obsessively. He'd never even seen another person with black hair and dark skin, and he often tried to imagine his mother. But with only Enkara's words to draw the picture from, the images he conjured up were evasive and fleeting. He could see a figure in the distance, walking alone, and when he tried to come closer, she became—dream-like—a younger and taller version of Enkara, but with black hair.

When Jem was very young, the other children had occasionally teased him about his "black eyes" and his "dirty hair", but they'd still included him, still treated him as another child. And there had been one boy who became Jem's constant playmate when he was six or seven. They'd done everything together. Jem vividly remembered the day the two boys found an old reindeer cow in a small pen next to a dwelling not far from the Birthing House.

Daring each other—and feeling very big and brave—they climbed onto the rickety corral fence, and from there onto the cow's bony, shaggy back. His friend latched his fists onto the long hair on the beast's shoulders—knowing that if he grabbed her antlers she could send them flying with a toss of her head— while Jem clung to him, and they rode the old cow around the muddy corral until she dropped to her knees and rolled them off, freeing their little hands from her coarse white hair.

Jem still remembered how she'd looked at them—sitting on her brown knees in the snow as she placidly chewed her cud with the sideways movement of her jaw, an almost patient expression in her somber brown eyes. And Jem and his friend had run off, laughing and triumphant, with nothing worse to show from their adventure than mud on their trousers and parkas.

Though he couldn't recall that boy's name, Jem had never forgotten his face. A round face with a pointed chin, narrow eyes like chips of ice reflecting the distant blue of the sky on a clear day, and fine blond hair that was always in tousled disarray. He, for one, had never pointed out Jem's differences—at least, not until the day he simply refused to play with him any more. They were both about nine years old when Jem went to find his friend and the other boy tried to avoid him. When Jem cornered him, the boy told Jem he wouldn't play with him.

"Why?" Jem asked.

"Be—because . . ." the boy stammered, looking down. "Because your hair's black," he said finally, in a strained voice that didn't sound at all like himself, and ran back to the other children, leaving Jem standing alone.

Since most adults had always seemed to see the shadowy image of what Jem was, rather than Jem himself, he was used to that, and had convinced himself he'd accepted it. But it hurt when the other children changed their attitudes toward him, slowly turning away and shutting him out, until even that boy with whom he'd shared so many little joys ended their relationship.

Now that Jem was older, he was conscious of his exclusion in a new way. Though no one his age spoke to him, he couldn't help watching them, especially during the Festival times, or when there were gatherings at the Women's House and many people came together. So he witnessed the boys and girls he had always known beginning to flirt as they played and chatted, and then to pair up—calling to each other in the street, meeting in a doorway, walking side by side. Knowing he couldn't hope to step inside that circle sharpened the old pain that had grown dull because he was so accustomed to it.

Sometimes he would imagine a girl sitting with him by the fire, walking beside him on his way to and from the station, or standing next to him when all the other young people were together, laughing. He couldn't see her clearly in his mind; she had to be unlike anyone else. But he knew her face was soft and round, like the face of a little girl he'd played with often and seen die from the Fever when he was eight. And he knew her eyes were a bright sky blue. But her hair—her hair was black, like his own. It had to be, or she wouldn't be with him. Yet just as it was difficult to picture his blood mother, it was hard to put together in one image what he knew she must be like—this girl who would actually choose him. Mostly he imagined her presence, and she was like a faint shadow cast only when the light of his secret wish shone through the clouds for a brief moment.

Often his wishes were for things to go away, rather than to come to him. He wished that the memories—of his friend and the day they rode the old cow, and of the face of the little girl who'd died—wouldn't return to him in moments like this, when he was too aware of being alone. He wished it would all fade, like some memories did, until there was nothing where they'd been but a white fog, like the soft, cold emptiness that crept in from the sea.

Jem stayed in the station that day until hunger drove him home—he'd missed a meal again, because of his absence. But despite the cocky defiance he'd shown Nadka, he dreaded seeing her again.

At the Birthing House he snuck back in the side door leading into the pantry, as he often did. Then he pulled open the wrapping around a loaf of gray bread, made from moss the children collected on the tundra east of the village. His fingers were working to tear away a piece of it when Enkara came into the pantry.

"Jem!" she hissed. "Stop that! Where have you been? I've been looking all over for you!" Enkara was almost two heads shorter than Jem now, but the tiny round-faced figure—so dear and familiar—was not small or frail to him. He couldn't see that she grew smaller in relationship to him. She was the only thing he could depend on; she could not change.

Jem's tight shoulders dropped in relief. He turned to face her. "I didn't eat," he said mournfully. "I'm really hungry. May I—"

She interrupted him, her tone sharper than usual. "If you had been here, instead of wandering off again . . . Oh, Jem! I don't know what to do. And there's a man here to see you . . ." Her voice trailed away. Then she sighed and regarded him with a mixture of exasperation and pity. "I'm sorry, but there's no stew left. You should have been here." She shook her head. "All right, all right, you may have some bread—but don't take too much."

"What man?" he'd started to say, but then was too busy pulling off a hunk of the dry gray stuff and cramming it into his mouth to get out more than a muffled expression of gratitude.

"Hurry. He's been waiting. Nadka didn't say it—I think she won't admit it—but I think she asked him to come . . . to come to see you."

"To see me? What for?"

"Yes," she answered coolly. "They want you to work."

Jem realized she was nervous. Puzzled, and feeling a twinge of nervousness himself, he gulped down the rest of the bread and followed Enkara out into the big room.

The old man stood with his arms folded across his chest and his narrow eyes staring straight ahead, as if he looked right through the half dozen women clustered around him. It was unusual for a man to come to the Birthing House, and it was evident, from the way the midwives were watching him, that this one wasn't welcome.

He was very short, and his bony frame was engulfed in a long, shabby, brown reindeer parka that went below his knees. The embroidery on the sleeves and hood of the parka was faded and colorless, the threads worn and broken. The man's hair was silver-gray and his wizened face was creased with a thousand wrinkles, his eyes almost lost in folds of pale skin.

Jem had walked into the room slowly, in the sullen slouch he'd perfected whenever he was sent or called some place he didn't want to go, always anticipating a scolding or a lecture. When he reached the old man and faced him, he wanted to recoil. This ancient little man was as vile as crumbling bones and decaying skins. He looked as if he should no longer be alive, and yet somehow kept on living.

The old man raised his head and looked directly at Jem, his deeply-lined face entirely lacking expression.

"This is Waltak," Enkara said very softly.

Though he'd never seen him before, Jem knew the man's name. He also knew that Waltak was the companion of another very old man—the infamous Avakab. From the stories they told about him, and even the way they pronounced his name, the midwives had all made it clear that they hated old Avakab.

He'd been one of the rebels who fought against the Sanndai, and after everyone was imprisoned in Kruvak, he'd tried to govern the village, becoming something of a tyrant. Although many of the people were too caught up in their day-to-day struggle to care, for a time Avakab had managed to gain control. After everything they'd been through, some had desperately wanted a leader to look toward, and the old Ongalak, Neskeb, had been so despondent during the first winter in Kruvak that he withdrew into himself. For five years he hardly spoke at all, leaving the people without any guidance when they most needed it—or so the story went.

But many also believed that the final revolt Avakab had attempted was the cause of their banishment. And they muttered darkly about how he showed no remorse over the fact that the others who'd acted with him in the rebellion had been caught and murdered by the Sanndai, while he'd fled to the coast, coming back to the village only after the Sanndai had left Kruvak.

Now that Avakab himself was elderly, he'd retreated into the imposing stone-walled fort he'd built as the stronghold for the rebellion, and rarely came out into the village. Though many at least pretended some respect for old Avak—perhaps out of fear, for he'd been a brutal man when he'd chosen to use force—it seemed to Jem that whenever people spoke of him, it was only to blame him for everything.

The man called Waltak looked Jem over, his eyes shifting. "You are big," he said, in a strange nasal voice that made Jem grit his teeth.

"What a brilliant observation," Trevga muttered sarcastically, and several of the others tittered.

Waltak ignored the women, his nervous eyes only on Jem, as if the tall, black-haired boy standing in front of him were the only other person in the room.

"Can you work hard?" he asked.

Jem glanced uneasily at Enkara, the realization of what was happening—what this meant—coming clear. Looking away from what he saw in Enkara's face, he swallowed and nodded.

He heard Nadka and one of the other midwives standing behind him chuckle and whisper to each other.

"If you'll do as you're told, I'll give you work," the thin, irritating voice said, as the old man continued to stare up at Jem with little expression. "You can live in the fort, too. You can be alone; no one will give you trouble. You can't go out with the other boys, you can't learn to hunt—none of the men will take you. Unless you are stupid, you know this." He stressed the word 'stupid' as if he actually intended to insult Jem, and he scowled bitterly, though his staring eyes now seemed to be looking through Jem as if he weren't there. "She knows it," he added, nodding coldly toward Enkara.

Jem fidgeted, feeling his stomach tighten. But the horrid old man was right. Though it was one of many things he'd pushed into a dark corner of his mind, Jem had known for a long time that Enkara wouldn't want him to join the hunting and fishing expeditions, or even to seek work at the reindeer pens, helping the herdsmen. Now that he was forced to face the issue, that cold hard knot sank down through his torso and seemed to settle at the very bottom of his being, as it had on the day he'd seen the captured images of the Sanndai faces in the station.

The expeditions journeyed to the rocky coast, bringing back seals, cod and herring—and occasionally strange blue fish from deep under the ice, which were called Natives, because they'd been there before the Ancestors came. These trips were grueling and dangerous, and men were sometimes lost. And staying with the herds was hardly easy or safe either. Because the reindeer were trapped in small corrals throughout the long, relentless winters—where they quickly destroyed the sparse grasses and moss under the snow—the need to find feed for their livestock led people to desperate competition and bitter confrontations.

Outside of the reindeer and what could be brought back from the coast, there were just a few other sources of food: running trap lines, which required possession of traps and a sled; farming potatoes and other root crops in little sod-walled plots; and raising the kiruna in the stone poultry houses. There were only a few people who did these things, and Jem already knew that none of them were willing to teach him, much less to share their resources with him.

No matter what sort of work was involved, there were plenty of quarrels and plenty of accidents happened. Nothing would be easier than getting rid of one gawky, ignorant boy. Someone could arrange for Jem to have an accident, or just accuse him of theft and kill him outright. Enkara would grieve alone, with no way of knowing what really happened.

Although it was painful to bring these facts up to the surface, they were things Jem knew well. And that knowledge simply reinforced his familiar sense of separation. Now the wretched little man was waiting for his reply, and Jem understood that he had no choice.

As long as these old men were willing to feed and shelter him, it didn't matter whether they really wanted someone to help them, or just wanted to keep an eye on him. Some people seemed to expect Jem to turn into a raging murderer any day, and to start doing everything dreadful the Sanndai had ever done. Since he knew much less of the Sanndai and their ways than any of the older people in Kruvak who'd actually encountered them, or even lived among them in the mining settlements, this notion seemed particularly absurd to Jem. Still, he couldn't pretend no one feared him. He could see it in people's eyes when they glanced warily at him, or in the way they chose a different path when they saw him trudging toward them on the same track freshly stamped into the deep snow after a blizzard.

Nadka, who was standing behind Jem, spoke up loudly. "If Avakab wants the lout, he can have him—he's too old to stay here, and we've no use for him."

"What does crazy old Avak want him for?" one woman asked coldly.

"Take him," Trevga said tauntingly, glaring at Waltak. "Whatever Avakab wants with him, he knows how to deal with *them.*"

The women laughed loudly. The cacophony made Jem wince and clench his jaw. Nearly all of them joined in except Enkara, until finally their voices dwindled down to giggles and muttering. Of the dozen midwives at the Birthing House, only a few were young, unwed women not strong enough to bear hard work. The majority were older women who'd long been widowed—and some had become widows during that ill-fated attempt at revolution.

"Come on, boy," the old man said. He still took no notice of the women, and turned toward the entrance without speaking again.

So Jem put on his mittens and pulled up his hood. He could retrieve his few other belongings later, or just leave them with Enkara; they were tucked into a bag she kept among her own possessions. He was sure no one would stop him from coming to visit Enkara, but he feared his visits might become infrequent.

It was hard not to fear that he was walking away from the only warmth and joy that still lived inside him. Yet the toughened part of him—the part that had built and reinforced the walls around that hidden center—reasoned that it made no difference where he lived, or what he did. He didn't care. He didn't want to fish or hunt seals anyway, and he certainly didn't want to stay with a bunch of squabbling old women for the rest of his life—he'd had more than enough of that.

As he followed Waltak, Jem heard the midwives laughing again. Laugh all you want, you stupid old hens, he thought— I'm glad to be rid of you, too. But he was acutely aware of Enkara's silent presence as she walked behind him.

Beneath the steps leading up to the outside door, she reached out and put her hand on Jem's arm. "Be careful, Jemren," was all she said, and there was a quaver in her normally strong voice.

"I will," he said, although he wasn't sure he knew how to do what he promised. He didn't look back at her, but turned to follow the old man up the shadowed wooden steps and out into the blinding blast of cold and white that was the world outside.

## IV

THE REBELS' FORT had been constructed with every material that could be used for building. The outer wall, rounded on one side and roughly straight on the other three sides, was made of gray stones. Within this barrier were walls of sod, reinforced with wood, bone, and antler, and roofed with earth, moss and skins. The sod rooms were built in a circle against the stone walls, leaving a large interior space without a roof.

When Jem first saw it, this space was filled with unmarred drifts of snow, as if no one had ventured out into it for moons. But he knew that the biggest room in the fort had once been a snow dome—the largest anyone had ever seen—rising from the center of an impressive cluster of snow-block structures, and he'd heard people say that it had been visible from outside the stone walls. The fort's odd structure may have shown that Avakab was opportunistic and practical, but it was also clear that he'd intended to impress his own people as much as the invaders.

It wasn't unusual to build several interconnected snow domes. They were warmer than any other kind of structure in the windy bleakness of the tundra winter. The old women taught the children that very long ago the people who lived in the coldest regions of the Motherworld—where there was snow and ice most of the year, just as there was in Kruvak—had learned to build houses made of snow. The old word for that kind of house was illu, and the snow domes were often called by that name.

Although it usually stayed so cold in Kruvak that the snow blocks slowly turned to ice, which was reinforced by each new snowfall, making the structures both strong and resilient, an illu had to be rebuilt with fresh snow if it began to settle and sag—and, of course, couldn't be used during the brief thaw of summer. So Jem wasn't surprised that Waltak and Avakab hadn't reconstructed the center of the fort every year. He doubted they could even manage to put up one small illu now. And it was also obvious that the entire fort was sorely in need of repairs. Jem figured he might make a couple of snow domes in the inner yard, although it wouldn't be a priority, but he soon found out that the crazy old men had different ideas.

Sullen but obedient, Jem had been following Waltak through the fort for some time, wishing sourly that the old man could move his scrawny carcass faster so they might get through the miserable place before nightfall. They finally trudged out of one of the dark, sod-walled rooms into the glare of the fort's open interior, and Waltak stopped abruptly. Jem narrowly avoided bumping into the old man's withered frame.

Waltak stood just outside the doorway, blinking his watery eyes. It was a few moments before he produced—from out of a pocket in his oversized parka—a map drawn on a piece of skin, like the ones the hunters used. He turned to show it to Jem. The drawing was a faded but clear diagram showing where the snow domes had been built. There had been seven of them, with the very large one, the meeting room, in the center. He told Jem that he was to build them—just as they were shown.

Jem took the map that the old man pushed into his hands. He stared at it only briefly before looking up to give Waltak an incredulous scowl. "You want me to build all of these? By myself?"

"What is the good of being strong if you do not work?" the old man answered.

Jem gave a disbelieving cough before spluttering, "Why? I mean—it'll take me a long time. It'll be spring, and the ones I've done will start falling, and I'll have to start all over when the snows start again. Besides, who's going to live in them?"

Waltak's lips twitched as if dimly remembering the action of a smile, and the nasal voice intoned, "It will keep you busy. Every winter, you can work on it. Perhaps you'll finish them next year, if you are too slow and lazy to do it this year."

Jem rolled his eyes and looked away, fighting down the impulse to talk back and venting his anger by kicking at a mound of snow at his feet. "What about the rest of the place?" he said instead. "It needs work too—you said you wanted me to fix the roof and some of those doors."

"You will do that also," Waltak snapped, as if he'd been very patient but now his patience was wearing thin.

When he opened a narrow door in the wall to their left, it revealed a small sledge that a man could pull, and a collection of tools—worn but serviceable—for cutting snow blocks. Then, walking very slowly, Waltak showed Jem several places where the sod walls that faced the open interior were in poor shape. Jem was to break down one small section at a time, then rebuild it, reusing as much as he could of the old building materials. It would be a slow process for one man working alone.

There were other chores to be done as well. Jem certainly wasn't surprised that the old men could no longer do much for themselves. "My back," Waltak muttered, "is not good." Jem simply stared at him, wondering why someone who barely looked alive needed to give a reason for why he was incapable of doing work. On top of that, Jem couldn't help but notice, when they went back inside and Waltak removed his mittens to light a lamp, that the thin hands were twisted and distorted by large, knobby joints.

As the old man's grating voice prattled on, Jem tried to pay attention in a half-hearted way, but by then his curious mind was dwelling on the mysterious non-appearance of old Avakab himself. But Waltak hadn't taken him into all of the rooms; they hadn't gone around to the far side of the yard. Jem supposed it was foolish, but he was actually eager to meet Avakab—to see the man everyone spoke of with such familiarity, even now that he was only a shadow of the past.

When it seemed Waltak was finally winding down, Jem started to open his mouth and ask where he was supposed to sleep, but the old man was ahead of him. "Now I'll show you where you will stay." With a gesture of his gnarled hand, Waltak returned to the door leading to the inner yard.

Jem sighed with relief. He'd seen enough of the dismal place now to feel confident that nothing else would be worse than he expected.

This time Waltak only leaned out the door and pointed— at the one room that jutted out into the empty circle, breaking the curved line of the interior walls. They hadn't gone near it when Waltak had taken him outside. As Jem stepped off the stoop and headed toward it, he slowed when he noticed what he hadn't seen before: there was a small door in the side of the wall facing them that had only a door flap—a sealskin blanket— covering the opening. He turned to scowl at Waltak, about to object.

The old man's wrinkled face had puckered up even more, and his lips worked nervously. "There is a body in there," he said. "You must take it out."

At first Jem thought he must have misheard. As Waltak continued, he knew he hadn't. "Take it far out. Not to the grounds—you don't have to go there. Just out, east, beyond the ridge, so no one will find it."

Jem had started back toward the old man. He stopped to stare incredulously at him, wide-eyed. The old fool was insane! "But-but—" he stammered. "Just leave it out there? In the open? What about . . . the wolves and . . ."

Waltak's expression hadn't changed, but he seemed exasperated. "It doesn't matter. It's that or burn it, and the fuel . . . There is no reason—it would be a waste. Just take it out. Far out."

Jem found his voice. "You can't do that! Who is it? No matter who they are, they have to be buried!"

"Don't argue with me, boy!" Now the wizened face reddened with anger. "He was hardly a man any more—he might as well have died years ago. There's no one who will know or care. Just do it!" He added, "You're not starting very well, are you, if you won't do the first thing I ask you to do? And don't use the sled—you're more than big enough to carry him—and clean out that room; take everything out there with him." The old man's eyes flickered over Jem's face before he turned away. "Though I don't think you have anything to fear." He disappeared inside, closing the weather-worn wooden door behind him.

Jem went slowly across the yard, hearing and feeling the crunch of the top layer of snow as it broke at each step, letting him sink to mid-calf. Reaching the slant-walled room, he pushed aside the door flap, having to stoop to get through the doorway. He wished Waltak had given him a lamp, for the interior was dim. He was afraid of what he would find, yet morbidly curious at the same time. Propping up the door flap with the stick that weighted its bottom edge, he stepped inside.

The room was very small. There was a fire pit in the middle of the floor, and a spot of light coming down from the smoke hole overhead. But there was no doorway connecting it to the room behind it; it was separate from the otherwise unbroken circle of sod rooms. There were a few skins on the floor, but most of it was bare. Against the back wall there was a sleeping platform.

The narrow earthen ledge was covered in skins. On top of the skins, partly covered by a woven red blanket, was the body.

Jem put one mitten over his mouth and nose and clenched his teeth, although there was hardly any odor in the cold dry air. He forced himself to approach. The short figure was face up, lying peacefully as if he'd died in his sleep, and when Jem looked down at the desiccated, slack-jawed face, he recognized it as belonging to a man who'd been at the Birthing House years ago.

Jem recalled him only vaguely—a fairly young man who'd been badly injured while hunting on the coast, falling and striking his head. He'd been brought to the midwives so they could care for him, in the hope he would recover over time. But the injury had left him a speechless idiot, capable of some simple tasks, entirely incapable of others. The children had alternately watched him with curiosity or repulsion, or ignored him altogether. When he'd disappeared, Jem hadn't thought to ask where he'd gone—the midwives cared for many, and people came and went.

So this was my predecessor, Jem thought wryly, relieved that the body itself was not as horrific as he'd imagined it might be. I get it now, he said to himself. This is where the unwanted people go—to help out a couple of old used-to-be's who are barely more than corpses themselves, and patch up a crazy old fort for no reason at all.

If it were true that he was no longer a child, as the other midwives kept telling Enkara, this—leaving the Birthing House to work at tasks usually done by adults—should have meant he was growing up. Why then did it feel more like sliding downward, as if he'd climbed into a passageway that smelled of ash and decay, only to find there was no floor beneath him?

After wrapping the blanket and the stiff furs around the body as well as he could—he had to tug them out from underneath the body and awkwardly maneuver the wood-like corpse—he lifted it off the narrow bed and carried it out of the room. When he reached the gate in the outer wall of the fort, he had some difficulty opening the latch while holding the body against his shoulder and trying very hard not to think about what he was carrying, what he was doing. Just move, just act, he told himself—don't think, don't feel.

Dutifully, Jem followed Waltak's orders. He trudged with his gruesome burden along one of the eastern trails, thankful that he saw no one on the way. Then he went out onto the open tundra, all the way out to where the East Ridge rose up and then dropped off, like a ripple in the expansive sea of white, so the land beyond it wasn't visible from the village. After climbing over the crest of the rise, he put the body down on the wind-sculpted firn, and gave in to an impulse to cover the face and tuck the coverings around the stiff figure. Then he headed back to the village, walking in his own tracks.

Clearly Waltak feared the mute had died of the Summer Fever, but Jem had seen enough of that disease in his childhood to conclude it was unlikely. In any case, it made no difference to him, as Waltak knew. Still, Jem had no intention of inhabiting the little space he'd inherited from the dead man. The floor was sunken less than half a meter below the outside ground, and the door was simply an opening, with no outer walls. Even with a wooden door, the room would hold little warmth. If he were supposed to be building snow domes, he could start now—and for his own comfort.

He picked a spot near the center of the courtyard, where the drifted snow was fairly level, and trampled down a circle. He had assisted in the building of snow-block shelters several times, when the rooms of the Birthing House were especially crowded, or when there was someone sick who needed relative isolation, quiet, and cleaner air—the air in most of the sod houses was usually tainted with oily smoke. The snow houses were often warmer as well, as drafts that came down the large smoke holes in the Birthing House wouldn't get into a well-constructed illu. Still, Jem had never tried to build one by himself, though he knew it was something the hunters and trappers did.

When he fetched the tools and began cutting blocks, his meager but adequate knowledge of the art came back to him, and he recalled how to shape the blocks with just enough angle that they fit snugly and grew higher in a slow spiral. The snow wasn't in ideal condition, being slightly icy, but the deeper layers, still soft but lightly packed, were suitable enough. Jem settled into the rhythm of his task with some enjoyment. The straightforward purpose, combined with its physical demands, made it absorbing and rewarding. Besides, despite the half-cocked ideas of that disgusting old man, he was actually doing something for himself—not for them. He hadn't even looked at the map in his pocket when he picked the location for his illu.

As Jem worked, the sense of accomplishment that grew within him made up in part for the disheartening elements of the day. He'd almost finished when old Waltak reappeared. He'd just lifted a block and was settling it carefully into place, and merely glanced across the courtyard at the figure. The light was beginning to fade, and he intended to complete his new home before it was dark.

He wasn't surprised to hear the nasal voice pronouncing, "You shouldn't have put it there—it's too far from the wall." It was some consolation that Waltak's tone didn't sound angry; it was, perhaps, more apathetically critical.

Jem shrugged. "The snow isn't very good. It looked like a good place—and I'm not sleeping in there." He nodded toward the little room where the body had been.

"Suit yourself," Waltak called. "Worried about the Fever, are you?" the old man added, both taunting and condescending, and Jem saw him smirk.

"He didn't have the Fever," Jem said, bending down for another block.

"How do you know?" the old man snapped suspiciously.

The boy shrugged again, rolling his eyes. "I don't—but I've seen it a lot. He wouldn't have looked like that. Besides, nobody's had it in a long time." Patting his next snow block into place, and checking the alignment of the curving wall, Jem paused, then spoke more loudly, anger rising into his retort. "Of course I'm not worried about it." Looking in the direction of the tiny room again, he added, "Maybe he froze to death," and didn't try to hide the sour smile that spread across his face.

Waltak didn't miss the implication, and he snorted. "Well, hurry up, boy. If you don't get in here and help me with the fire, you can sleep in your fine new illu with an empty stomach. The old women said you eat too much as it is."

Jem was spared from having to respond because he'd ducked down inside the dome to lift the last few blocks into the opening he'd been standing in. One person making an illu alone had to build themselves into the structure—he would finish by digging out under the wall and constructing the entryway.

If Jem didn't eat much better at the fort than he had at the Birthing House, his situation was certainly no worse. He discovered that being allowed to fill his own bowl from the pot of stew meant he could take more than he would have been allotted at his old home, as long as he didn't get too carried away. The pantry in the fort was twice the size of any of the other rooms, and Jem was very surprised to see the quantity of food stored there. At first he entertained thoughts of sneaking in and taking extra food, but it was immediately clear that Waltak knew exactly what was in the pantry—he was very specific in his instructions when he sent Jem to fetch something, and when they were both in the pantry, Jem saw him counting under his breath as he looked over the racks and shelves.

After several days at the fort, Jem had begun to feel settled, in a dull but not unpleasant way. There was an odd security in the walls and dark rooms of the strange, old place, and he was already beginning to feel a sort of nonchalant tolerance mingled with his dislike for Waltak. After hearing the old man's whining voice so many times, every screeched order and deadpan comment had begun to sound familiar. Jem had spent two fairly comfortable nights in his cozy new illu, although the oil lamp Waltak had let him have was quite small and gave off only a little light and warmth. He'd collected several old reindeer skins and one seal skin; one skin he'd salvaged from the floor of his predecessor's room because it looked too new to discard—he didn't tell Waltak—and the rest Waltak had grudgingly given him.

When the wolves sang at night, the sound was louder than Jem had ever heard it before—probably because the Birthing House was in the village's center, while the fort was near the eastern edge of the settlement. He was glad they were closer, he and his fellow unwanted spirits. Though he'd always heard a deep sadness in their voices, it was soothing to be swept up in the eerie magic of the music that filled the darkness around him.

On the morning of the third day, Jem was in the courtyard patching one of the sod walls when Waltak popped his head out the door and called to him. Jem had been musing over his new theory—that Avakab was actually dead, and perhaps had been for some time. And Waltak would be keeping up the pretense that he still lived in order to retain some of the grudging respect that his old friend had warranted.

Jem grunted in answer to the old man's call and got to his feet slowly. He wiped his palms on his thighs of his trousers, leaving streaks of dark mud on the pale tan reindeer skin, then walked across the yard to the leaning door, where he ducked under the lintel and stepped down into the dark interior.

"Come in the kitchen," Waltak directed, going out the other end of the room as he spoke. There was one room between this one and the larger space where they did the cooking, which had a deep floor and wide platforms around the fire pit. The kitchen was where they spent most of their time when Jem was inside the fort with Waltak, cutting up dried fish and potatoes for the stew, and drying their clothing—mostly

Jem's, since he was the only one working outside.

Jem dipped his head to go through the doorway—as he had to do with all the doors. Orange light flickered over the room, and the thick odors of meat and fish mingled with the oil smoke from the two large lamps. Immediately Jem knew that the figure seated on the platform behind the fire, with his head bent over his lap, was not Waltak.

With a sharpness of movement that betrayed keen senses and instinctive wariness, the old man looked up. Through the shifting light and the haze of the smoky air, his piercing clear eyes met Jem's, and it was as if he'd reached across the room and struck him a physical blow. "Ah, there you are," he said. The voice, although not loud, was strong and unwavering.

Jem felt a shiver run through him. He opened his mouth, but was unable to speak.

"Come closer," Avakab ordered. Jem obeyed, coming around the fire pit until he stood only a couple of meters from the seated figure. The man's features were not unlike those of Goplak, the poultry keeper, though perhaps he was even older, and his thin hair was as white as new snow. But beyond that he was no ordinary old man. His eyes held Jem with an incredible force, and a kind of accusation; the boy felt as if that gaze could split him open and see inside of him.

It seemed only fitting when Jem noticed, as a glint of firelight glanced off the blade, that one of the thin hands held a dagger. The other held a piece of wood the old rebel had been carving, but both hands were strong and supple—unlike Waltak's—and it was all too easy to imagine them holding the knife for another purpose.

The old man made a soft sound in his throat, though whether it meant disgust or merely disapproval, or even humor, Jem wasn't certain. The intense eyes narrowed, and Avakab said, "How old are you, Sanndai?"

Jem struggled to swallow and managed to say, "Fifteen."

"Hmm," the man said, this time clearly with wry

amusement. He smiled strangely. "Ah, yes—I suppose you wouldn't look quite so tall if I were standing in front of you. No doubt you'll grow taller still. But I remember well . . . your people. I've seen many of them. And for some who saw me, I was the last thing they ever saw." The menacing smile had gone, but there was still dark humor in his expression.

So much for my theory, Jem thought. He forced himself to take a deep breath, embarrassed by his reaction.

"I hear you've been seen around the Sanndai station." The eyes shifted from Jem as the hands resumed their work, the knife flashing as strips of wood peeled away under its sharp edge.

Jem nodded, feeling his heart quicken again. This man is nothing any more, he told himself. He's the one the old women sneer at. But now he understood why there was that uneasiness, that presence of a respect born out of fear, that filled a room whenever Avakab's name was spoken. Here was someone whose true power was his own will and, in spite of everything, he would never lose it.

When Avakab lifted his eyes from the carving, again Jem felt his gaze like a knife blade pressed against his flesh. "I got them out of there—did you know that, boy?"

Jem shook his head.

The old man shifted and recrossed his legs, settling himself like one of the midwives beginning a story on a winter night. "It was the height of the Dark Moon. We had been watching them come and go in their sinister white ships like seabirds blown astray across the tundra, scurrying in and out of the station and grimacing at the cold in their flimsy clothing. They are fools who try to deal with Nature by tricking her and changing her, instead of working with her, learning her secrets. They think they can change worlds, make them better. Instead they only destroy them—and destroy themselves as well.

"Because they think only of controlling and changing, they aren't looking to see and understand. They have little awareness of what is outside of themselves, and that makes them easy to fool. I saw this, and knew I could use it. Rastok and I, we planned it, though some of the others argued. I knew we had to move fast, and they were at their most vulnerable in that moon, for they feared the weather and the land itself."

Jem stood motionless beside the fire, his eyes watering from the smoke, mesmerized by the rhythmic power of the voice.

"One night we crept out to the station—from this fort, which we'd just finished building. There were eight of us, all dressed in white fur. We brought four rifles and several bows. Everyone had at least one knife, and had filled his pockets with stones or balls of ice." He glanced up at Jem again, with a smile. "Those were all the weapons we had. Simple, primitive weapons, your people would say. Not like their precious light guns and knives with fire in them. Oh, they scoffed at our weapons . . . And they died when we used them, just the same.

"It is not the weapon, but the hands wielding it that matter. They don't understand that, because they don't understand the natural world—only devices, only their wicked toys of power. So on that night we used the drifts that the land and the wind had built—the land we knew, the wind we knew, as well as we knew each other. We worked with them to build shelters, so we could wait out the night. We knew the Sanndai would see nothing, would notice nothing, even if they came outside to their flying ships to bring supplies into the station, or to check on the storm in their own blind way.

"In the morning we approached the station, and Rastok and I crouched outside the doorway, with the others flanked around the sides of the dome. We waited and waited. When the door opened, I whistled—that was the signal—and I knocked down the Sanndai in the doorway, cut his throat with my knife, and stepped on his face as I entered. Rastok was right behind me and got another—knife in the heart—and the big bastard died where he fell. We stood on his body and aimed our rifles at the rest of the Sanndai, and told them they must surrender or die. The rest of our men came in behind us, but none of them even had to draw a bow. The cowards dropped to the floor and groveled in front of us, begging us not to shoot them."

He chuckled and looked Jem full in the face, causing the boy to wince. "Not one of us got so much as a scratch. It turned out they were all just sitting down to their morning meal, and they had no weapons on them. I learned once that they only carry the sacred light guns when they are going into a battle, and it is against their laws for men who are not soldiers or great leaders to possess one. So the power of their devices is useless to most of them. It's mind-boggling, is it not, that they are so proud to have created such things, and yet they withhold them from most of their own people?"

Avakab studied Jem's face for a silent moment. Jem was managing to breathe more slowly. The fact that the story was engrossing helped to calm him, taking him out of himself. The thought had formed in the back of his mind—in a queer, detached sort of way—that now he knew what had made the brown stain on the floor of the station.

"We forced them to get up. To parlay with us and agree to leave. We scribbled out a treaty, and made them sign it." The old man chuckled dryly. "I was young enough to hope they might respect it, although I did have serious doubts." He paused and sat back, still watching Jem closely. "They didn't, of course. We should have killed them all, but perhaps that would have changed nothing. They sent more—with light guns and other weapons—two days later. They searched the village, patrolling up and down every street in the flying ships, dragging people out of every dwelling they could find, torturing those who wouldn't answer their questions with the answers they wanted to hear.

"Rastok's wife warned us in time. We left the fort and fled to the coast, taking his son and two of the other men who'd been with us when we attacked the station—we couldn't get to the others in time. We found out later that they were all caught and executed—at least one was tortured for three days, because they were trying to get him to tell where I was. But he was a good man, an honorable man—something they know little about. He told the black-eyed bastards nothing.

"One of the men who came with Rastok and me died when we were on the ice going up the coast to our camp. The other," he paused to give Jem a whimsical smile, "was Waltak. Rastok and I quarreled—for the first and last time—because he didn't want to take Waltak with us. Waltak had been feeling poorly, and Rastok was afraid he'd slow us down. I believe he was jealous as well, and wanted me to lose him. No matter—I brought him in spite of everything Rastok said. I tied his skis together and pulled him most of the way. It was risky, yes, but I did it anyway. Perhaps you've heard people say that I'm heartless and brutal and care for no one. I know there are those who see me that way. But they're wrong, of course. No one is that simple. In truth I am a deeply loyal man, and I am not incapable of love. That is my little story in my defense."

Avakab began whittling the wood again, and fell back into the rhythm of his storytelling voice. "When we came back to the village—and Waltak proved his mettle when I sent him in ahead of us to find out what had happened and where the Sanndai were—we learned that they'd abandoned the station and closed all of Kruvak, so we were not to leave, and their people were not to enter. A mixed blessing, one might call that.

"But the Sanndai had killed Rastok's wife, Riisa. Her sister told us that the Sanndai had claimed it was an accident, and that she 'got in the way' when they were trying to capture a man they were pursuing, but we all knew they had deliberately killed women and children before. I think someone became foolish with fear and told the Sanndai her husband was one of the rebels, and they killed her out of spite—or because she also would not tell them where we were.

"The night after we returned to the village and Rastok

learned she was gone, he took his clothes off and walked out to the East Ridge. The wolves found him before his son did. I didn't go to see what remained of his body—I am a warrior, and proud of it, but I had seen enough. Rastok was the one who stood with me throughout the rebellion, the only man I ever called my equal, who shared my vision of freedom and my abhorrence of inaction. In the end, I don't know if what he did showed weakness or a greater strength than my own."

Jem had forgotten where he was, who he was. He was both terrified and fascinated by this old man, but found himself unable not to like him. He was glimpsing another world, as he had while wandering in the station and trying to imagine the world of the Sanndai.

Avakab had paused and was watching Jem again, while the boy bit his lip and tried to keep the burning gaze from rattling his composure. The old man raised the hand that held the knife and said with a smile, "This very knife—I put it through the back of a Sanndai's neck once. From ten meters away. They never figured out who did it, but it caused quite a stir, believe me. I was only a little older than you." He raised his eyebrows and rocked back, looking up at Jem with a ghostly smile.

"If I'd been any older and wiser, I would never have risked it. Odd, the things one can do when one doesn't know enough to know they can't be done. I was on skis, you see, and I figured that if I missed I would lose my knife, but I could get away and not be caught. He was a Contact officer, who was meeting with us over some issue regarding the mines, and he and one other had come and talked to some of the elders, and he was very rude—especially to my father. I said I was heading out to help with the herd, but I skied around the back of the drying shed. I knew that man was leaving but the other one was staying, so he would come out alone. When he walked out of the house, I came out from behind the shed and threw my knife at his back.

"I suppose I was lucky, but I was also good—and a man

doesn't need fancy weapons if he knows how to use simple ones. He only made a little sound, a sort of gargle as if he'd started to yell and could not, and then fell face down, his hand trying to reach the back of his neck. I sped over to him and pulled my knife out and was gone long before anyone discovered him." He chuckled. "I didn't even admit to my father that I was the one who'd done it until several years later."

Jem swallowed and fidgeted, and Avakab fingered the edge of the knife, the enigmatic smile still lingering on his lips.

"Rastok used to call me 'Avak the savik'; savik is one of the old words for knife. He thought it suited me, and found it amusing that it rhymed." The old man looked up at Jem and said, "Are you afraid of me, boy?"

"I . . . don't know," Jem said awkwardly.

"You just behave yourself, and do what Waltak tells you, and no one will harm you here."

Jem swallowed again and nodded. "All right," he managed to say.

Avakab went on. "This was Walt's idea—not mine. But he's right, you are strong, and as he says, if we don't make use of you, you'll simply go to waste. A shame—after all the trouble Enkara's had over you. She shouldn't have saved you, of course, but a wise man does not argue with a woman over a child. Especially when that woman has lost everything. As you perhaps know, they had lost three children, and she was with child again when Nihkul died, and then she lost that one to the Fever—only moons before you came. Who could blame her for wanting a child who wouldn't die?

"And she was always a brave and loyal woman; many a fellow envied Nihkul. If I'd wanted to marry, I would have picked her myself, though I doubt she would have had me, even after Nihkul was gone. I could impress most of the girls— though I only did it to make friends or rivals jealous—but I don't think I ever impressed Enkara."

It was strange to hear him talk about Enkara. Jem had never tried to imagine what she'd been like before she was an old woman living in the Birthing House. And he'd certainly never imagined that Avakab had known her well. Strangest of all, she'd never really told Jem about her children. Yes, he knew she'd had children, that they were gone, and that one had died not long before he was born. But he hadn't known how many there were, or their names or anything else about them, because she never spoke of them. Neither had he heard the name of the man she'd been married to—the man she had loved.

"No, I couldn't criticize her, and those who tried to persuade her not to keep you were wasting their breath. Likewise, I will never argue with Waltak when he's got an idea in his head." He smiled again. "He finally developed a mind of his own, and considering how long it took him, well . . ." He laughed, and it wasn't an unpleasant sound. "I usually let him do as he will. He takes care of most everything, as you've seen by now. And you—well, I don't think you're dangerous." Tilting his head, he looked up at Jem, studying him with what appeared to be both disdain and amusement.

Jem shook his head. "I don't know anything about . . . the kinds of things you were talking about. I've never even been in a fight."

"Well, that is wise of you—considering what the inevitable result would be, regardless of whether you instigated it."

"I know," Jem said, his usually defiant attitude when dealing with adults slowly beginning to resurface.

"Good," the old man said. "Not that I trust you," he added, again splitting Jem wide open with his eyes. "You are what you are."

Jem shrugged. "I think you know a lot more about them than I do . . . Sanndai, I mean."

"Oh, yes," Avakab raised his eyebrows and rocked back, seeming to look down at Jem even though he was seated below him. "Much, much more. There's no question of that, boy. Though I wish I could forget all that I know about them, I'm afraid it's burned into my brain." He added, "But no matter how much more I know of them than you do, you *are* one. And I'm very thankful that I am not."

When Jem winced at these words, it had nothing to do with the old rebel's unnerving presence; it was because it always came back to that—his shame at being what he was.

But he thought of the stain on the floor of the station, and found himself thinking: so you've done terrible things, too, old man. Even if they started the whole mess and they'd done worse things, you still ambushed and attacked unarmed people. So doesn't that make you like them?

For as long as Jem could remember, Enkara had told him to ignore the insults and taunting, rather than returning the same treatment he received—because if he did, he became no better than his tormentors. If he didn't play their game, they couldn't touch him. It was a good theory, but he'd learned it was very hard to put into practice. Still, he thought about it now. Avakab could call the Sanndai murderous black-eyed bastards, but he'd put himself on their level and become a cold-blooded murderer as well. So who was he to imply that Jem was innately evil, when he'd never done anything worse than boyish pranks and theft? And yet Jem couldn't simply ignore the old rebel's treatment of him, and believe he was a better person. He couldn't despise Avakab the way he could despise Waltak. This man still commanded his respect, and probably always would.

But he was relieved when Avakab dismissed him. In spite of how the old man had affected him, Jem went out into the cold feeling light and refreshed, and very grateful to be alone. There were times when his own company was simply comforting—like a pair of warm mittens made just for his hands, when there were no others that would fit him in all the world.

V

THE SUBTLE CHANGE in the icy air signaled the passage of night and nudged Jem into awareness. Morning was beginning to fill his senses when he heard Waltak's nasal voice. "Boy! Get up! Now! Come to the pantry."

Jem shivered out from under the shabby reindeer hides and stuffed dry liner into his well-worn boots. He squirmed into his parka and pulled on the boots, then crawled out the short tunnel that was his doorway. There was no sign of the old man.

He took the narrow passageway that ran inside the stone wall and bypassed most of the rooms. When he reached the pantry, he saw that the wide door leading to the outside of the fort was open. White light reached into the depths of the large, fish-scented room.

Standing in the doorway, at the top of the earthen slope leading down to the floor of the pantry, were three men. They were all wearing light-colored parkas that must have been fairly new—they were unsoiled and unweathered—and the tallest one wore a square-topped white fur hat. Because the light was so bright behind them and Jem was standing in the dark, it was hard to see their faces.

Waltak stood some distance below them, and he looked up and saw Jem. "It's about time, you oversized geatki. Can't get up in the morning, eh? Get over here and help bring this food in." He added, muttering, "'Lazy as a Sanndai' they say—it must be true."

Jem paused, heedless of Waltak's insults. Squinting up at the men, he could see now that there was a sledge outside the door, with bundles on it. He walked slowly across the pantry, sullen and defiant, and didn't acknowledge Waltak. But now he was facing the newcomers, and he could see the taller one in the middle clearly.

The man narrowed his eyes and a muscle twitched on the side of his jaw. "Oh," he said, in the coldest voice Jem had ever heard. "Don't tell me. This would be the brat one of the old bags at the baby house was raising . . . Wouldn't it?"

Waltak grunted, and Jem realized he wasn't just being his usual unpleasant self, but was defensive and on edge. It was obvious that Waltak didn't like this man at all.

"Yes, Rulskar," the old man intoned carefully, as if speaking to a child he expected to explode into a tantrum. "But you needn't call Enkara an 'old bag.' I don't like her myself, but she's a clever woman, and having seen her when I went for this boy, I don't believe she's grown feeble."

Rulskar chuckled, and it was a strange, manic sound, with no humor—so unlike Avakab's laugh, which had warmth despite the bitterness. "She's not an old bag to you, Waltak, because *you* are an old bag."

The two men who flanked him laughed as if on cue. It was artificial sounding laughter, and Jem saw one of them glance at the other; they seemed uneasy.

Jem could tell by Waltak's posture and by the way his usually expressionless face had tightened that he was very angry. "You're an insolent pup, Rulskar. You should be careful, or the ice under your feet may crack."

Rulskar laughed. "What? Is that a threat or something, old man? I'm not afraid of you. I'm not afraid of Avakab, either. And speaking of the old jalla, where is he? I haven't seen him in ages. I'd like to see him."

Jalla—that meant fox, Jem knew. An appropriate enough term for Avakab.

"He doesn't like you, Rulskar," Waltak said with his jaw clenched, which exaggerated the nasal quality of his voice even more. "I don't know how many times I have to tell you. And as you so often point out, he and I are getting on. We'd like a little peace and quiet. Why would he want to listen to your nonsense?"

Rulskar gave a short snarl, as if the old man had touched a sore spot. "Fine. Have it your way. And you can say Avakab doesn't like me, but I happen to know what my grandfather really thought of you, because he told my father, and my father told me. Did you know that? So I know the truth. My grandfather didn't like you because you were a whimpering coward, and you were always sick. If Avakab hadn't been foolishly attached to you, they would have left you behind from the first. Left you behind and left you to die, stinking like the rotting old fish you are. And I know that most of them—my grandfather included—would have thought it good riddance. You can't deny that, because it's true."

"You know nothing about me, and it beats me how you can keep going on about your grandfather when he was dead before you were born!" Waltak spat. He added sharply, "And from what I've heard about you, you shouldn't be speaking of cowardice."

"Blah, blah, blah, old man," Rulskar scoffed. "You know, my mother's father was a great man, too. Very strong, very smart. Both of my grandfathers were brave, intelligent, resourceful men—the best sort of men. That's the blood in my veins. So what if I never met him? You—your entire family was weak; that's why they all died! You just got left out by sheer meaningless luck. I look at you, and I see nothing. Nothing at all. So I really don't care what you think of me. I don't care at all what you think."

"Well, good for you!" Waltak retorted, seeming to have regained some of his composure. Then the shrill voice rose even louder. "Now let this oversized boy help you, the sooner you may get out of my sight!"

Rulskar turned his gaze to Jem, and Jem shuddered. There was something odd about this man's eyes that he couldn't identify—a combination of shiftiness, a strange glimmer, and a manic intensity. He scowled at Jem, pushing his lower lip forward, and then said, "All right, ugly—we'll let you do it. Why should we have to work when we have such a big strong servant at our disposal?" His cronies laughed at this—the same mechanical laugh.

Jem shouldered past them and began lifting bundles off the shed and bringing them down into the pantry. Squinting in the light when he stepped outside, he blinked in the darkness when he came back in and deposited the bundles at Waltak's feet.

Rulskar stood with his arms folded on his chest, and watched Jem with a look of smug superiority. As Jem took the last bundle off the sled, ducked through the doorway, and started down the passage, he heard the cold voice say, "Very useful, Waltak. When you old bags are done with him, let me have him."

Waltak coughed disdainfully. "What would you do with him?

"I'll make a bag . . . out of his scalp."

The other men laughed again.

"If I hadn't made a mistake," Rulskar added, "he wouldn't have lived to grow all that ugly black hair. So I've a right to it." More tense laughter.

Waltak spluttered, "I don't know what you're talking about, you impudent tibiak! If it weren't for the memory of your grandfather, I'd have nothing to do with you." A tibiak was a weasel—but Jem couldn't say that comparison was as fitting as calling Avakab a fox; though they were wily, ruthless hunters, surely no weasel was ever as vicious and full of hatred as this man.

"I told you, wimpy Walty—Grandfather didn't like you."

Waltak folded his arms, his wizened face pinched even tighter. "You won't impress anyone by acting like an ill-mannered child! And now, since *my* helper has finished *your* job, you are dismissed. Get out."

"Hah, hah—I'm just terrified of you, old man. Can't you hear my teeth chattering?"

The three men laughed and laughed, reminding Jem very much of ill-mannered boys. Then Rulskar sauntered over to where Jem stood. Stopping directly in front of him, he reached out and gave Jem a hard shove.

"As for you, big and dirty, I suppose I'll let the old men keep you awhile. Let them turn the tables—make you be their slave instead. But I've got a job to finish, and I'll do it. You can count on me. The world won't have to endure your ugliness much longer." He chuckled, his mad eyes glittering, and turned on his heel.

The two men that flanked him followed, with a precision that would have been comical under different circumstances.

Jem stood rooted, his whole body tight with anger and uncanny fear. He could see the back of the sledge from where he was; it started into motion as Rulskar gave a shout to the reindeer. Then the large sledge vanished from sight, bearing all three men—Rulskar driving, the other two standing on the runners behind him.

Hearing Waltak make a muttered growl released Jem. He gulped and turned around.

"A most unpleasant fellow, that Rulskar," the old man grumbled, bending over the bundles at his feet.

Jem nodded. "His eyes are strange," he heard himself say, feeling dazed. "He doesn't look like he's . . . well, sane."

Waltak had straightened up, and for the first time he looked directly at Jem's face, meeting the boy's eyes. "I think you're right. I'm not sure he is." Just briefly they were equals, fellow human beings, and it was strangely comforting to Jem. The moment lingered long enough that when Waltak spoke again it was in a more conversational tone than he normally used. "Here, pick this up and I'll show you where we'll hang it."

From then on the subject of Rulskar was the one thing Waltak and Jem agreed on. But for Jem, the gratification of that understanding was sadly overshadowed by the chilling feeling Rulskar had given him. He couldn't forget the disturbing way the man had looked at him, the thinly disguised rage he'd sensed when the hand had shoved him. A vivid image had appeared in his mind: an image of Rulskar knocking him down and stabbing him with a knife. It was followed by a vision of the man in the white hat holding a long rifle, pointed straight at him.

Some instinct warned Jem that this man could easily do it—just as easily as another man might butcher a reindeer, twist the neck of a kiruna hen, or shoot a prowling wolf. And it was one thing to know that many people wouldn't mind having an excuse to end his life when that idea was only an abstraction. This was something different; this had been real. Much too real.

When Rulskar again came to the fort with food and supplies the following moon, Jem was determined to ignore the man, feigning cold disinterest as he yanked the bundles off the sledge. He knew if he actually looked at Rulskar—saw his face and his strange, mad eyes—he would be afraid. So he would pretend Rulskar wasn't there, and simply wouldn't look.

Trudging back to the sled for the second load, Jem was brought back to the moment by the sight of a young dog scratching in the snow between the runners. He hadn't noticed the dog when he first approached the sledge, intent on shutting out everything but his task. It was a half-grown pup with a white coat and a few orange markings. It looked up at Jem, cocking its head curiously, and the boy smiled. The way the pattern of orange fur capped its head and pointed ears suggested half a mask and a crooked hood, and gave the puppy an amusing quizzical expression.

Jem turned away and took his load down into the pantry. As he stepped back into the light from the open door, he saw that the pup had followed him. He paused as it sniffed his boot.

"Hello, puppy," Jem said softly. As he bent over and reached his hand out, the curl of the dog's tail began to tilt from side to side, and a red tongue flicked out of the small white muzzle as the puppy sniffed—and then licked—his hand.

In that brief moment Jem had forgotten himself, and he flinched as if he'd been struck when Rulskar's icy voice came down on him.

"Don't touch my dog!"

The puppy jumped, startled, and looked toward the sled, as Jem stood up quickly. "I didn't," he said indignantly, keeping his eyes on the dog to avoid looking at the dog's master, who had stepped around the sledge and was standing next to it imposingly.

"You'd better not!" Rulskar snarled. "You've got a place here, ugly—and you're place is the bottom. The absolute bottom rung of everything. Everybody in the whole village is above you—and that includes every dog."

One of his companions laughed loudly. "If he touches a dog, he might dirty it."

Rulskar chuckled nastily. "That's right—every shit-eating dog in the world is cleaner than a filthy Sanndai." Then he called to the dog, and his tone of voice, though firm, changed markedly. "Trika! Come, Trika."

The puppy scurried back up the passage to join him, and Rulskar looked down and spoke in a soft voice touched with genuine warmth. "Good girl, Trika." He nodded at the man standing nearest him and said, "She's going to be really good. Did you see her trying to move those cows yesterday? This young, and she's already got it—she's got the drive. You have to give them room and plenty of time at this stage. Just be patient. That's the way to get a superior worker in the end."

The other men nodded, and they all began to chat easily about dogs.

Jem looked up, surprised to hear Rulskar speak in such a different manner. Blinking at the tall man, Jem saw him transformed into a completely different person. The rage had melted away, leaving a man who seemed gentle and reasonable, even though there was still something unnerving about his eyes. And Rulskar's companions seemed to have changed, too—perhaps because they were relaxed, and the tension in their manner was gone as well.

Allowing himself only a moment to stare curiously at this startling revelation, Jem took the opportunity to take the last of the goods off the sledge and hurry back down into the pantry. When Rulskar was gone, Jem was left with an odd feeling of puzzlement. It seemed absolutely incongruous that someone who could be so hateful and irrational could turn around and, moments later, seem not only perfectly sensible, but even warm and charismatic. Judging from Waltak's relationship with him, however, it wasn't just Sanndai who set Rulskar off and brought out the demon in him.

Jem never tried again to speak to the little orange and white dog. He only watched her, with a touch of wistfulness, from a distance. And it wasn't long before it was clear that she was completely focused on Rulskar and paid little attention to anyone else. Whenever Rulskar appeared, Trika wouldn't be far behind.

But learning that the man could be pleasant to his dog— and to his friends, when he chose to—did nothing to ease Jem's dread of Rulskar; nothing happened to change his conviction that the man with the mad eyes wanted to kill him. Most of Rulskar's taunts toward Jem were merely insults—sometimes elaborate and absurd, as he could take a long time to embellish a comparison of Jem to excrement or a pile of entrails, making his companions laugh uneasily. But after the ridiculing, Rulskar would drop a barely disguised threat that Jem couldn't miss: "If he's around much longer," or "But we can clean up this mess."

By then Jem had learned the names of the men who always followed Rulskar—Fenak and Gumak. Gloomy Fenak almost never smiled, even when he laughed, and often looked as if he wished he were someplace else. Gumak smiled too readily—a fierce, hungry smile.

Jem heard the midwives gossiping about Gumak during one of his visits to Enkara; the story was that Gumak's wife had put him out of the house because he'd struck her.

"Gumak!" Trevga snorted. "His name should be 'kumak' instead."

The women laughed together. Even Enkara looked amused when she said that it was curious that the man's name was so similar to that word—a word that meant 'louse' in one of the old languages.

Jem almost smiled himself when another woman wondered aloud why Gumak and Fenak followed Rulskar around like dogs, and Trevga said that Trika was surely the smartest of the tall man's three devoted companions. "A louse and a mouse—that's what those two are. You'd think they had no minds of their own, men like that."

Though it briefly made him feel better, knowing that the old women scoffed at Rulskar's friends couldn't help Jem either. For he'd also learned from Enkara that Rulskar, who owned many reindeer that he'd inherited from his well-liked father, was still a respected man in the village, even if some muttered about him for reasons other than the company he kept. What Jem had sensed about him at their first meeting— that the man had the potential to be brutally violent—was hardly a secret.

Perhaps what infuriated Jem most was that he was hiding away from the world in the dull emptiness of the old fort, yet he wasn't safe there either. The one person who was surely the most inclined to harm him knew exactly where he was. It was only a small consolation when, several moons after Jem's arrival, Waltak produced a large ring of tarnished brass keys, and took Jem on another tour of the strange fort to show him how to lock and unlock the doors.

Of course the entrances in the outer stone wall had locks, but so did most of the doors between the sod rooms and the narrow passageway that encircled the fort, and some of the smaller ones connecting adjoining rooms. Waltak explained that, except for the entrances to a few of the rooms they never used, the doors hadn't been locked for some time. He then added that perhaps it would be best if they began to do so again. Jem only guessed that this had something to do with Rulskar and his cronies; he didn't ask.

Since his chores meant he moved around the fort a great deal more than the old men did, Jem solemnly accepted the responsibility of carrying the keys. From that day on he wore them attached to his belt. Although he knew it had little meaning, it gave Jem a small sense of importance to be the bearer of the keys—and he allowed himself to indulge in the feeling.

But he probably pushed a little too far when, shortly after Waltak gave him the keys, he asked the old man if he might have a good sharp knife for his own use. His own was a very small, very old blade Enkara had given him, which never seemed to hold an edge. Waltak had specifically prohibited Jem from taking the large knife from the kitchen box—a superior blade that made easy work of slicing potatoes and tough salted meat—telling him that if he caught him using it for any purpose other than cutting up food he would throw him out of the fort.

Jem wasn't quite sure how seriously to take Waltak's threats, but the thought that the simpering old man could probably get his companion to back him up was deterrent enough. So Jem gave up when Waltak snarled at him that there was no reason he couldn't make do with the knife he had, and didn't bring up the fact that it would be a lot easier to cut leather for mending if he had a better knife.

He went sulkily back to his work. But when he was alone he made himself laugh by imagining that someday he would have the sharpest, most amazing knife anyone had ever seen, and then he would sneak up on Waltak while he was asleep and shave off all of the nasty old man's hair without waking him, for the blade would be so flawless it could slice off each hair at the root without the old fool feeling a thing.

Yet it wasn't so funny the next time Rulskar cornered Jem and shoved him against the side of the pantry door, saying he would string him up by his heels and hang him next to the bundles of seal meat if it weren't that his Sanndai stench would cause all the food to spoil. Because the only thing Jem could think of when he stared into the icy blue fire of the madman's eyes was how badly he wanted that perfectly sharp knife; he could almost feel it in his hands.

## VI

DAY AFTER DAY, moon after moon, the pattern of life at the old rebels' fort followed a quiet and solitary routine. The only breaks in that routine were Jem's forays into the world outside—his regular visits to the abandoned station, and his occasional visits to Enkara. He made longer visits, spending most of the day with her, during the Spring and Autumn Festivals, and when it was the Singing Time of the Dark Moon, he crept in after everyone else was settled and sat in a shadowed corner, beyond the reach of the firelight, to hear Enkara perform some of the songs and tales.

Enkara changed very little, and the changes came slowly. Only after several years had passed did Jem see that she had a few more wrinkles, her eyes were less clear, and she seemed smaller. But a smile always lit her face when she welcomed him warmly, clasping his large dark hands with her small pale ones. Then they would sit and talk, mostly about little things that happened in their daily lives, occasionally about gossip in the village.

One day when he was particularly frustrated with Waltak, Jem snuck out of the fort and ran all the way to the Birthing House without stopping, using the exertion to vent his anger. He'd been trying to replace some fallen stones in the fort's outer wall, but his fingers were sore and he was sick of struggling at the task; it wasn't as if anyone had ever taught him how to build a stone wall.

When Waltak had shuffled out and asked him why it was taking him so long, Jem bristled and said he didn't know why he should bother, since the stones would only fall out again.

Waltak spat out, "Just do as you're told, ropmi!"

Jem glowered back at him. "What does that mean?" He guessed that Waltak liked to use the old words Jem didn't always know because it made him feel superior—and also because he knew it irritated Jem.

"As if I would tell you!" the old man sniffed indignantly, and tottered away.

It was late spring and there were patches of bare earth in the streets, and the icy snow was streaked with mud. In his flight to the Birthing House, Jem slipped several times and splashed mud on his trousers, but he kept running until he reached the familiar building. His chest heaving, he paused to scrape his boots in the crusty drift against the north wall, thinking it was curious that he already felt much better, as if the distance he'd put between them had already diminished the crabby old man and the recalcitrant stones so much that they could no longer trouble him.

When he was settled near Enkara's knee on the soft skins spread beside the little orange fire—and had pulled out his loop of string and started practicing a new string figure Enkara had shown him on his last visit—Jem asked her what the old man's word meant.

Enkara didn't look up from her weaving. She was making a red and white belt with a design that looked like antlers—or were they branches? A girl named Sofia, whom Enkara was teaching, sat at her other side, frowning over her own efforts, and the old woman paused to give her a soft reminder and a word of encouragement.

Then Enkara said slowly, "I am not sure that keeping the words of the old tongues alive is a reason to use unpleasant ones, but I suppose it can't be helped."

"So what does it mean?" Jem repeated.

"In the language of the boazu people—the people who followed the reindeer herds on the Motherworld—'ropmi' means 'ugly'.

Jem laughed. "Well, that's no surprise."

Sofia glanced up at him curiously. She was the niece of the midwife, Karya, a solemn but kind woman who'd always been a dear friend of Enkara's. The girl was near Jem's age; she'd been one of the children he'd played with before they'd all excluded him. Now she was respectful towards Jem, and sometimes she was almost friendly, perhaps because she was also close to Enkara. But earlier that moon he'd seen her walking with another young man their age, and she'd looked right through Jem as they'd passed, as if she hadn't even seen him.

"Who called you that?" she asked.

"Waltak," he said, untangling his failed attempt at the string figure.

As Sofia's eyes dropped back to her weaving, she giggled. "That old man? He has a lot of nerve—calling anyone that."

Jem laughed again.

But Enkara's busy hands grew still, and she said in her soft, strong voice, "Even if he is unkind himself, it does not make it less unkind to do as he does."

For a precious second Jem and Sofia's eyes met, acknowledging their shared chastening. Enkara was right of course. She was always right.

"I know," Jem murmured. Remembering that Enkara herself had shown her amusement when the women had all laughed about Gumak's name being similar to the word meaning 'louse', he added defensively, "But it's still kind of funny."

Perhaps to cover her embarrassment, the girl watched Jem wind the loop of string around his hands and restart the figure, and used the opportunity to change the subject.

"Enkara, it was the other people—the ones who made illus and fished through the ice—who first made the string figures, wasn't it?"

"That's right." Enkara laughed softly. "When my grandmother talked about them she always used to say 'boazu people' and 'natik people'. Reindeer people and seal people. She said she could see them in her mind that way—imagine what they were like." She glanced over at Jem, and though she was smiling, the sadness showed in her eyes. "They say that the seal people had thick black hair, just like Jem's."

But Jem hated being reminded of his differences for any reason, so he kept his gaze focused on the string webbing his fingers, as if he were trying to recall the next step of the pattern, and pretended not to hear.

For the first couple of years after Jem moved to the fort, Enkara cut his hair for him when he came to visit her. One day he declined her offer, partly because he felt she shouldn't have to care for him any more, and partly on a whim. He laughed and told her he'd decided he was going to let it grow—it would keep him warmer. Enkara laughed with him, saying she would just have to make do without the hair clippings to use in her embroidery—for she often saved the trimmings from his hair and used them to accent details in the stitching with black.

Much of the yarn was made from dog hair, often spun together with the wooly tufts shed by the reindeer in spring. The only black animals to be found in Kruvak were some of the dogs, and although they looked glossy black, the soft undercoat they shed was smoke gray. Black was not a hue that could easily be found, and the best dyes from the lichens were the ones that made blue and red.

Enkara had also made a long woven belt with small black diamonds in the center of a blue and white pattern. She'd worked on it over many years, using the hair she saved when Jem had gone longer between haircuts. She had always said his black hair was beautiful, and admired how much thicker it was than the other children's, though the compliments meant nothing to Jem, who could only feel resentment that his hair was unlike everyone else's. And after the day he told her he was letting it grow, he never asked Enkara to cut his hair again.

After a time Jem understood that his uncivilized hair reflected his identity as a being outside of ordinary bounds—a being who belonged to no one, like any wild creature. And oddly enough, his new appearance garnered approval from Avakab—an approval that was in keeping with the relationship they'd developed, which Jem felt he could tentatively call friendship. At the least it was mutual acceptance and respect, though the latter was mostly on Jem's side.

It was the ongoing project of building the snow domes that unexpectedly formed a narrow bridge between Jem and the intense old man. Jem found that he enjoyed the challenge of working on the illus and began to see the task as his own, rather than as a duty assigned to him by the old men. In fact, Waltak had scarcely mentioned it after that first day; his orders involved maintenance of the rest of the fort, or food, or clothing. Jem was disappointed that he'd only started building the base of the large illu when the thaw began, and he found himself eagerly looking forward to the end of the brief summer and the return of the snowfall.

When winter reclaimed the village and turned the world white again, Jem soon discovered what he'd suspected from the beginning—that building such a giant illu wasn't going to be an easy endeavor. So he rebelled and came up with his own design, which was a cluster of linked illus that included two larger ones—though each much smaller than the big one on Waltak's faded map. The old men chose one of the small domes to sleep in, and nothing was said, but neither seemed impressed by Jem's accomplishment. And by the following year, in the third winter after his arrival, Jem had become adept enough at constructing the illus that he wanted to build them according to the map, including the largest one, if only to prove that he could.

As soon as there was a deep enough blanket of snow in the courtyard, Jem started cutting the blocks. And there was a reward for his efforts that he hadn't anticipated—he wasn't always alone when he worked. Often Avakab would come out into the courtyard and sit on a reindeer skin spread out on the snow, picking a spot where he could watch Jem's progress. And while the old man watched, he told stories, or simply spoke of his thoughts and feelings, opening the door to his mind—as if Jem were his equal.

So Avakab was there on the morning when Jem started on the big illu for the second time that winter. The circle he'd trampled down after measuring the space was surprisingly large, and he'd cut a staggering number of blocks out of it. On his previous attempt, he'd gotten only halfway up the height of the dome before seeing it wasn't going to stand. Little imperfections in the shape or slant of the blocks seemed magnified, and he would work his way around the circle to find that the blocks he'd set on the prior layers were leaning in or bulging out. Finally he'd groaned and shoved the whole thing down.

The weather had just cleared after two days of snow, and now he was hoping that having a fresh start and plenty of deep layers to work with would make the process easier. Avakab was seated cross-legged on his reindeer skin rug, next to the round white wall of one of the smaller illus Jem had already completed, talking in his soft but clear and rhythmic voice. He'd said he would tell Jem about the largest Native fish he'd ever seen.

"We were ice fishing some distance off the coast, after the end of the Dark Moon. I was quite a young man—not much older than you, come to think of it. We had just begun fishing when one of the men pulled it up—a Native as long as his arm. We all gathered around, speechless. Like all Natives, it had blue scales. But, perhaps because of its size, the blue was a deeper hue, and yet the scales also had a transparent quality—we could make out the shapes of the organs and bones inside the fish. The eyes were huge and silver, and seemed to glow as if a light shone inside the creature's head.

"Even the older men, who'd probably caught thousands of Natives, were spellbound. Not only was the fish immense, it had a great presence—and it seemed to be looking back at us even as it struggled to breathe outside of its element. Without any discussion, everyone in the party acknowledged a shared reverence and sense of awe. It was understood that the Native must be returned to the sea. I remember having a feeling I'd never had before—the feeling that we were only visitors, and had violated the world of this ancient creature. And as I looked at it, I wondered what understanding such a creature might have, and what its kind had thought when the Ancestors put all the sea life they'd brought with them into the Natives' world—for up until that moment, the sea had belonged only to them."

Jem knew that the Ancestors had brought many fish—and seals and other sea mammals—and that only some had survived to become permanent inhabitants of this world. Before that, the only denizens of the sea had been the Native fish, the bitter blue seaweed, and the tiny, scarcely visible threads of life that fed the smallest fish, living in an ageless arrangement. They had been specks of life in an almost empty sea, and the Native fish usually stayed deep in the frigid dark waters below the omnipresent ice.

"Is it foolish to speculate on the thoughts and feelings of such beings?" Avakab wondered aloud. "Or is it a valid question? Now that I have time to think, and to look back over experiences I couldn't reflect on while they were happening, these are the things that rise up in my mind—the odd little questions that seemed only passing fancy when they first occurred to me."

It was often those odd reflections that drew Jem into the stories most of all, making it even more impossible for him not to like the old man. As Jem worked, listening to the hypnotic rhythm of the voice, it was as if the storyteller had taken up residence in the back of his mind, and no longer lived a separate existence outside of him.

But the feeling disappeared abruptly, leaving only a faint echo in his mind, when Avakab stopped talking and made a sound that was half disapproval and half amusement.

Jem looked up from the wall of snow blocks in front of him, biting his lip, his sense of the old man's presence shifting back to a place where there was a level of wariness. "Well?" he said. He didn't want to risk angering Avakab, and so far he hadn't done so. Although he asked questions and sometimes asserted himself in small ways, he was always on his best behavior with Avakab, and never showed him the disrespect he so often showed Waltak.

Avakab chuckled. "I'm enjoying this, you see. I want to see how long it takes you to make it work."

Boldly, Jem asked, "Will you give me a hint, if you won't tell me how it was done?"

The old man looked away, still chuckling softly. "And spoil the fun? No, my unhappy Sanndai, you will not get any hints."

Jem felt momentary annoyance, followed by an even greater sense of determination—he was going to build the cursed thing if it took him the rest of his life to make it stand. But the very fact that the old rebel was laughing at him suggested that he needed to do something different, rather than trying to build such an enormous illu in the same way that smaller ones were built.

He ended that session by giving up on the structure once again, and deciding to take a different approach. If he built all the other illus first, he told himself, perhaps he could use the walls of the adjoining smaller domes to help support the base of the big one. Salvaging most of the blocks, he spent a few days completing the rest—soundly beating his own time record for the task—and left the big circle empty.

Feeling the need to take a break, he went out to the station, but he was still thinking about the big illu. Lying on his back on the padded floor, he pulled out a strand of yarn he'd saved from a mending task and began one of the string figures Enkara had recently taught him. It was something they'd always enjoyed together, and she often had one or two new ones to show him when he visited her. As Jem watched the string weaving around his fingers, studying the patterns it formed, he was reminded of something he'd once found intriguing: the fact that multiple strands that were all pulled straight could cross each other in such a way as to form a curved line.

It dawned on him that this could be a clue to the giant snow dome. The focus of his gaze shifted; he looked through the web of coarse beige yarn, up to the ceiling. He'd never paid much attention to the structure of the roof of the station. But although the alien dome looked perfectly smooth and round from the outside, there were bands running across the ceiling that were visible inside—bands that cut the form into triangles and arches. And those shapes were made up of lines and angles that were straight and symmetrical, like almost everything in the Sanndai world. What's more, each section at the base of the walls was a straight line, which was why the interior rooms were square; nothing in the dome's underlying structure was actually curved.

Sitting up quickly, Jem looked around him, forgetting the tangle of string in his hands. Balance and symmetry. The big illu didn't have to be perfect, but it did have to be balanced enough to support itself. So he needed to divide the structure into pieces he could measure and match up all around the circle, in spite of the distance between them.

Back at the fort, he found Avakab sitting in the same place he'd chosen before, cross-legged on the small skin rug, with another reindeer skin draped over his shoulders. He was carving a piece of wood—just as he'd been doing the first time

Jem saw him. Jem asked the old man if they might have some old ski poles, or parts of a worn-out sled or meat rack, that were straight and solid. When Avakab looked up, Jem thought he saw a hint of approval in his expression. He told Jem to check in the storage room where they kept the old sled and the tools for cutting snow blocks.

Once his eyes adjusted to the dim indoor light of his lamp, Jem found some wooden poles of various lengths lying against the wall; they were behind the sled, which he'd never had occasion to use, so he hadn't noticed them there before. After he selected several that were fairly short but seemed sturdy, he took them back out into the dazzling brightness of the courtyard. Sitting close to the old man, he cut his piece of string with his knife and used it to bind the poles together. He created a right angle with two of the shortest pieces of wood, and he also made a triangle with matching corners and sides.

With his new tools in one hand and his knife in the other, he crawled through one of the small domes to get back into the open center. Then he began to work his way around the circle, cutting marks in the packed snow at measured intervals. When he was halfway around, he glanced up, and was rewarded by a glimmer of satisfaction—or was it just humor?—in Avakab's cold blue eyes.

"I'm just trying something," Jem said with a shrug, as if he'd given it little thought. If his conjecture turned out to be wrong, he didn't want the old rebel to think he'd spent much time or effort on it.

"Good for you," Avakab answered. His soft, slow voice was sometimes hard to interpret when it wasn't clearly menacing or full of sardonic humor.

When Jem got back to where he'd begun, he measured the amount needed to compensate for the odd distance left over, and cut some notches in his measuring tool. As he started the marking process again, rubbing out his original marks as he made new ones, he heard the old man speak behind him.

"I've noticed your hair hasn't been cut in some time. Makes you look like something other than what you are—a new race, perhaps." He chuckled. "I never saw a Sanndai whose hair wasn't closely cut. Every hair on their head short and even, and never a patch or a visible mending on their clothes—hardly even a spot of dirt. When I observed this, as a very young man, I came to the conclusion that it had to do with their need for control. Dirt and hair are part of the natural world they believe they must dominate, you see.

"But now here you are—and there is something about this look. A dark man, with long black hair. Almost like black feathers. It's a picture from another world and time, that doesn't speak at all of your parents' kind, or their ways. I believe I like it. Seeing you like this, it's easier to imagine you're something different altogether."

Jem felt warmed by this. He was pleased that Avakab could see him that way. And surely the old man was right, and he *was* something different altogether. For he wasn't like the Sanndai who'd done such brutal acts, who didn't care for the natural world, and who used strange tools and flying ships and lived among things he couldn't name. Nor was he like the people around him, as everyone he'd ever known had made so clear to him—even Enkara. He could see his differences in the pain in her eyes when she looked at him, mingled with the affection and tenderness that shone there.

After reaching his full height, he was larger and taller than any other man he'd seen—any other man in Kruvak. The black hair that now grew freely was blunted only by the cold wind whipping it around his face, and by the weight of his own back and shoulders tugging on the strands when they trailed across the furs he slept on, and it reached well below his shoulders. Although the ends were ragged, the body of it was thick, with a faint, purple-brown sheen. His wide, long-fingered hands were dark, olive tan, although they were more of a dull, dirty brown when he'd been working a lot with his mittens off.

He knew his eyes frightened people. Even Enkara gazed into them as if they held some mystery she wished—yet perhaps also feared—to discern. Waltak almost never looked directly at him, and Avakab rarely looked long at Jem's face. When he spoke to Jem, he often appeared to gaze off into a distance only he could see.

Still it seemed that something passed between Jem and the old man on the day when Jem attempted once again to build the giant illu and finally met with success. Once he'd marked regular intervals around the circumference, he borrowed a long skein of yarn from Enkara and stretched it across from one side to the other, using his tools again to make more measurements. Then he began by building partial walls that jutted into the circle at opposing points around the space, and cut these walls so they sloped at exactly the same angle all the way around. Only then did he begin the actual spiraling construction of the outer wall, building it up against the supporting walls until the interior became a series of wide arches, with bases that extended partway into the center of the large space—which was as vast as the big room at the Women's House.

Now Jem quickly made progress, and although the old man said nothing, he sensed from Avakab's manner that he'd hit upon the right thing. It gave him a deep satisfaction he hadn't expected—a satisfaction arising more from Avakab's approval than from the accomplishment itself.

Then it was necessary to interrupt his construction long enough to rummage for more scrap wood, and to build a small platform he could climb onto, to increase the height of his reach. He came up with something like a miniature drying rack he could easily move about. It was a bit wobbly, but it nearly doubled his height when he stood on the top rung. Standing on the top proved necessary when he was finally placing the last blocks in the center of the illu, maneuvering them up through the shrinking hole and cutting their edges with his knife until they dropped into place, wedged tightly against the blocks beside them.

On the day Jem completed the giant dome, Avakab had been watching him, but some time after the sides of the illu grew tall enough to obstruct their view of each other, the old man had gone back inside. Waltak hadn't called for him all day, so Jem had been left to work on the task in solitude. With the snow barrier blocking the wind, the efforts of his work made him so warm he had to open the neck of his parka as far as it would go, and a little later he'd been able to take his parka off.

When the last block was in place, Jem brought in buckets of snow and filled in all the chinks, until he'd satisfied himself that the walls of the immense snow dome were snug and secure. Climbing again onto the top of his platform, he cut out several small air holes high up on the walls, and then stood gazing down and around at the amazing room he'd created. The light was very dim, and the small lamp on the floor below him provided little illumination. There was a strange peace in the shadowy space and the bluish-white walls.

It was nearly dark when he'd finished digging out the last of the doorways between the smaller domes and the big one. When he crawled out and surveyed the scene, the giant illu stood flanked by the others like a mother kiruna with her chicks crowded around her, and the walls of snow glowed in the gloom of night's beginning.

In the morning when Waltak came out, he was soon joined by Avakab, who usually didn't make an appearance until later. Then both men went back inside and returned with utensils and tools to set up a fire pit in the new dome, and the kitchen was relocated—but only after the illu had passed inspection. Part of that inspection was having Jem climb up on top of it.

Jem knew that a correctly built illu could support the weight of a man standing on the top, and if this one weren't capable of bearing his weight, it would be unwise for them to trust it to stand over their heads—especially considering the consequences if so great a number of snow blocks were to collapse on top of them. But Jem had felt the balance and solidity of the structure when he'd finished the interior, and he wasn't worried when he bellied up onto one of the largest of the other domes, then climbed up the broad curve of the white wall until he stood on the very top of the giant illu.

He'd never been that high off the ground before, and it was a heady thrill. He was able to look out over the stone walls of the fort to the tops of all the buildings and occasional snow domes near the fort—and was surprised to see how small everything looked. He could see the smoke rising from the roofs as people added fuel to their fires, and even see the tracks in the snowy streets between the dwellings. Climbing down, Jem slid off the flank of the great illu onto one of the others, and from there to the ground. Then he joined Avakab and Waltak inside, and took over the breakfast preparations.

He found himself absurdly pleased by the old men's approval. Avakab now admitted that the original illu had used additional walls for support as well, although they'd been somewhat different in design. Then he pulled out his knife to show Jem how the inner walls could be trimmed to minimize the amount of space they took up, without compromising the strength of the dome. But best of all, Avakab didn't hide the fact that he was impressed with Jem's handiwork—at least somewhat—and Waltak was being almost pleasant. Not since he was a small child had anything happened to Jem that had made him feel this good.

A few days after the large illu was completed, both old men were sitting beside the new fire pit. Jem was a little way off, mending one of his boots, when he ventured to comment, "I still don't understand why it's warmer in here than in the sod rooms. Since sod is heavier and more solid, why doesn't it hold in more heat?"

"Ah," Avakab said. "But it's not that simple, young man."

(Jem liked it that Avakab sometimes called him that—Waltak never did, as if he didn't think Jem really qualified as a man; when he didn't call him 'boy', he called him animal names, like 'geatki'—wolverine—or 'amarok', which meant wolf.) "Do you know what makes the best barrier against cold?"

Jem frowned momentarily, then shook his head, not wanting to say the wrong thing.

"It's air."

"Air?"

"Yes, air." A faint smile touched the old rebel's face.

Waltak glanced at Jem and chuckled, as if enjoying seeing his puzzlement. He was always more at ease with Jem when Avakab was with them.

"A good layer of fresh snow is full of air, and that is why it can help to keep you warm, as it does for the reindeer and other animals." Avakab said. "That is also why the best sod houses have double walls, with a space between them—you know that, don't you?"

"Yes." Jem had known about double walls, but not that the space between them was important.

"Now one reason illus are warm has to do with the round shape. There is always air moving through an enclosed space, you see, and the illu's shape helps to guide it in such a way that the warmest air, which comes from our own bodies as well as from the fire and the lamps, tends to stay in the center, rather than rising to the top. And, as you know, the ice that forms on the inside creates a tight barrier. But it is also likely that even when the snow in the blocks is packed very densely, it still holds more air within it than a sod wall that is frozen solid. That would also make the outer wall of snow, on top of the ice layer on the inside, superior to sod when it comes to keeping in the warmth and blocking out the cold. Do you understand now?"

"Yes—I think so." Jem stared up at the walls and ceiling of the giant illu, his brow wrinkled. It seemed so odd that both the air circulating around them and the air inside the frozen walls he'd built was helping to shelter them—that it was the emptiness within the walls that made them work so well. In a curious way it seemed a perfect metaphor for everything he'd done these past few years, alone in this strange, forsaken place with two old men whose pasts were haunted and violent. What was he now but a builder of empty walls? Walls that shielded him, but had no real substance.

Except for Enkara, the other midwives, and the children who stayed at the Birthing House, Jem saw almost no one besides the two old men; he could hardly count his ephemeral encounters with people he passed in the streets. He saw Waltak every day, and often felt weary of the sight and sound of him— the shriveled features and nasal voice hadn't grown any less unpleasant with the passage of time. But Jem might go several days without seeing Avakab at all, since he didn't always come out into the big illu to eat, and Waltak would take food and tea to him instead. Jem imagined that sometimes the old man simply preferred to keep to himself, and to be alone with the bittersweet company of so many memories and shattered dreams.

When Rulskar and his cronies came to deliver food—an arrangement that had apparently been agreed upon some time ago, although Jem didn't know why—Jem usually tried to wait beside the inner door to the pantry until they'd gone. But sometimes Waltak called him in to unload the sled, either on his own accord, or because Rulskar goaded him into it. When that happened, the insults and crude remarks were inevitable. Jem never tried to retort back. With Waltak standing at his elbow and muttering through clenched teeth, it seemed wisest to grit his own teeth and do his best to ignore the hateful man.

Unfortunately, ignoring Rulskar seemed to irritate him more, causing the unhealthy gleam in his eyes to burn brighter, and causing him to shove Jem harder when he didn't manage to duck out of the bully's reach on his way back into the pantry with a bundle in his arms. Then Rulskar would rattle off more outrageous insults, and Fenak and Gumak would laugh dutifully. Rulskar also had a penchant for loudly telling boastful stories about his grandfather, which were obviously intended to annoy Waltak.

Rulskar was one of the tallest men in Kruvak—although still almost a head shorter than Jem—and that helped make him easy to recognize from a distance. He also stood out when he was bare-headed, since he was one of a handful of people in the village whose hair was a sandy light brown, rather than pale blond. Up close, his features were ordinary—round face, wide cheekbones, narrow eyes. Those eyes were distinctive only in that disturbing glimmer that hinted at madness—in color they were the same crystalline sky blue as almost everyone else's; only a few Torviks had eyes of a greenish hue, which were referred to as 'eyes like the sea'.

But another identifying feature of Rulskar's was that his mouth was usually set in a scowl, with his lower lip pushed up. When he smiled at Waltak it wasn't really a smile, but more of a sneer. Only when he turned to speak to one of his companions, or to the dog, Trika, did his face soften, showing the opposing side of his character that Jem found so startling.

One morning Avakab made both Jem and Waltak laugh when they came from the pantry after a delivery, and Waltak was so vexed at Rulskar he was still muttering to himself.

Avakab chuckled soothingly as he looked up from his carving. "Rulskar again, eh?" Flashing a malicious smile, he said, "I noticed once that his face has changed little since he was a small child; I do believe that for most of his life that poor fellow has kept the very same expression he had the first time I saw him—that of a whimpering baby who just spewed all over himself." He chuckled again. "And, as I recall, all over his poor father, who was holding him up to show him off."

Sometimes Jem tried to slip away and go to the station when Rulskar came, but if Waltak saw him leaving he would rail at him and threaten to deprive him of supper. On one occasion he carried out that threat, and Avakab was sitting by the fire pit in the big dome that night and affirmed the sentence when Waltak pronounced it. Since Jem wasn't about to challenge Avakab, he couldn't ignore the punishment. He decided it was better to go hungry than to jeopardize his situation, and went off, swearing, to crawl inside his own small illu and sulk.

Lying on his stomach, he buried his face, still hot from his anger and from sitting close to the fire, in the cold soft skins, and tried to push away all thoughts of food. He tried to summon up the tenuous image of the girl who only existed in his mind—the girl with black hair and eyes like the sky at the end of summer—and to imagine her there, beside him in the close silence of the walls of snow he'd built to shelter his own dreams.

Although he usually didn't stay as long at the abandoned station as he had in the moons after he'd discovered it, when he still lived with Enkara at the Birthing House, now and then Jem still wandered through the familiar space, put his hands on the alien objects, and lay on his back on the floor, staring at the oval lights in the ceiling. Those lights continued to come on and off when he pushed the raised spot on the wall, though several of them had gone out and gone dormant, as one had on the day he first entered the place.

For some time after hearing the first story Avakab ever told him—about the attack on the station—Jem had walked uneasily around the brown bloodstain on the floor. Later, as if in further defiance of all taboos, he would sit directly on the stain, and put his naked hands down on the padded surface, and tell himself that someone who looked like him had died right there, right on that spot.

Though he always tried to avoid being seen when he went in and out of the station, Jem knew a few people had seen him, and some must have figured out he was going inside.

And one day when Rulskar came to the fort, he leered at Jem and said, "Well, if it isn't huge and ugly! You're actually here. I expected you'd be skulking around that unnatural tumor the other demons left for you to hide in—a fitting place for a walking piece of disease and filth. I've been thinking about finding a way to dig that thing out of the cursed ground under it. When I do, maybe you'll shrivel up and die."

Jem grimaced and looked away, trying not to listen. After that he was even more cautious about looking to see that no one was watching when he came and went from the station. He now carried the odd rectangular key on a thong around his neck, hidden under his shirt where the old men wouldn't see it.

But Avakab also mentioned on one occasion, as he had when they first met, that he'd heard that Jem had been seen around the station.

"Have you been inside it?" he asked Jem.

Jem couldn't think of a good enough reason to lie, and felt, as he always did around Avakab, that the old man could see through him. If he lied, surely Avakab would know. So he simply said, "Yes."

"Find anything interesting?" the old man asked then, as if he were testing Jem.

Jem shrugged. "Weird things, mostly. Some dishes and clothes and stuff it looks like they left behind in a hurry. I can't tell what some of the things are, but they don't look important or anything. And there's a table and chairs," he added, knowing Avakab would have seen them when he and his men had been inside and made hostages of the Sanndai.

Avakab nodded. "Logical. I'm sure they wouldn't have left anything valuable to them. I was told that when they came back—and started rounding up people to torture—a couple of them went back in there briefly. But they didn't spend much time there; they brought bigger ships, and stayed inside them instead. Not that I care what they left behind—I never had any use for their fancy gadgets. Rastok and I certainly proved that our primitive weapons were more than sufficient on the day we flushed them out! Of course, we'd known that all along; we never coveted their precious light guns."

"But . . . even if you had their guns, you couldn't shoot them anyway, right?" Jem ventured. "Since only they can use them? Only Sanndai, I mean?" He added quickly, "Or is that just a story?"

A hint of a smile twitched across the old man's lips as his eyes flickered over Jem. "No—it isn't just a story. But your people are not nearly so clever as they think they are. There are ways around their vain gimmicks. In this case, one might say there are ways of fooling those weapons into 'thinking' they are in the hands of a Sanndai, so that anyone can wield them." He snorted softly and added, "Even Rulskar figured out that little trick, and I certainly wouldn't credit him with more than average cleverness."

Then Avakab looked straight at Jem again. "But I'm sure you haven't put yourself at risk by going into that place." He displayed one of his threatening smiles and added, "Unless you fear ghosts. I recall that Enkara wondered at first if a baby born here and not raised among them would still be immune to the Fevers, but you put the question to rest in a few moons. In any case, I doubt there are more of their evil contagions in that place than what's already been spread around this village."

"That's part of the reason, isn't it, that everyone's afraid to go near there?"

"Yes, it is. But few would want to enter a dwelling made by the Outsiders, especially when some of those alien men died in there—that would surely invoke bad luck, wouldn't it?" Avakab had shifted his gaze away, to Jem's relief, and didn't seem to expect an answer—and Jem suspected the old man didn't believe it himself.

Jem had noticed that the old rebel seemed to disregard superstitions, and it was one more thing he admired. It fit with his own desire to be untouched and untouchable, and with the pride he felt in defying the taboo of the abandoned station. And even if Avakab's own defiance hadn't led to success, Jem understood now that part of defiance was hope—the hope of breaking free from dark places, bitter pasts, and ever-present shadows.

# PART THREE

# THE REBEL'S BOW

## I

IN EARLY AUTUMN of the fourth year that Jem lived with the old rebels, there wasn't enough snow yet to build snow domes—the bare brown earth was still exposed in several places in the courtyard of the fort—but it had turned very cold. With the days growing shorter, it was gloomier than ever inside the dark fort, and the old kitchen between the walls of stone and sod had a low ceiling and was always smoky, which made them all cough, especially Avakab, and put whiny Waltak into a particularly unpleasant mood. But venturing outside of the gray walls wasn't much more appealing, with the air painfully cold and the frozen mud in the streets grooved with deep ruts that made walking difficult, running impossible.

Jem was in a foul mood himself as he poked about looking for things to do, wishing over and over that it would snow so he could work on building the illus instead. As he wandered through the fort, he entertained a daydream in which he tricked Rulskar, trapping him alone in the pantry, and stole the fine rifle the madman always carried over his shoulder. He pursued the morbid fantasy through several different conclusions, debating how best to kill the man—using the rifle itself wouldn't work, since someone might hear the shot—and dispose of his remains in some clever way so no one would ever suspect him.

Largely thanks to Rulskar, fantasizing about rifles, knives, and axes was one of Jem's favorite past times, though he knew many of those fantasies were childish. And sometimes they were gruesome, and he was ashamed when he imagined what Enkara would think if she knew he had such thoughts. But that didn't stop him from fervently desiring a weapon. So when he made a remarkable discovery in one of the small storerooms, it was hard not to feel that his wishes had been answered.

He'd found a hole in one of the interior sod walls, where a family of voles had made a nest. When he came around to check the room on the other side, the pale yellow light of his lamp revealed an old wooden trunk constructed of wide solid planks—the kind of wood that was scarce in Kruvak—pushed into the corner adjacent to the wall he was mending. As the lamp's glow stretched the trunk's rectangular shadow up the earthen wall, he saw something wrapped in cloth that was partly concealed behind it, leaning against the crux of the corner.

Jem raised the lamp to look closely at the faded red cloth. It was wrapped around something made of pale tan reindeer skin that showed through a gap in the covering. When he touched it, he found a solid smooth shape. His fingers closed on it and he tugged it out, lifting it over the top of the trunk. There was a soft rattling sound, and his eyes grew wide when he saw what it was.

He was holding a quiver full of arrows. The quiver was light but solidly made, covered in the skin of a reindeer calf, with two embroidered gray bands around it, one near the bottom and one near the top. The mouth was trimmed with silver-gray fox fur, and it had a narrow shoulder strap made of smooth leather. The arrows—there were eight, he found, as he pulled them out one by one—were well-crafted wooden arrows fletched with brown and white kiruna feathers. The tips were all intact, and quite sharp, and only a couple of the arrows had minor damage to the fletching—small gouges in the otherwise perfect outline of the cut edge of the feathers.

Jem stroked the shafts of the arrows, fingered the fletching very lightly, and then put each one back into the quiver with the same painstaking care he'd used when he took them out. Holding the quiver by the strap, he looked at the corner where it had been hidden and saw something else there, wrapped in the same faded red cloth—something long and thin.

Eagerly Jem reached out and gripped the cloth—and felt what seemed to be a curved wooden bar. He drew it out and pulled away the cloth. It was a bow.

Made of silvery beige wood, it was carved in a symmetrical arc with the tips curving back gracefully. The hand grip was swathed in tightly wrapped gray yarn. For at least fifteen centimeters above the grip, the wood was covered with soft tan reindeer skin that was nearly the same color as the hide on the quiver, and it bore a pattern of interlocking white diamond shapes, each with a dot in the center. The last diamond was elongated at the top so it looked like an arrowhead. The bowstring was still attached at one end, and wrapped loosely around the body of the bow—a smooth and tightly spun string that appeared in perfect condition, without a single frayed spot.

It was by far the most beautiful bow Jem had ever seen. Not that he'd seen that many up close—he'd only played with a small child's bow at the Birthing House a few times. A couple of rustic bows had been among the toys the old women kept in the house, though the last one had been broken by some overzealous child by the time Jem was ten. But he didn't need to be an expert to see that this was a skillfully made weapon.

He let his breath out slowly, aware of how rapidly his heart was beating, and glanced nervously over his shoulder. He was quite certain the old men wouldn't want him handling this weapon, and almost equally sure it must have been the bow Avakab used in his prime. He'd heard that the old rebel had traded all the rifles he'd owned, so others could use them for hunting. Obviously he no longer had any use for them himself. But this—this he must have kept for some sentimental reason, which might mean he would be even more angered at the thought of Jem touching it.

Jem knew he should put it back, but he gave in to the desire to hold it for just a moment, raising the bow in his left hand and holding it out with his arm straight, imagining himself nocking one of the arrows onto the bowstring and setting it in flight. His hands were trembling as he stepped back into the corner by the trunk, picked up the red cloth, and did his best to rewrap the bow and its companion quiver the way he'd found them.

Returning to his chores, the image of the bow and the feel of it in his hands kept circling through his mind. By the next day the thought of it was like a burning ache inside him. No matter how many times he told himself the object was forbidden, he couldn't get the idea of returning to that room and looking at it again out of his head; it simmered there until he knew he had no choice—he had to do it.

He chose a time in the afternoon when he was sure both elderly men were resting. The room they stayed in was on the other side of the fort from the place where Jem had found the bow and quiver, which made him feel marginally better. Though he still felt a powerful uneasiness, the equally powerful urge to handle the weapon again made him steel himself and slip silently into the dark room.

He set his lamp on the floor and went to the corner where the wooden trunk sat. Fumbling in the dim lamplight with nervous hands, he found the cloth-wrapped objects and carefully carried them to the center of the room. He sat cross-legged beside the lamp, with the precious artifacts in his lap. He ran his hands over the graceful bow, and took the arrows out of the quiver and counted them again.

He wondered why old Avak had kept this bow, hidden

away, and whether he'd ever killed anyone with it, as he had bragged about killing with his knife. And then he let that slip from his mind and thought only of himself with the bow. The daydream swept him from the dark room and the flickering light, to a bright, clear place where he was a strong and talented hunter. A hunter whose arrows could strike anything—or anyone—with unequaled skill and precision, always piercing their target within a hair's breadth of where he wanted them to go.

But after Jem put the bow back in its place, he found that giving in to the urge to handle it had only made him more obsessed with it. Over the next moon the act became the guilty pleasure he rewarded himself with every chance he got. And each time he took the bow out without anything terrible befalling him—that is, without Waltak or Avakab discovering what he'd done—his cockiness about his transgression grew.

Though it still made him nervous, it was like entering the abandoned station—his uneasiness about it gave him a rush that only made him wish to do it more. And it wasn't as if he had much excitement in his life, other than trying to avoid meeting Rulskar and not always succeeding. But those encounters left him with a sick fear in the pit of his stomach that had nothing redeeming about it.

It wasn't long before the satisfaction Jem got from handling the bow and the arrows began to wane and a more daring plan took form in his mind. The brutal cold and dry winds had finally turned to snow, and though the wind had sculpted the drifts in the courtyard into erratic waves, Jem had been able to build one small illu.

As he was reinforcing the walls of his new snow dome after a fresh snowfall, patting handfuls of powder into place and beginning to feel the cold through his thick mittens, he glanced toward the sod room that jutted out into the yard—the room where he'd found the mute's body. And he saw that if one were standing along the inner wall behind it, the back wall of that room would be in a perfect position to use as a target. There was plenty of open space in between, and several doors that were close enough to be readily accessible for ducking out of sight. He had the answer he'd been looking for.

More snow and harsh winds forced Jem to put off his first attempt at his plan, but finally there was a day that dawned clear and bitterly cold. That meant it was unlikely the two old men would venture out of doors—especially not Waltak, who was the one who'd be checking up on him at any rate. And since Jem hadn't yet been able to build more illus, the old rebels were still staying in one of the sod rooms in the fort's outer circle.

Finishing his morning chores, Jem added fuel to the fire in the kitchen and went out to the courtyard. With an oil lamp burning beside him to warm his hands, he sat in an open doorway to take advantage of the outside light. He'd been gathering pieces of old skins and scraps of leather, and now he arranged those remnants into a roughly rectangular shape and tied them together. Then he took a lump of charcoal he'd taken from the fire and drew a large circle on the lighter side of the skins.

Jem blew out his lamp, pulled up his hood, and carried his shabby creation out into the biting cold. Braving the pain of taking off one mitten, he dug a handful of rough pins made of bone fragments from his pocket, and used them to stake the target to the back wall of the leaning sod room. Satisfied that it was secure but could still be pulled down with one quick tug, he went to retrieve the bow.

It took him a few moments to get it strung, but it helped that he'd recently seen one of the herdsman do it. He'd been passing the Men's House and paused in the shadows, preferring to wait until the men standing on the stoop of that building started down the street ahead of him. While he was waiting, he'd watched one of them restring his bow.

When Jem finally stepped out into the courtyard with the

beautiful weapon and its matching quiver in his hands, the cold was made more bearable because his heart was racing and his face was flushed. He set the quiver down carefully and took out one arrow. Trying to remember the correct way to position his hands—and, as always, uncomfortably conscious of how large those hands were—he nocked the arrow and pulled back the bowstring. Though his bulky mittens added to his clumsiness and made hooking his fingertips over the string a little awkward, they also provided padding.

He was surprised at how hard he had to pull, but he knew this confirmed what he'd suspected—that it was a very good bow. When he released the arrow, it went only a short distance, careening off to the left, and landed in the snow against the inner wall of the fort. Glad that no one was watching, Jem drew another arrow from the quiver and tried again. This one at least went into the wall that bore his target, but just barely, catching the outer edge of the sod barrier and sticking out at a cockeyed angle.

When he let go of the string on his third attempt, the arrow plopped into the snow right at his feet, and through the thick sleeve of his parka he felt the bowstring slap the inside of his left arm. He cringed, both wondering what he'd done to make that happen and feeling doubly thankful that he was doing this in secret with no audience to bear witness to his bungling.

By the time he'd fired all eight arrows four times over, the exposed parts of his face were numb, but on the last round several of the arrows had struck his target, one even coming close to the center. Deciding it was a good point to end on, he took down the skin target and carried it back inside with the bow and quiver. When he put them back where he'd found them, he hid the target behind the same trunk.

Then he hurried to the kitchen, stirred up the orange embers in the fire pit, and knelt down beside it, leaning over the low, hissing flames. He spread his bare hands directly over them and brought his face as close as he dared, breathing deeply and even relishing the pain as the intense heat restored sensation to his icy skin.

After that it became part of his routine—sneaking the bow out to the courtyard whenever he had the chance, and practicing for as long as he dared. Once he'd built all the illus, including the giant one—following the old map as he had last year—he had to listen even more carefully for any sound that might betray Waltak's approach. Luckily the old man always came out the entrance of the large illu, which faced the wall opposite the mute's abandoned room where Jem hung his target. It also helped that Waltak's appearance was always preceded by a faint muttering, the crunch and shuffle of his boots, and the scuffing of his long parka as he stooped to come through the narrow entry.

Jem soon became adept at dividing his attention so his hearing was fully trained on picking up those distinctive, soft sounds, while the rest of him was focused on shooting the bow. Proficiency at the shooting itself didn't come so quickly. Though he pushed himself hard each time he practiced, sometimes he noticed no improvement in his skill for days and days. Then, the next time—often coming after a lull when he'd been unable to practice for a while—it would all seem easier, and his arrows would find their mark with greater frequency.

Still his progress was steady enough that every few moons it would occur to him that he was no longer making the mistakes that had plagued him before. In the beginning, the humiliating shots where the arrow dropped straight down out of the bowstring happened half a dozen more times, and they seemed to come out of the blue. The odd thing was that Jem could never tell what he'd done wrong—whether he'd released the string too soon or too late, or if there were some fault in the way he'd positioned his hands. Surely something that ridiculous was caused by a blatant beginner's error. But one day he realized it hadn't happened in moons—and after that it never happened again, though he never did figure out what he'd been doing to cause it.

At first his efforts made him sore; he could feel the muscles in his upper back and shoulders from drawing the bow again and again, and for a little while the base of his left thumb was tender at the spot where the bow pressed against it, especially on the days when it wasn't so cold and he tried shooting with his mittens off to see if it improved his dexterity. There was also a spot on the left sleeve of his parka that was scuffed where the bowstring sometimes struck it, creating a smooth patch.

But in time the process of shooting began to feel natural and comfortable. Even when he practiced for a long time he no longer felt any muscle soreness, and the arrows cooperated more often than not. He never had any more shots that went wildly awry, and even the ones that seemed to fly straight only to duck around the target at the very last moment—as if they'd changed course in midflight—stopped happening as well.

In an open space near the center of the village that was sometimes the site of friendly contests—including archery competitions—Jem occasionally saw a target or two set up, and a few young men and boys practicing. He would stop to watch them, lurking in the shadow of one of the nearby buildings.

One afternoon when he was coming back from visiting Enkara, he saw half a dozen boys half his age taking turns with their bows while a couple of elderly hunters coached them. Some of the weapons were obviously no more than toys, like the ones he'd played with years ago at the Birthing House.

"No, no—always stand at a right angle to your target. That's right. Fold your thumb down on the grip. Keep your elbow up. Pull harder—all the way to your chin."

Jem stood still, concentrating on catching the old man's words. Most of the points he already knew, but as he watched and listened he picked up some he'd forgotten, or hadn't heard before. He was so engrossed he didn't notice that one of the boys, who'd stepped a few paces away from the group to play about in the snow while awaiting his turn, was now watching him.

Suddenly the boy called out, "What are you looking at, ugly?"

Pulled out of his concentration, Jem realized the youngster was addressing him. Of course, he thought sourly—who else got called 'ugly' by everyone in the village, even by stupid little boys who knew nothing about him? He shook off the inevitable prick of pain from the insult, and tossed off a taunt of his own.

"I bet a little smelt like you can't even hit that target."

"I can too!" the boy retorted indignantly. It was his turn next, and when he released the string of his little bow, the arrow landed in the snow behind the target.

When the boy glanced in his direction, shame-faced, Jem laughed and called, "See, I knew you couldn't hit it!" and sauntered off, enjoying the crunch of his large boots in the crisp snow—and shoving aside the small voice that popped into his head to chastise him for being mean. And when he practiced again, he remembered to think about everything he'd heard the old men tell the young boys.

On the day when every arrow from his first round struck deep into the center of his tattered target, Jem stood and gazed at the tight array of fletching protruding from the charcoal circle, holding the bow at his side. Along with the satisfaction he always felt when he made a good shot—compounded by having made eight excellent shots in a row—a thought rose in his mind. A thought he hadn't really considered before: how many of the men in Kruvak could do this?

Probably most of those who regularly hunted with bows were pretty solid shots, but some had to be better archers than others. And what he'd just done was far from shabby in any case—no one who saw such a feat would have reason to criticize it. He hadn't told Enkara what he'd been doing, so there was no one to share this with. Not that he wasn't used to that. But there was something about the way this made him feel that was new.

Getting into the station, for what it was worth, had given him a sense of accomplishment, but it hadn't taken moons of dedicated effort. More importantly, it was nothing that anyone he'd ever met would see as an accomplishment. Winning the old rebels' approval by learning to build the big illu was the only thing he'd done that had felt at all like this—the satisfaction was much deeper because it had meaning to someone else. And now it wasn't just about winning the approval of two eccentric old men. Every man in the village would agree that he'd acquired an important skill.

He was jarred from his reverie by the too-familiar sound of a thin nasal voice. "Boy! Where are you, boy?"

His heart hammering in his ears, Jem raced to his target. He always took pains to handle the arrows carefully—grasping them close to the target and avoiding the fletching when he pulled them free—but his haste made him clumsy and he dropped two into the snow at his feet before all of them were safely returned to the quiver. He swore and yanked down his target, then bolted for the nearest door with the quiver slung over his shoulder and the bow still in his left hand, stumbling over his own frozen footprints.

In the storeroom where his borrowed weaponry was supposed to be resting in concealed retirement, he rewrapped the bow in its familiar cloth covering. Annoyed that his hands were shaking, he tried to force himself to act calm. Once everything was back where it belonged, he crept to the door and listened.

Even if Waltak had come out into the courtyard looking for him, Jem would have a few moments to regroup and pretend he'd been busy mending something before answering the old man's summons. So when he heard the voice call out again and it was clear Waltak had left the shelter of the illus, he waited a moment longer, trying to give his breathing a chance to slow. He pushed his trembling hands deep into his pockets before sauntering out as casually as he could.

The grating sound of the old man's voice led him to the door of the main passage in the fort's outer circle. Waltak was probably headed for the pantry. As Jem trudged in after him, pausing to pick up a small oil lamp, the alarm still reverberated through him. He hated that he could go so quickly from feeling good—even feeling strong—to feeling as frightened as a child caught thieving. And all it had taken to spoil the moment was hearing Waltak's call.

When he reached the old man and stood before him in his habitual slouch, it occurred to him that if he stood up straight he would tower over the frail little figure even more. Looking at the wizened face illuminated by the flickering yellow light, seeing the way the woeful watery eyes stared out of the mask of deeply-lined skin, it seemed absurd for anyone to be intimidated by such a person.

Why am I afraid of this man? he wondered. Why am I afraid of anything? But that was a foolish idea. As appealing as it had sounded when he was a child, it would be dangerously stupid to be like an unnaturally brave hero in a tale who felt no fear at all. No—he just wanted to always feel self-assured, yet still be wise enough to be cautious.

As the moons passed, Jem's skill with the bow increased until he had to come up with new ways to keep his practice sessions challenging. He put additional small circles on his target, and sunk an arrow into each one, creating patterns in a specific order. Then he worked on shooting more and more rapidly. With the quiver over his shoulder, he would reach up and grab an arrow and nock it to the bowstring in one smooth motion, then draw and release in one breath. Again and again, always pushing himself to be even faster, even more accurate.

Although the sound of Waltak's voice breaking the spell of his concentration could still make him feel panicky, he became more complacent about the bow and quiver, sometimes taking them into the small illu where he slept, or leaving them just inside the door nearest his practice site, rather than putting them back in the storeroom where he'd found them. He imagined that neither of the old men had good enough eyesight that he need worry about the fact that the wall where he hung his target was peppered with holes—holes obviously made by arrows.

One moon several storms followed each other in succession, each on the heels of the one before it. Jem was weary of sitting indoors, alone or across the fire from the old men, trying to be useful and patient, running out of things to be useful at, and running out of patience. As his thoughts wandered while he brooded, it came to him that there was plenty of space inside the station to shoot the bow. He hadn't practiced in so many days that he missed the feeling—the rhythm of the so-familiar movements, the satisfying pull of the strong bow flexing in his hands, the leap of the arrow speeding from the bowstring.

But if he took the bow to the station, it wouldn't matter if snow blurred the air as the wind buffeted the falling flakes to and fro—inside, with the strange oval lights in the domed ceiling shining above him, he could shoot in perfect comfort. And there would be no distractions.

Still, he'd have to carry the bow and quiver there secretly, and bring them back secretly, and trust that Avakab and Waltak wouldn't miss them in the time he was gone. But he rarely saw either old man venture into that room. Perhaps Avak had even forgotten where he'd stashed the bow, and would never look for it again.

With the snow falling thick and fast over the village, few would be out and about, walking or skiing through the streets. Jem knew his way to and from the abandoned station so well he was confident that as long as he could make out a familiar structure here and there he would find his way.

So he slipped out of the fort with the quiver under his parka and the bow slung over his back with the bowstring across his chest, as he'd seen hunters carry their bows. Snowflakes stung his eyes as he trudged through the dense white curtain, and he saw no one. It was as if he were the only person in the village, moving between the shadow shapes of the buildings that showed dimly behind the veil; sky and earth were one, harmonizing in the song of white.

In the empty quiet of the station, he wiped the snow from the bow and set it on the soft gray floor, then shrugged out of his parka and set the quiver down beside the bow. He used a chair and a thick padded square he'd found on one of the beds to create a target against the wall at the back of the main room. Then he picked up the bow and stood just a few paces from the doorway, which put him a good distance from the target.

By the time Jem had finished, the brand new target was thoroughly decorated with punctures, and his shoulders were sore in a way they hadn't been for a couple of years. But it felt good—as if being deprived of the activity and the sensations that went with it had put a new weight upon him, and now the weight had been dispersed, leaving him light and cheerful. And it wasn't often that he felt cheerful.

He took the bow to the station regularly after that, but only under the cover of snowfall, when he could be fairly certain no one would see him with the weapon. When both sides of his indoor target were too ragged to hold the arrows, he poked about in the station, searching through the unnamed Sanndai objects, to find other things he could shoot. He appropriated more bedding, and also cut a piece off one of the padded chairs with his old knife—not an easy task. But the place had become more and more his own—though there were still things he didn't care to linger over—and he felt little guilt over using the objects for his own purposes. Besides, it wasn't as if anyone else were using them now—or would ever use them again.

Jem would have liked to think the same thing applied to the bow—tucked away in that storeroom, no one else was using it, so why shouldn't he? But he knew that was very different. Any man in Kruvak who laid eyes on that bow would covet it, and most of them would have a real use for it. Learning, practicing, but only shooting at tattered targets made from worn-out skins or abandoned alien comforts—was that really a proper use for such a well-made weapon? Even if it were, it was a purely selfish one.

But then, the old men were being selfish to keep the wonderful bow hidden away, weren't they? For a brief time Jem entertained the idea of telling them he was using the bow and arguing that it was a shame for such a weapon to sit idle in a dusty corner. But that was fraught with risk—they had no reason to care for his opinion, and he knew he never wanted to anger Avakab. And even if he'd convinced himself he wasn't intimidated by Waltak, there was no question that Waltak shared everything with Avak.

One day when he was standing behind Waltak, Jem was once again acutely aware of how much bigger he was than the old man—he saw how little there was of the man himself under the shabby parka hanging on his small frame like an empty skin. But then he thought about how the size you were on the outside didn't always matter. It was the very thing he'd realized about Enkara ages ago.

She was small and frail too, but she was the strongest person he knew. There was something deep inside her that nothing could change—something that remained through grief and hardship: a source of light and warmth that could never be put out. It was like looking up into clouds heavy with snow and seeing that the sun still burned through, a single bright spot in the white sky.

That was what he wanted—that strength. It was part of the feeling that had come with knowing he could do something well, something meaningful. Exactly as he'd felt when all his arrows pierced the center of the target. And he wanted to be able to keep it, to hold onto it with the core of his being so no one could take it away. Not Waltak or Avakab, certainly not Nadka or any of the other midwives. Not even Rulskar.

## II

SEVEN YEARS after Jem's arrival at Avakab's fort, the familiar routines he lived by slipped away from him in the span of a few days. It was hardly a surprise that it began with a confrontation with Rulskar. But Jem could never have imagined how it would end.

Like Enkara, the two old men had changed very gradually. Jem would realize now and then that something was different, but couldn't recall when it had happened. Waltak's hands grew more crippled, and he developed a slight limp. Avakab also moved more slowly, sometimes having difficulty getting up and down from his seat by the fire pit, and he seemed to grow smaller, with his features fading behind more wrinkles— although his burning eyes never lost their intensity.

There were days when Waltak's alternating indifference and suspicious resentment infuriated Jem, and other times when he felt a pity that verged on fondness for the both of them, though he would only admit to himself that he liked Avakab—not Waltak. Jem was sorry when Avakab came to spend less and less time outside, and the old rebel only occasionally told stories when they were sitting together at the fire.

Jem was also aware that Avakab had developed a persistent cough. Though the illu the old men slept in was on the opposite side of the big dome, he could often hear them, and there were nights when he lay awake, listening to the faint sound of coughing. And sometimes the two men talked softly in the silence of the long nights. Waltak's voice carried well, perhaps because it was a high nasal tenor. After waking to hear coughing, Jem would hear Waltak talking to his companion for a long time, though he usually couldn't make out the words. Only rarely did he hear Avakab's soft voice.

For a time Waltak had seemed more amenable toward Jem. But shortly after Jem noticed that Avakab's condition had worsened, the sullen little man who ordered his days grew cold and irritable again. Jem took revenge for this treatment in the only way he could, by being insolent in his manner and frequently talking back. But that solved nothing, and only increased the tension between them.

One day he came into the big illu and found Waltak sitting by the fire with a strange thing in his hands—an object made of shining metal that reflected the firelight with startling brilliance.

Waltak glanced toward him. "Fetch another bundle of that dark tea from the pantry, will you, boy?"

"Sure," Jem said, but paused and took a step closer. The object had a long, rectangular barrel, and its color was part silver and part gold. It appeared to have been made for larger hands than Waltak's small, gnarled ones, red in the firelight.

"What is that?"

"No business of yours," Waltak answered. He lifted the object off his lap—almost as if he intended to threaten Jem with it—but then he set it down again and began stirring the stew in the pot over the fire.

Jem was more fascinated than intimidated, and immediately guessed what it was. "It's a weapon," he said, confident enough that he didn't put it as a question. "A Sanndai weapon."

Waltak's suspicion was so obvious it was easy to imagine

the hair on his gray head standing up. "How did you know that?" he demanded sharply, glaring in Jem's general direction, as he often did, without actually looking at him.

"It has to be. And it looks like their things. I've seen . . . some Sanndai things." He'd already told Avakab, so he could brag to Waltak now; what difference could it make? "I've been in the station. I've looked at the things in there."

This seemed to cause Waltak some discomfiture, but he picked the object up in both hands again, awkwardly turning it over; Jem could tell it was very heavy. He also saw what looked like a filthy rag tied around the metal shape, at the juncture of the handle and the barrel.

"Why is that rag tied around it?"

Waltak chuckled softly. "That, boy, is necessary to make it work."

Jem was skeptical. Avakab had said there were ways for non-Sanndai to use the sinister weapons, but a strip of cloth tied around the thing could hardly be one of them. "How could a dirty rag make a Sanndai weapon work?"

"It's not the rag—it's what's under it." Waltak sat up straighter, and Jem thought he detected a hint of smugness. "Do you want to see?" Again he looked up toward Jem, but not at him, with the hard bitterness set on his pruned face.

Jem could scarcely imagine the decrepit old man using the heavy weapon, and he wasn't afraid, but there was something in Waltak's tone of voice that made him apprehensive. "Yes . . . Are you going to show me?"

Waltak's answer was to place the object down on his lap again and begin prying at the knotted rag with his stiff fingers. Watching, Jem thought perhaps he wouldn't be able to untie it, but it didn't take too long before the stained piece of cloth slipped off and was lifted in one twisted old hand. That hand was then thrust toward Jem—with the rag draped across the palm.

Jem bent down to look at it. His mouth opened in surprise

tinged with horror. In the center of the strip of cloth lay a long hank of dark hair. It was quite like his own hair, and parts of it were nearly pure black. But much of it appeared matted with dirt. Or rather, Jem realized—looking at the color of the stain on the rag—it was likely that the hair was crusted with dried blood.

"Why . . ." Jem had to pause and swallow. "Why does that make it work?"

Waltak smiled, though his eyes still shifted uneasily as he looked past Jem. "Because this evil thing can't tell the difference between hair and skin. It reads the hand that pushes the trigger—even you know that, I think. And with this bound to it," and he raised the rag and its contents again, making Jem lean away, "it always reads this instead."

With his hands gripping his knees, Jem stared down at the thick lock of hair. "So then it thinks the person holding it— shooting it—is the person who . . . that hair came from?"

"Yes, boy!" Waltak snapped, and began rewrapping the stained strip of cloth around the alien weapon. "The bastards' evil magic can be tricked by just a little thing. They're so stupid!" he hissed. In a low mutter he added, "And I know how to use it."

Jem watched him warily; he could think of nothing to say. Waltak put the weapon—with the rag around it—down inside his parka, and turned toward the fire, his back to Jem. Swallowing and clearing his throat, Jem simply asked, with less cockiness than usual, if he could bring anything else from the pantry.

He was disturbed by what he'd seen—more so, he thought, than he ought to be—but he wasn't frightened by the thinly veiled threat. He wondered if he should have been frightened; perhaps such a weapon required no strength or skill to make it swiftly deadly, as Avakab had implied, though it appeared Waltak had difficulty even lifting the thing up. The old men would be sorely in need of help without his presence, but he sensed that Waltak was more nervous than usual, and wondered if age and poor health might make the old man act irrationally.

Still, it was the image of the lock of dark hair that bothered him most. It kept resurfacing in his mind for the rest of that day, forcing him to shove it away and try to think of anything else. And that evening, as he stared at the little yellow flame quivering over the shining oil in his lamp, sitting beside it with his arms clasped around his knees, he remembered what Avakab had said about Sanndai wearing their hair closely shorn. The hair Waltak had shown him was definitely long . . .

Jem closed his eyes and tried again to squeeze the image from his mind, but it was no use. Finally he blew out the lamp and dropped face down onto his bedding. If he were going to fret over something, he told himself, there were certainly more serious things to dwell on—like whether Rulskar or Waltak would be the first one to try to kill him. He groaned and wondered how he ever managed to sleep at all.

Then he heard the howl of a wolf. The sound started low, then slowly rose up. Another joined it, and then another, until the whole babbling, aching chorus filled the night air beyond the empty walls of Jem's little illu. He exhaled, then whispered a thank you to the owners of the haunting voices. The sound was a balm to his spirit, to the clutter and pain in his mind. As the chorus dwindled, then rose again, now farther away, he let the song lift him and carry him to a quiet, lonely place—a place where he could imagine the feeling of peace.

In the morning he decided to go out to the station. After building up the fire and adding some fish to the potatoes already simmering in the pot, then speaking to Waltak just long enough to tell him that the stew was ready, he slipped out the side gate and hurried away. He was only halfway to the abandoned dome at the south edge of the village when he saw the ominous shapes of three familiar figures in the cross street ahead of him.

Though their ruffed hoods were pulled close around their faces to shield them from the chill wind, Jem would have known them even if their identities hadn't been confirmed by the presence of the dog who trotted behind them. He swore quietly and kept going, pretending he hadn't seen them, and wishing he could vanish like a puff of breath on the wind.

"Hey, Sanndai!" Rulskar called loudly. "Where are you going, dirt face?"

Jem knew he could quickly outdistance them if he ran, since the men weren't on skis. But he was sick of playing the coward. He was sick of retreating in response to the insults that were hurled at him, with only the small consolation of getting to commiserate with Waltak over the one thing they agreed on. So he slowed his pace to a less-hurried walk, and looked casually in the direction of the approaching men, pushing his hands deeper into the pockets of his parka.

When the men reached the point where their paths had to cross, Gumak spoke in a snarling voice that was nearly as hostile as Rulskar's. "Hey, ugly. Want us to stick your dirty face in the snow and help you wash the shit off?"

All three men laughed. The dog, Trika, cocked her head at the sound of the laughter, looking as if she were amused as well.

"What's the matter?" Rulskar put in, turning to step in front of Jem, and walking backwards when Jem didn't alter his pace. "You afraid we'll find out it's stuck on so thick it won't come off?"

Meeting the strange blue eyes that gleamed like living ice, Jem tried to speak as nonchalantly as he could, determined to pull off the impression that he was unshaken. "Oh, it's the lunatic."

"Lunatic? Who told you I was a lunatic?"

"No one. It's obvious." Jem continued to walk forward while Rulskar walked backward, so close now that Jem could have reached out and touched him.

"You have a smart mouth, for an ugly alien." The man's face twitched in a swift grimace of hatred, like a parody of a smile.

"Alien. Sure. I never asked to be born in this body," Jem countered, in his well-practiced apathetic voice.

"No, of course you didn't. And you didn't ask to be born on this planet, either."

"No, I didn't. So it's not my fault. If you don't like to look at me, why don't you just leave me alone?

"I'll leave you alone after you're dead. How's that suit you?"

"It doesn't."

"Well then, wouldn't it have been better if someone had stomped on your mother's belly when you were inside, so you'd never been born?"

Jem stopped, his anger flaring like sparks bursting from a glowing ember struck with a hard blow. "That's disgusting—you're sick."

Rulskar stopped as well. His expression was triumphant, as if succeeding in riling Jem were a kind of victory, and he laughed loudly again. Gumak wore his vicious grin; Fenak, as usual, was expressionless, just staring at Jem. The wind whipped around them, rippling through the silver fur that framed their hoods, and stinging the parts of Jem's face left exposed by his own hood.

Then Rulskar spoke again, slowly and deliberately, as if to stress the weight of each word. "If I'm sick, black eyes, your people gave me the illness. I'm merely a poor victim, you see."

"And I'm not?" Jem retorted without thinking.

Rulskar chuckled, an eerie grin spreading across his cold-reddened face. "Well, we could arrange that. In fact, that's just what I had in mind—making you into a victim. Fenak," he said simply, as if it were a cue.

There was a flash of movement. Fenak had pulled a long shining blade—the kind of knife used for butchering meat—out of his parka. Before Jem could react, Rulskar lunged at him, clamping one hand onto his arm.

The hand was strong, but Jem wrenched away from its hold. He whirled and ran, shouting every awful curse he'd ever heard. Trika barked excitedly as the men's voices shouted a jumble of words. Though they followed for some distance, shouting after him, they couldn't match the stride of his long legs. Jem soon put distance between them, praying all the while that Rulskar wouldn't stop and attempt to use his rifle—which was slung over the man's back, as it usually was. Jem's lungs burned from the bitter air and his legs throbbed, the snow pulling at his boots with every flying step.

But he was rattled most of all by the words that were flung after him: "I know where you hide, filthy coward! Go ahead—run! I'm not afraid of that place—I've had the Fever, and I'll bet your unnatural kind don't even have spirits!"

Looking back to confirm that his pursuers had stopped, Jem caught Rulskar's last words, faint on the icy wind. "Run, you ugly bastard, run! I'll finish you yet!"

When Jem reached the station he was trembling with fury as much as exertion. It took him a moment to get the alien key into the slit in the lock.

Throwing himself down on the floor next to the brown bloodstain, he exhaled loudly, then let out another hate-filled curse. He'd wanted so badly not to run, and they had made him run anyway. They'd turned him into a panicked child, and shook the thick walls inside him until they rattled like dry bones.

For the next couple of days Jem's sullen mood made him feel like hiding in the fort and sulking, angry at everything. But soon he longed to get out—whether to go to the station or just to walk for a while. Since the weather was mild for late winter, with a cloud cover keeping the air from growing too cold, yet no immediate threat of a storm, it seemed a shame to confine himself within the motley walls of the old fort. But when he thought of how Rulskar and his men had pursued him, his stomach churned and his face flushed with anger again.

In the end, knowing it might be foolish—and fully aware it might bring worse things than being threatened with a knife—he decided he would take the bow with him. But this time he would carry both bow and quiver in plain view, and walk down the middle of the street like a man who feared no one. He was more than capable of defending himself—why pretend he wasn't? Why cower and run like a child? He was no child—he was twenty-two now—and he had a skill any man would be proud of.

On the way to the station, he only passed two young women with a child. They scarcely glanced at him, and perhaps didn't even notice he carried a weapon—or wouldn't have cared if they had noticed. Inside the dome, Jem practiced shooting for a little while, adding more holes to his latest ragged target. To get as far as he could from the target, he stood just inside the door with his left foot on the bloodstain.

When he decided to head back, thinking of a couple of chores he wanted to get out of the way while the weather was cooperative, his mind wondered as he walked. He'd nearly forgotten he was carrying the bow—until he saw four familiar figures: three men and one white dog with orange markings.

Jem swore under his breath.

Then he swallowed hard and made a promise to himself—he wouldn't run this time. No matter what happened, no matter what they said or did, he was never going to run from Rulskar again.

He walked on, heading straight toward them.

## III

IT WAS TRIKA who alerted Rulskar and his companions to Jem's presence; she cocked her head and looked down the street at his approaching figure. Though her coat wasn't as smooth and she had a few nicks and scars that showed she was no longer a young dog, she still wore the endearing quizzical expression that had charmed Jem when he first saw her.

The three men were standing in the street, a few paces from the door of the Men's House. When Rulskar glanced up to see what the dog was looking at, it was obvious that he murmured something to the others when he nodded toward Jem. As the others turned around, one of the men made a jeering remark. Jem didn't catch the words, but they were all staring at him, clearly doing nothing but waiting for him to come closer.

"Well, here's big, stupid, and ugly," Rulskar called out, his savage grin spreading across his face. "But what's he got over his shoulder?"

Once again Jem tried hard to act calm and casual as he continued to trudge along, altering neither his path nor his pace. So he was walking home—what of it?

Rulskar's eyes widened. "Well, look at that, boys! He's armed. A bow and a full quiver, too."

Jem kept going until they blocked his way, spreading out

so he would be in arm's reach of at least one of them unless he turned around. Trika, her curled tail tipping from side to side, stayed close to her master, but looked curiously up at Jem as if she thought they were about to engage in some kind of game.

It was a game all right, Jem thought wryly. A game he wished he could finish, so he'd never have to play it again.

"Is that old Avak's bow?" Rulskar asked, apparently deciding to adopt a casual attitude himself. "Does he know you have it?"

Jem looked at him blankly and shrugged, as if he'd given it little thought.

"It is," Gumak said. "I recognize it."

"So what?" Jem countered sullenly. "It's not as if he uses it any more."

Rulskar chuckled, the light dancing in his mad eyes. "It's not as if you can use it either. We all know you're as clumsy as you are ugly. Bet you couldn't hit this wall from where you're standing." He gestured at the sod wall of the wide, low building on the north side of the street.

"I can shoot better than you." Jem bit his lip and glowered at Rulskar, his heart quickening.

He knew he shouldn't have said it—it never helped to provoke the hateful man, and it was likely his viciousness at their last encounter had escalated because Jem had insulted him. Yet at the same time he was glad he'd said it—because he was almost certain it was true. What's more, the clumsiness he'd been stricken with for so long had ceased to give him grief in the past year, perhaps because he was no longer growing much, if at all; he'd been wearing the same pair of sealskin trousers for moons.

But all three men were laughing, shaking their heads and looking at Jem as if he were the crazy one.

"Why don't you show us then?" Rulskar taunted. He pulled a short knife from his belt and stepped over to the wall, where he used the knife blade to draw a large circle in the crust of the gray-brown surface. "Let's see you put an arrow into this circle—from over there."

Jem coughed incredulously. "Do you think I'm stupid?"

"I know you're stupid," Rulskar said with his ugly sneer. "You're a Sanndai."

Rolling his eyes, Jem retorted, "Well, you're stupid if you think anyone would fall for that trick." He nodded toward the rifle slung over the madman's shoulder. "If I draw this bow, you'll just shoot me with your rifle and say I was going to shoot you. Not that I think you'd even wait for that excuse, after the other day," he growled bitterly. "So forget it—you can just wonder how good I really am. I'm not touching this bow in front of you."

He didn't know if this were madness too—if this parrying would only get him further into trouble.

"The other day? Oh, you mean Fenak's little knife?" Rulskar grinned scathingly. "If you weren't so stupid, you'd know we were just playing—trying to scare you. And it worked, didn't it? Since you went flapping off like a kiruna." They all laughed again, Fenak and Gumak with that stiff, forced laughter that made them sound like young bullies.

Jem glowered again and said nothing, wondering if he could just step around them and walk away. What would they do if he did?

"Here," Rulskar said. "I'll put my rifle down, and Fenak can lend me his bow"—Fenak was the only one carrying a bow—"and we'll have a little contest. If you're going to go around saying you shoot better than me, you'd better be prepared to prove it. Right, boys?"

Fenak was scowling, but Gumak grinned and nodded. "That's right—you can't say that and not back it up, ropmi."

As Rulskar pulled the rifle sling over his head, his mittened hand closing on the barrel of the weapon, Jem's ears were filled with the pounding of his heart—for a moment he could hear nothing else. Even as Rulskar turned away and propped the gun against the wall, refuting the image that had flooded Jem's mind—the image of the rifle being pointed straight at him—the fear didn't release its powerful grip. And when the madman took the bow from Fenak's reluctant hands and swung his friend's quiver over his shoulder where the rifle sling had been, the picture in Jem's imagination changed accordingly—to show an arrow aimed at his chest.

For what was to keep Rulskar from shooting him anyway? He could so easily place the rebel's bow into Jem's dying hands, dropping an arrow in front of him to make it appear that it had been nocked onto a drawn bowstring, and tell everyone, 'See, I told you this would happen—the Sanndai went mad and tried to shoot us with the old man's bow!'

Jem tried to breathe slowly, to bring the world back into focus, but all he could see were Rulskar's crazed blue eyes staring at him over that too-eager grin, and all his instincts told him that the sensation of terror that had swept over him was warranted. As he took another deep breath and his heart slowed a little, its drumbeat was trumped by the sound of approaching voices.

Jem looked over his shoulder. Four men were coming up the street behind him, their voices drifting like smoke through the cold air. A tide of relief rose up to wash away the fear.

As the men drew nearer, Jem recognized the one in a brown parka as a man named Vechnor. He was one of the few people in the village who would say hello to Jem, and sometimes even smiled at him. But he was a relative of Enkara's—he always came up and spoke to her when there were big gatherings at the Women's House. His kindness to Jem, like that of the girl named Sofia, was probably just for the old woman's sake.

The foursome slowed when they reached Jem and his antagonists. It was Vechnor who spoke first.

"What are you fellows up to this fine afternoon?" Looking at Jem—who was wearing one of his blackest scowls—he asked gently, "Is everything all right?"

Jem felt a wave of gratitude, and his heart started to return to its normal pace. This man was not only looking at him as if he were fully human, but actually seemed interested in his welfare. Even if it were true that this was only because of Enkara, it gave Jem a warm, solid feeling to see the paternal concern on Vechnor's pleasant face.

But before Jem had a chance to speak, Rulskar chuckled and announced, "Well, as you can see, our resident Sanndai has taken to parading about with Avakab's fine old bow, and he's just claimed he can shoot better than I can. We think he ought to prove it and have a little contest with me. But as soon as I suggested it, he became quite reluctant." He grinned slyly at Vechnor and the others. "I can't imagine why, can you?"

Vechnor looked curiously at Jem. Jem had seen that look before; sometimes when the man graced him with a smile, something in his eyes suggested that he found Jem intriguing. He clucked softly and said, "Now, young Jem, I'm sure Enkara's taught you that nothing good ever comes from boasting." His voice was low and gentle, his tone conversational rather than accusing.

But now his kindness made Jem feel childish, even embarrassed. "I'm not boasting," he said quickly.

Vechnor's brows lifted. "Well then, why not agree to have a friendly little contest? There's no shame in being proud of doing something well."

Several more men had stepped out of the Men's House. They were just in time to hear Vechnor's words, and after a few greetings were exchanged, they joined the crowd, perhaps curious to see if there would really be a contest.

Jem glanced at the unsettling grin on Rulskar's face, saw the predatory gleam in his eye. Like a weasel about to pounce on a vole, Jem thought sourly.

"I don't trust him," he told Vechnor.

Rulskar laughed, but it sounded false, as if he were trying

to act unconcerned. "He seems to think I'll shoot him instead of the target, Vech."

His fellow bullies added more forced and unnatural laughs, while a couple of the others apparently found this genuinely amusing.

But Vechnor turned back to Jem and said, "I'm sure he wouldn't do that." He glanced over at Rulskar with an expression that seemed to both expect and doubt confirmation of that statement—as if what he didn't say aloud was, 'Tell me you wouldn't think of doing such a thing.' Seeing this didn't do much to make Jem feel better.

Rulskar laughed again. "He scares easily, our poor lost Sanndai. Perhaps he has a guilty conscience." He sneered and added, "But I suppose that's inevitable—if it's not on account of something he's done himself, he has so many reasons to feel guilty for all the evil deeds of his kind."

Though there was more laughter, some of the men frowned, as if they thought Rulskar's remark inappropriate.

"Now, now, my friend," Vechnor said. "You know the boy can't help who he is. And perhaps he wouldn't be so skittish if you didn't bully him so much."

This was another surprise for Jem. It hadn't occurred to him that anyone besides Enkara noticed or cared when he was bullied, much less that they would be aware of how often Rulskar taunted him. In truth, he rarely imagined anyone else thinking of him at all.

Then Vechnor addressed Jem again. "Will you accept Rulskar's challenge if we observe to ensure that the competition is fair? I'm sure we'd all enjoy watching a bit of shooting, and it's a fine, calm day for it." He glanced upward, squinting at the bright day through the pale brown fur rimming his round cap. Though the entire sky was white, the cloud cover was high and thin, and the crisp air was still.

Jem's relief was followed by the tingling touch of anticipation. This was just what he'd wanted—a chance to show the men of the village what he'd learned to do. "Sure," he said. "I'll do it if all of you watch." As crazy as Rulskar was, Jem couldn't imagine him shooting him in front of all these men; he could sense that Rulskar respected some of them, especially the older ones like Vechnor, in the same way that he still had respect for Avakab.

There were murmurs of satisfaction, and momentarily someone added to the circle Rulskar had drawn on the sod wall, using a knife blade to etch out three circles embedded within each other. It was decided that the outermost circle would be worth one point, the second two points, and the inner circle worth three points. To Jem, who'd been working on shooting thumbprints he made on his targets with charcoal, the circles were overly generous; the one in the center was nearly two decimeters wide.

He caused raised eyebrows when he took two large steps back from the line Fenak had begun to drag in the snow with the toe of his boot, and said, "No—back here."

The man who'd drawn the target scratched a large R near the edge of the wall, then glanced over his shoulder and said, "What's his name? Enkara's boy?" When no one answered him immediately—they were chattering among themselves—he said, "Oh, never mind," and wrote an equally large E.B. next to the R.

"It's Jem," Jem called out, but no one seemed to pay attention. He was stuck with being 'Enkara's boy'. It was rather funny since not only was he too old to be called a 'boy', it was very obvious that he was taller than everyone else there.

The preparations complete, Vechnor turned to Jem and asked if everything was agreeable to him.

Jem answered, "Yes. Except the target's kind of big," and favored the kindly man with one of his rare smiles. He wasn't surprised when this brought a murmur of surprised—and mostly skeptical—laughter.

"How about a wager?" someone asked.

"Oh, yes—there's a wager," Rulskar said, with a nasty smirk. "If I win, the Sanndai gives me the old man's bow." He narrowed his glittering eyes so they bore into Jem. "And I'll be sure and tell him that I've got it—and how I got it. If the Sanndai wins, he can have this bow"—he raised Fenak's bow in his right hand—"and we won't tell Avak his naughty servant has been playing with that one."

Fenak made an indignant sound. "Rulskar! That's *my* bow, and you know I need it! You can't wager someone else's property."

Rulskar snorted. "Don't be such an old woman—your bow is quite safe." He dropped his voice, although it was still audible over the murmurs of the other men's conversation, and said rapidly, "When have you ever seen that monstrosity show as much coordination as a sopping wet calf?"

Jem bit his lip, trying to ignore the inevitable rush of anger. He turned his attention to Vechnor, who gave him another one of those curious, questioning looks.

"Does Avak know you're using his bow?" he asked Jem.

As before, Jem evaded the question, looking down as he checked his arrows and then repositioned the quiver over his shoulder. He shrugged and repeated the words he'd said to Rulskar. "It's not as if he uses it any more." Then, because he both respected and liked Vechnor, he added, "I'm always very careful with it."

Vechnor smiled and placed a hand on Jem's shoulder. "I'm sure you are, cousin."

"Cousin?" one of the men echoed.

Turning toward the man who'd spoken, Vechnor said, "Well, he is my cousin, you know—after a fashion." He smiled broadly, appearing to be amused by the expressions on the other men's faces. "You know Enkara's my aunt."

But Rulskar the weasel pounced, displaying his cruelest sneer. "After a fashion? Whatever 'fashion' that is, keep it to yourself. I'd die before I claimed any ugly Sanndai for a cousin." He paused to shake his head in mock sadness. "Ah, poor Vech—it's about your beloved Uncle Nihkul, isn't it? But even if he was married to that foolish little woman, do you really think he would have wanted you to call this piece of dung your 'cousin'?" His laughter was loud and brutal.

Vechnor shook his head and his countenance changed; he grew uncharacteristically stern. "You're entitled to your opinion, but I would be careful of your tone of voice when it comes to speaking of my uncle."

Rulskar seemed to sense that he'd come too close to crossing a line, and he turned his most ingratiating smile on the older man. "You know I meant no disrespect to your uncle, Vech." But he spoiled the show of humility by saying, "Besides, he wasn't there to talk his foolish wife out of making that dreadful mistake. I imagine he would have tried—even if she wouldn't have listened to him."

"I don't wish to pick a quarrel," Vechnor replied, "but it's hardly fair to call someone as wise as Enkara 'foolish' for having compassion." He cleared his throat and added, "Nor is it fair to treat this young man"—and he paused before and after the words 'young man', making his view of Rulskar's crude insult quite clear—"as if he were to blame for all the crimes of his race."

Jem looked away to hide his smile.

"Come, come," one of Vechnor's companions said, either wanting to dispel the tension or simply tiring of the banter. "Let's have this little contest before the wind picks up."

Everyone backed up behind Jem's chosen line. Rulskar, being the challenger, went first, putting the toe of his left boot just behind the groove in the trampled snow as he nocked an arrow onto the string of Fenak's bow.

His first shot went into the smallest circle, halfway between the center and the edge. Appreciative sounds came from the observers, helping to ease the sudden flutter of nervousness in Jem's stomach—he'd been gripped by the realization that he was about to shoot in front of other eyes for the first time. If they're impressed by that, he told himself as he took Rulskar's place at the line, I've got nothing to worry about.

When Jem let the bow down and stepped back, the familiar brown and white fletching was no more than two centimeters from the exact center of the target. Again there were murmurs of praise, and when he glanced warily at the little crowd—wishing he'd hit the bull's-eye dead center, since he knew so well that he could—he saw piqued interest on the men's faces. Hopes had been raised that this might turn out to be an entertaining competition.

Rulskar's next shot also hit the inner ring, but off to the left. Jem's second arrow landed a hair's breadth from his first one. There were matching marks on the scoreboard, and the onlookers were clearly enjoying themselves now.

Jem was annoyed when Rulskar's third arrow landed on the border between the inside circle and the next, and after a brief discussion there was mutual agreement that he'd squeaked by, and the shot was still worth three points. After Jem took his shot, all three of his arrows were huddled together, while Rulskar's were spread in a wide, patternless array across the inner ring, and yet their scores were still tied. It was obvious that between the size of the target's rings and the point system they'd chosen, the contest would downplay the variance in the contestant's skills.

But Jem couldn't complain that it wasn't fair—perhaps Vechnor and the others had assumed he'd be taking a beating, and hadn't wanted him to look too bad. Or perhaps not. It didn't really matter. A warmth was spreading inside Jem, moving out through every limb. Though he tried to focus only on his shooting, every time he stepped away from the line he saw eyebrows raised higher and more excitement in the exchanged glances. Whenever someone caught his eye, his gaze was met with honest approval—though often balanced by equally genuine surprise.

The contest was still tied after the fourth round. Rulskar's fifth shot landed well out in the second circle, eliciting both sympathetic groans and laughter from the audience. The groans were louder when his seventh arrow pierced the line between the middle and outer circles. Again they all agreed to give him the higher score. So Jem was ahead by only two when Rulskar drew back the bow for his last shot.

It went deep into the center of the target, right alongside the tight cluster of Jem's seven arrows. As Jem stepped up to the line and nocked his last arrow, he could feel every pair of eyes on him; he knew they all wondered if the pressure would finally bring an end to his consistent performance.

Jem pulled the string back to his jaw, flexing the powerful bow, hearing only his own breathing, seeing only the target and the arrows that decorated it. His arrow hit the earthen wall in the exact center of the three circles. The splintering sound as the point bit into the shaft of the arrow that had preceded it was loud in the still, cold air.

As boisterous exclamations rose behind him, Jem felt the powerful surge of pride and relief above all else. Yet when he saw how all eight of the familiar brown and white-fletched arrows were in a tight clump with the unmatched white one hanging by its shattered shaft in their midst, as if its assailant had wanted to drive it out because it wasn't its own kind, he winced, knowing how few good arrows were left in the village.

There'd scarcely been a centimeter of empty space in the center of the target, but knowing full well that he was capable of that precision, Jem had aimed to sink his last shot snugly up against the other arrows; he was genuinely sorry that missing by merely half a centimeter had caused him to break Fenak's arrow. But it couldn't be helped now. And he had won.

Jem filtered the voice of one of the men from the jumble of murmurs and laughter. "Well, I'll be! Looks like the boy wins—twenty-four to twenty-two." And the last mark was now on the scoreboard, confirming that E.B. was the victor. A couple of the men walked past him and began to pull the arrows out of the wall.

To Jem's satisfaction, Rulskar actually looked chagrined; he displayed a faint, incredulous smile and shook his head as he watched them take down the arrows. But the feeling of vindication was brief. Seconds later Rulskar crushed it by saying, "Well, only two points. He just got lucky."

For a moment Jem was unable to make a sound, choked by the rage and indignation that leapt up inside of him like a cornered animal lunging at its attacker. "Lucky?" he spluttered in disbelief.

One of Vechnor's companions came up to him, holding Avakab's eight arrows in a neat array. Jem saw them in a blur as he slid them back into their quiver, then heard himself say, "Wait a moment."

Returning to the line where they'd stood to fire their shots, Jem took another large step back, raising his bow. "Stand back, everyone," he demanded, his voice hard and clear in the renewed silence.

He took a deep breath, then let it out audibly. Bringing his right hand to his shoulder, where the fletching of the arrows protruded from the top of the quiver, he drew another slow breath. Then he began.

Nocking and firing without the briefest pause between shots, he sent each arrow speeding into the sod wall. The sound of the bowstring and the 'shunk' of each arrow marked a perfect staccato rhythm. Each arrow struck exactly the same distance from the outer edge of the wall. Each was exactly a hand's breadth below the one above it.

In seconds the quiver was empty, and all eight arrows were arrayed in a vertical line down the wall, the pattern made by the brown and white feathers as flawless as the stitches in a line of Enkara's embroidery.

"How's that for 'lucky'?" Jem declared defiantly, and turned around.

Mouths were hanging open.

A heady warmth rushed through Jem. Now the feeling was complete, with the reward of his victory increased beyond measure by knowing he'd shown what he could really do—and by seeing his triumph painted on the faces of the men who'd seen him do it. He weighed nothing, and all the light in the white sky was focused on him. He would never forget that moment—nothing could ever take it away from him.

He didn't even care that the only jaw that wasn't gaping, and the only eyes that weren't watching him with genuine awe and respect, were Rulskar's. Instead his opponent bore a strange, hard expression, with an odd satisfaction in those burning eyes.

"Well, my dear fellow," Vechnor proclaimed as he turned toward Rulskar. "I'm afraid you've been soundly beaten; there can be no question who the winner is."

An unsavory smile spread across Rulskar's face. Clearly he'd seen a way to gain some advantage for himself from Jem's accomplishment. "Perhaps," Rulskar answered, gazing past Vechnor as if seeing something else in his mind. "But perhaps I win in another way."

"How's that?" someone asked.

The smile grew more sinister. "Well, our wild Sanndai has just proven how dangerous he is . . . hasn't he?" Rulskar paused. "Maybe that means he isn't the winner."

"Dangerous?" Vechnor echoed. "I don't think he's dangerous."

Jem recalled that it was exactly what old Avak had said to him when they first met: "I don't think you're dangerous." For a moment he was swept back to that day; he saw the orange light in the smoke-filled kitchen, saw the knife in the old man's strong hands, felt the uncanny force in the old man's gaze.

Returning from retrieving his arrows, Jem approached Vechnor, who was looking at him with that curious expression again, now complimented by a playful twinkle in his eyes.

"You're not dangerous, are you, Jem?" he asked. Jem thought he sounded amused.

"No," Jem said. "I would never harm anyone on purpose."

Gumak was standing a few paces away, and he sneered at Jem, curling up his lip in a fair imitation of Rulskar's signature expression. "Not even someone who was trying to scare you?"

Jem shot him a dark look. "Especially not someone who was just ridiculing me." Turning his back to Gumak, he addressed Vechnor. "I'd defend myself if I had to, but I'd still try not to hurt anyone. Enkara says if you don't respond in kind to people who are cruel, it makes you stronger than they are."

Vechnor's smile was like a splash of light piercing the clouds in midwinter. "That's right, cousin," he said. "You just listen to Enkara. Don't pay attention to what anyone else says. Enkara is the wisest person I know."

Pleased but a little embarrassed, Jem murmured, "I always listen to Enkara." It was nearly true—and he wished it were completely true.

Rulskar gave a skeptical snort, shaking his head as he walked past them. He barely slowed as he thrust Fenak's bow into Jem's hands.

Jem blinked—he'd forgotten the wager—and looked up to see the aggrieved expression on Fenak's sullen face. Stepping in front of Fenak and blocking Rulskar's path, Jem held out the bow.

"It's all right, Fenak—I don't want to take your bow." Feeling awkward, he added, "I know you need it. I don't—not really. And I'm sorry I broke your arrow."

Fenak looked surprised, and Jem was still more surprised to see a touch of gratitude in the man's eyes. "Thank you," Fenak murmured as he clasped the grip of his weapon, his voice barely audible.

Rulskar turned away and barked, "Come on, fellows, let's go." The threesome strode off, pausing only for Rulskar to pick up his rifle. As he pulled the rifle sling over his shoulder, he looked back at Jem, the cruel gleam bright in his narrowed eyes.

"Well, congratulations, young man," Vechnor said, again placing his hand on Jem's arm. Jem was so unused to gentle physical contact—or any contact at all—from anyone other than Enkara, it seemed odd that someone might actually want to reach out and touch him. "You certainly have reason to be proud of yourself today."

It was hardly as if Jem didn't already know that, but having someone else put it into words added to the power of what he felt—it validated those feelings, lifting them up beyond dispute. When he thanked Vechnor, his own words didn't feel adequate enough.

Then Vechnor told him cheerfully, "I hope we get to hunt together someday, cousin. Perhaps when Avak's gone you'll come stay with us. Take care of yourself."

Jem delayed heading back to the fort for a few moments. Standing where they'd left him, he watched—and listened—as Vechnor and his companions walked away, their voices rising just above the crunch and squeak of their boots on the well-packed snow.

One said, "Of course I'd like to hunt with that boy myself, but you know Rulskar's right about him being dangerous—not to others, but to himself—because of those who see him that way. If something happened when you took him out with you, how would you feel? It would be awfully hard to tell Enkara, wouldn't it?"

"Yes—and he's the only cousin I have left!" Vechnor replied with a soft laugh, his voice touched with sadness. "But you're right—it's the reason I didn't take him in the first place. We were afraid I'd put him in danger if I took him to the coast. And if I didn't, what would be the point? He'd be left sitting at home with nothing to do. I don't have much else to teach him." He chuckled. "Besides, at the time I didn't think he'd be that good at it."

"He used to be rather awkward, didn't he?"

"Yes—a bit. He's not any more, is he? It's the situation that's still awkward. It may well be impossible. I hope it isn't, but we'll have to see."

As their voices began to fade, Vechnor glanced back. Seeing that Jem was still standing in the middle of the white street, he raised a hand in a simple gesture of parting. Though he smiled, Jem saw the hint of sorrow—and resignation—in his expression.

Logically Jem understood that he shouldn't hold onto the hope that Vechnor would ever take him in. It was likely his situation hadn't changed—or might even be worse when everyone in the village learned of his skill.

But none of that could bring him down now. He still felt full of warmth and as light as falling snow.

Putting the bowstring across his chest and the quiver's strap over his shoulder, Jem ran, racing wildly like a boy, all the way back to the fort, not caring how the cold air burned his lungs.

IV

TWO DAYS AFTER the archery contest, the morning dawned clear and cold. Jem was looking forward to taking the bow to the station—now that everyone knew about it and there was no need to hide it—to practice in comfort. When he came into the big illu, he was surprised to see that Avakab was up earlier than usual and had come out to sit on his pile of furs next to the fire pit; lately he'd been staying in the small illu where he and Waltak slept much of the time.

Then Jem noticed something odd about the smell of the smoke. At first he couldn't identify what it was. Then it came to him that it was the scent of burning wood. It wasn't often that they had any wood to burn.

Murmuring a greeting to the old rebel, Jem knelt beside the fire. On the raised platform beside Avakab was a handful of cut feathers. For a second Jem simply wondered why the feathers were there, and what the old man was doing with them. But when he realized the white and brown kiruna feathers looked oddly familiar, he felt a twinge of apprehension.

And when he looked amid the yellow flames rippling over the bed of coals, he saw shapes that were clearly burned wood—straight wooden sticks, mostly turned to ash, and a glowing red-orange piece that looked like a flattened, curved branch. Jem's eyes moved back to the old man. On his other side, resting on the dark furs, there was a tangle of gray yarn and some thin strips of soft beige reindeer skin.

The final clue was a piece of string loosely coiled on Avakab's knee. Then Jem knew, even before he saw the empty quiver lying just behind the old man, what had been put into the fire.

The blood rushed to his face. For a moment he was speechless, with his mouth hanging open like the men who'd watched his performance after the contest, and he could do nothing but watch the low flames burn. Then he turned to look at the old rebel's pale, quiet face.

"Your bow . . ." he murmured incredulously. "But why?"

It seemed a long time before Avakab answered. He began to loop the bowstring into a small skein, winding it around his fingers. Finally he spoke, in a soft, level voice.

"I was afraid it would cause trouble for someone I care about. From a little story I heard yesterday, perhaps it already has."

It took even longer for the meaning of the words to fully register in Jem's mind. They hung suspended in the cold silence, like pieces of moss in a half-frozen bucket of water.

Me. Jem thought. He means me. Scarcely able to wrap his mind around this astonishing idea, he latched onto the most obvious, and most shameful, element of the crime.

"But—but you could have just given it to someone else," he stammered. "Someone who could have put it to good use!"

Avakab spoke as if he were musing to himself, the way he sometimes had when he'd told Jem stories in the courtyard. "Everyone in this village has been saying for years that I'm a selfish man. No one should be surprised when I do something that proves it."

Jem stared into the coals, his eyes on the so-familiar curve of the piece of wood being slowly devoured by the flames. Then he looked instead at his own large hands, studying the calloused palms and dark brown backs as if he'd never seen them before.

Finally he said, "But if you'd just told me not to use it again . . . if you'd told me to put it back and never touch it, I would have done it. I would have promised."

The old man breathed out audibly, and coughed several times before he spoke. "I believe you. But perhaps it's better if there is no temptation."

There was nothing more to say. Tearing his gaze from the fire, Jem brewed a pot of tea and prepared some potato gruel for the old men.

Waltak shuffled in, sniffling and looking vacant, and sat beside Avakab. The three of them ate in silence; Jem hastily gulped down the soup and half a bowl of tea. When he returned the bowl to the weathered kitchen box beside the fire pit and stirred up the coals, small bursts of sparks sprayed from the remaining fragments of wood.

Then Jem got up and went out without a word. Since the old men sometimes came and went in silence—though Avakab usually acknowledged Jem, if only briefly—it didn't seem rude, and being rude wasn't Jem's intent. But he needed to get away from that strange quiet under the blue shadow of the dome, and try to make sense of his thoughts—to make some sense of the world again.

He walked with little purpose, though habit placed his feet on the route to the Sanndai station. With his head down, he stared at the crisscrossing footprints in the snow, saw the familiar shadows of the brown and gray walls flanking the streets he passed through, felt the familiar bite of the cold air on the exposed parts of his face.

Ever so slowly, it began to sink in: the wonderful bow—and all eight arrows—were gone. He wouldn't hold them again. He would not even see them again, either tucked away in their old hiding place, or coming to life in someone else's hands. They were gone.

Knowing all too well that they didn't belong to him hadn't stopped them from becoming a part of him—an extension of his own body, as familiar as hands and arms. And now his grief was tangled in the confusing strands implied by the old man's words, like a seal pup caught in a fishing net.

Had Avakab really sacrificed the bow to protect Jem? And if he had, did it make any difference? There were plenty of other bows in the village—surely those who thought Jem 'dangerous' would have no difficulty imagining him stealing another weapon. But perhaps it was just an excuse. Perhaps when the old man heard that someone else had been using his bow, he realized he still felt possessive about it, and wanted no one else to have it when he was gone—and the fact that Jem was the person using it was merely incidental.

Still, Avakab wasn't the sort of man to make up stories to please anyone. Why would he have said he cared about Jem if he didn't? It would make no difference to him whether or not Jem was angry at the loss of the bow. Avak had feared no one when he was young, and he had nothing to lose now, did he?

Jem was only a few meters away from three figures walking toward him when he looked up, pulled from his thoughts by an image he'd caught sight of out of the corner of his eye—a white dog with orange markings digging in the snow banked up against a shed. Then he was facing Rulskar and his companions once again.

Perhaps they'd noticed Jem's preoccupation, for there was something different in the way the threesome regarded him— even Rulskar. Jem saw curiosity blended with the usual distaste and suspicion. And Jem thought Fenak looked wary— or perhaps guilty—when he glanced at Jem's face and then averted his gaze.

Only Rulskar's uncanny eyes fixed on him steadily, as if he were surveying Jem, looking for the best way to launch his attack. But when he spoke, a touch of the curiosity lingered in his cold expression, and all he said was, "No bow today?"

"No bow," Jem said flatly, and walked on, not looking back.

They did nothing to stop him.

When Jem reached the outskirts of the village, the domed station was a welcome sight. He picked up his pace, lengthening his stride as he crossed the street that made a wide curve around the abandoned alien structure, then began to push his way through the deep, unmarred snow on the other side.

There was surprising comfort in just seeing the familiar half-eggshell shape, and in the anticipation of the odd peace that came when he was inside of it. And even if it were foolish, at that moment it helped immeasurably to think of the place as his, and to be certain it was the one thing no one would take from him. In his mind he laughed bitterly at the thought. No one would take it because they neither wanted it for themselves, nor wanted him not to have it for any crazy reason—whether that reason was well-meaning or selfish.

As he trudged up to the doorway, Jem reached into the neck of his parka to pull out the leather thong holding the key. Then he saw that the door wasn't fully closed. He stopped.

For a moment Jem couldn't even draw a breath; he was so shocked by the realization of what that meant he felt as if someone had grabbed him by the throat. But seconds later his overriding emotion became pure anger. Though he hadn't acknowledged it, the loss of the bow had already put him on the brink of grief-born rage.

Furiously he lunged forward and grabbed the side of the door where the lock was. Even at a glance it was obvious something had been done to it: the edge of the metal plate that covered the keyhole bore a curved gouge, and above it the surface of the door was raised and blistered. And when Jem forced himself to focus and look at it closely, he could see that a piece of severed metal—a thick silver bar that must have been part of the lock—was still in the edge of the door frame.

He felt a terrible sense of violation. Someone had broken into his private domain, his little world—the one place where he could always feel safe, always know he'd be alone. And because they had literally broken in, the door would never be locked again.

Pulling off one mitten, he ran his bare finger over the edge of the door and the severed piece. The cut surface of the bolt was perfectly smooth, as if it had been forged that way. And a file could not have been slid between the frame and the edge of the alien door; they fit so snugly that no light and very little air reached through the crack.

As everything spun through his mind, the first idea Jem could pin down was that it had to be Rulskar. The man had said he didn't fear this place—didn't fear Sanndai ghosts—and had threatened to follow him here. Rulskar and his faithful companions had been headed toward the center of the village when they passed him—could they have just come from here? Could they have broken in to taunt him, and to see what damage they could do? Or even to leave some kind of trap for Jem?

Yet there had been nothing in the behavior of the three men that suggested they'd just committed such an act. If they had, he was certain they would have been more smug, more eager. Surely Rulskar, who was always prone to saying too much, would have dropped some rude remark that hinted at what awaited him here. More importantly, how could they have cut the bolt like this? Was there even anything in the village capable of leaving such a mark on solid metal?

Jem gave the damaged door a violent shove to open it the rest of the way. He was about to swear loudly when a chilling thought struck him. If Rulskar hadn't done this—if it were someone else, perhaps someone who didn't even come from the village—what if that person were still inside? He did swear then, but only inside his head. Oh, how stupid he was! Stupid enough that at any moment he might be dead.

He stopped and stood absolutely still, praying he hadn't already made enough noise to give himself away. Then he took a deep breath and stepped inside. The lights were on—and he always turned them off when he left.

Two careful steps and he paused, both feet in the middle of the bloodstain. A faint sound made him freeze, biting his lip. He'd begun to take the next step when his eyes caught movement on the left side of the room.

Another pause to silently let his breath out again, then one more step forward. Now his view was no longer obstructed by the largest piece of white furniture.

The figure was seated on the floor, in front of the metal drawers in the wall—the ones with silver handles that wouldn't move no matter how hard Jem pulled or pried. Several of them were open. One revealed two rows of silver objects arrayed on a surface that looked like blue fur. But this—the contents behind the mysterious panels—seemed of little importance now. What was significant was the person who sat with his back toward Jem, apparently still unaware of his presence.

Everything visible on the figure was black. Not dark gray, or dark brown, but as black as total darkness. The clothing—of a smooth material that appeared molded to his back and shoulders—was solid black. And the glossy, short hair on the back of the uncovered head was black—even blacker than Jem's own long, wind-tattered hair . . . Or the hank of hair tied to the Sanndai weapon.

A voice spoke, hushed and breathless, and Jem realized it was the sound he'd heard. "Wow," the voice said rapidly. "Triple wow! This is unbelievable." And then, louder, came a strange laugh and more words. "Nobody—nobody will ever beat this! Not in a million years! Ha! By all the stars in the cosmos, I'm the luckiest ape that ever lived!"

Jem understood the words, but not immediately—the pronunciation and rhythm were strange, drawn out with an odd lilt.

The intruder was bent over something he held in his lap. Without turning around, he jumped to his feet in one motion. He was very tall, with long limbs.

Jem glimpsed a large bronze-colored hand as it lifted another one of the silver objects out of the drawer—another, because that was what the stranger held in his other hand. And having clearly seen the rectangular shape, Jem knew what it was.

For a crazy fleeting moment, Jem could think only of how badly he wanted the old rebel's bow back in his hands. Then, in a desperate impulse, he pulled his short knife—the only weapon he possessed—from his belt.

"Don't move," he hissed loudly.

The stranger jumped and let out a yelp of surprise. Jem saw one hand drop the silver weapon back into the drawer and grip the edge of the open panel as the man's head snapped around. Jem couldn't see his other hand, or the other weapon. But Jem wasn't thinking of the weapons any longer.

His mind had emptied of all but one thing—the eyes. The eyes in the tawny-skinned face that were fixed on Jem with a look of stunned disbelief. They were dark. So dark that the pupils weren't distinct. Deep and unfathomable, they were eyes that should only have belonged to an animal. But despite the alien color and features, the visage they stared out of was the very human face of a young man.

# PART FOUR

# PIECES OF NIGHT

I

FOR A MOMENT neither Jem nor the intruder moved. The stranger simply stared at him, breathing hard. Then Jem watched the expression on the impossible dark face change, slowly but with surprising clarity, as fear and alarm were replaced with relief. And the relief was followed by puzzlement.

The young man furrowed his brow, then wrinkled his face in an incredulous half-grimace that made him look very youthful and boyish—to Jem's amazement. Jem was still more surprised when the tall stranger spoke abruptly, with no evidence of caution. "Who are you?"

Jem stared back at him, his jaw clenched, determined not to show his own fear. Then he said, "Show me both hands."

It was a foolish charade—even if the intruder were as young as he appeared to be, he had to know it was a bluff. And even if Jem had spent the past several years practicing with a knife instead of a bow—and become as adept at knife-throwing as Avakab in his youth—he would have been in no position to make demands of someone standing next to a drawer full of weapons. From what little Jem knew about them, the Sanndai's light guns didn't need to be reloaded before each use.

The intruder lifted his left hand, still holding one of the silver weapons, and with an exaggerated motion he set the object down on the open drawer with the others. He held out both hands—surprisingly large hands—with the broad, unmarred palms turned up. "No trouble, 'kay hossti?"

Jem realized he was holding his breath and released it. Chewing his lip, he loosened his death grip on his knife but didn't lower it.

The young man ran one reddish-bronze hand through his short black hair, tousling it. He cocked his head, with the hint of a smile. "You're not like . . . guarding these, are you?" When Jem didn't answer, he added, "So can I ask who you are and what you're doing up here?" He pronounced some of the words oddly, and his voice was languid—a drawl with a lazy singsong rhythm.

Jem was thrown by the accent. He heard only the sound of the words first, with the meaning registering a moment after the stranger had spoken. Finally he said, "What are *you* doing here? You tell me first." He let the hand that held his knife drop to his side.

The intruder wrinkled his brow again, and bit his lower lip much in the way Jem had just been doing. "Why?" he said. Now that he'd obviously recovered from being alarmed, his lack of wariness was coupled with a shade of impudence.

Baffled by this audacity, Jem tried to speak again and found that his throat was tight. He swallowed, then said in a cold, hard voice, "You don't belong here. And this place . . ." He stopped himself from saying the place was his. "I'm the only one who comes to this place. Nobody else."

This increased the perplexed look on the lean, tan face. In spite of the exotic angularity of his features, the boy's open display of emotion made him appear curiously childlike. "You're living here? I heard this place was abandoned ages ago."

"It was. But I found the key. I don't live in here."

"Where do you live?" The boy made the same exaggerated expression of bewilderment that involved wrinkling up half of his face. "Northlite, or that other place?"

"I live in the fort. And it's no business of yours," Jem snapped, irritated that he'd been so easily conned into revealing that much, while his own question hadn't been answered.

"The fort? Here in Kruvak, you mean? With the Torviks?"

Jem nodded. His heart was still thudding hard in his chest.

"But why?"

"I was born here."

"You mean your parents are here? Your family?"

"My blood mother is dead. There's no one like me here." Hearing his own words, Jem winced. Why was he telling this stranger—this Sanndai—anything at all?

"By all the stars, this is amazing!" the boy exclaimed, taking a step toward Jem. "Where'd you get those clothes—from the Torviks?"

Jem scowled. "They're my clothes. I made them."

"Really? Wow, that's something. Explains why you talk like a Torvik, though, donit?" The young Sanndai grinned then—a startling, broad, and very white smile that transformed his face and made him look even more alien. "Shesh! But you know, you look familiar. Your face, I mean . . . It's funny." He laughed. It was a boyish, happy laugh, as if there were no shadows in his life. "Well, obviously we haven't met before. And if we had, I'd have remembered the accent, anyway! No offense, hossti—but this is *weeeird*. You being here, I mean."

Jem swallowed uncomfortably again. Then he returned to his own question, grasping for control like a dog guarding a bone when it knows someone wants to take it from them. "Tell me why you're here. Why did you break the door to get in?"

The boy shrugged. "Well, I had to cut the lock to get inside. That's obvious, aynit? And I'm here 'cause I'm looking for old stuff—relics and techfacts. I'm a member of the Order, you know, and we have this sort of—well, contest. Competition. For anybody who helps remove interference—cultural or tech or both—from any place outside the System. It can be something you find out about and help change, or physical stuff you actually take back. Or you can just look in old collections and find relics that have to do with Zennix—the Order gives points for that too. And wow!" He started to laugh again—a loud, unrestrained laugh. "Did I just beat everybody for all time!" He stopped and gave Jem a funny look. "Well, unless you're supposed to be guarding all these 'Z's or something, and won't let me take 'em."

"I don't know what you mean." The flood of meaningless information had brought back the queasy sensation Jem had experienced the first time he came into the station.

The young man turned to gesture at the contents of the open drawer. "All these Zendi guns, hossti. See, I read a report that hinted they left all kinds of stuff here—like the person who filed it didn't want to flat out say a lot of things got left behind. So I kept digging into it, and discovered some monkey leaked a story out of Guardian files 'bout an entire issue of 'Z's that was sent up here on account of the Torvik rebels, and how there wasn't any record of them being brought back! Whoever knew about it wasn't in a position to come find out if it was true, I guess, and Bakraga's not that accessible any more. It's real expensive to get out here. So I decided I was gambling on it, 'cause if it was true—by Zennix, nobody'd ever beat me!

"I'm going to be in big trouble for draining my card, that's for certs, but it'll be worth it." He grinned impishly. "I'm not supposed to be here. I knew there was no way in a million lights they'd give me a trip autho for anywhere on Bakraga—and the Torvik Closed Zone's supposed to be shut tight anyway. So I lied about my desty to get jumped out here. Came the last few lights on a really small transer, but it went smooth, you know. So, you don't know anything about these? The Zendis, I mean?"

Jem shook his head. "I didn't know they were here. Those drawers wouldn't open."

"Oh, yeah—I had to cut those locks too." The young Sanndai glanced about the room, gesturing with his chin at the space and its tattered furnishings. "This place is kind of scary, you know? People died in here."

This comment struck Jem as very odd; he'd imagined that any real Sanndai would be comfortable here—more comfortable than he ever was—just because this was a Sanndai place, and the building and the artifacts it contained would be familiar to them. But he only said, "I know. That blood on the floor was from a man who died there."

The boy blinked and looked alarmed. "Blood?"

As Jem loosened the neck of his parka with one hand—it was always warmer in the station—he pointed with his knife, indicating the large brown stain. "There."

The stranger made a childish face. "That was blood? Eeeuw!"

Although Jem managed not to laugh, he had to smile. It seemed ludicrous that the first Sanndai he met should act so squeamish when everything he'd been told portrayed them as violent people.

The boy gave him a strange look, perhaps offended by the smile at his expense. But he turned back to the weapons in the drawer, lifting one out in both hands and gazing at it with an expression bordering on rapture. "I just can't believe this, you know. Now I've gotta figure out how we're going to get 'em back to the System."

"What will you do with them?" Although Jem knew it was foolish, he felt a sense of responsibility for the station—it had been abandoned until he'd claimed it, after all. And just being a Sanndai didn't necessarily give this youngster any rights to the place, or what was inside it. Besides, he could be lying—he could be a thief who was violating the rules of his own kind. He'd admitted he wasn't supposed to be here.

The boy turned around. "Oh, we'll try to get them into the Order's Collection, but they might have to go back to the

Guardian armory. They're illegal now, of course. They've only issued them for one martial incident in the last ten years, and only for a few days. These were standard Guardian issue once—but not for a long time now. They wanted to make the laws so tight there'd be no way civils could get them. That's why even Guardian personnel don't get them any more." He stopped, apparently noticing the confusion on Jem's face as he struggled to follow the words. "You've never seen one before, huh?"

Jem snorted. "Oh, I've seen one. I know someone who has one, and he showed it to me. Trying to scare me, I think." He pointed at the object held loosely in the boy's large hands. "Same shape as that, but different looking—with yellow metal, too, and designs on it. It looked bigger, but maybe that was because it was . . . in smaller hands than yours." Jem shrugged indifferently, but as he raised his eyes from the shining weapon to the dark face above it, he saw that this report had elicited a profound reaction from the young Sanndai.

The boy slowly closed his gaping mouth. Then he hissed, "You're kidding!"

Jem shook his head warily.

"If it's gold and silver, and has engraving on it . . ." He paused for Jem to confirm this with a cautious nod. "It's a Shonan Zendi, then. They're the only ones that look like that!"

"Shonan Zendi?" Jem repeated. "What does that mean?"

"Shonan!" the boy exclaimed. "High Council members—the people who run the System! You know 'bout Shonans, don't you? They all have Zendis. They're ceremonial ones, but they work the same as the others of course, and Shonans are never supposed to use them either—not unless someone tries to kill them or something. But they get to wear them all the time. That's the most important badge of their office, 'cause of what it means and all. My father's a Shonan, and he's let me hold one of his a few times. He taught me to shoot with target 'Z's, too. They have them at some of the game rooms. So you can learn how to shoot without using a real 'Z'. They have a—well, it's a special screen with moving targets you shoot at. I can't really explain it without getting real techy—you wouldn't understand anyway. No offense or anything."

Jem could think of nothing to say in response, and since the boy seemed to want to talk, it was easiest to let him go on.

"Shonans get to practice shooting with target 'Z's, and Guardian personnel who might have to use them do too. Not that they're difficult to shoot or anything—I was eleven the first time Hada took me. You just aim and push the button, really." He lifted the weapon in his hands and pointed to the square indentation on the top of the handle. Jem could see that the shape of the thing, even the position of the trigger, was simple and efficient—almost elegant in form. All the sinister complexity that must have been inside the weapon was well hidden.

The boy grinned again. "Only hard thing for an eleven-year-old was how heavy they are—I remember it was hard for me to hold it up high enough, and Hada helped me the first few times. It's the power source, see. Again, I won't try to get techy on you; I don't know all the specs anyhow. I'm way ahead of most folks my age, 'specially in physics, but I'm still only in First Course. Anyway, the stuff inside 'Z's is really, really dense—that's why they're so heavy. That's also why, if you tried to take more than a couple of 'em in your cruiser and fly outa here, you wouldn't get through the port without getting checked down. The screens would detect them, even hidden in the lock box in your cruiser." Watching Jem's face, he laughed suddenly. "Ay . . . Am I boring you?"

"No. But I don't understand a lot of the . . . these things you're talking about."

"Well, that's smooth," the young Sanndai said. "The important thing is, see, we need to get these 'Z's outa here, so we can take 'em back to the System where they belong. And I can get the points I've got coming to me for making it all the way out here and finding them, too! But like I said, there's no way I could take them all with me in my cruiser today. So I can probably take two, and then I'll have to come back, and see if I can get four other people with their own cruisers. If each of us take a couple, we should be able to get 'em all out! Shesh! I've gotta get cracking. Except . . ."

His face lit up and the haunting dark eyes glowed as he displayed his broad white smile. "If there's a Shonan 'Z' here too, I'm not leaving without it. That would be totally sacrilege! So you gotta tell me who has it—and how I can get it."

Jem scowled. "I can't do that."

"Why not?"

"Because it belongs to someone. An elder. It's not my business."

The Sanndai boy put down the weapon in his hands and approached Jem—causing Jem to take a step back. It was alarming that this stranger appeared to have no qualms about walking right up to him—and standing much closer than most people would when talking to someone they knew intimately. Running one hand through his black hair again, the boy shook his head and let out a dramatic sigh.

"I'm sorry, my friend, but you've got it all wrong. No Zendi ever belonged to a Torvik, 'kay? And no Torvik could ever have the right to one. I don't know how they got it, but it wasn't honestly—that's for certs! So taking it back wouldn't be stealing it or something. You know what I'm saying? No Zendi belongs anywhere on this planet."

Jem took another step backward, instinctively trying to evade the alien presence violating his personal space. "No Sanndai belongs here either," he said coldly.

The boy looked up, meeting his eyes. "Oh, yeah! I agree with you completely on that, hossti. No argument there. We don't belong on this planet. But that's part of the deal. That's part of Zennix's principles, of course—that's what the Order works to defend. No interference with other kinds of people, other worlds outside the System. That's the big issue. All the

Contact colonies should be granted total independence. Like these Torviks—they should be let out of this ice prison and given their whole planet back before they die out. It's totally and completely wrong—all the stuff that happened on this planet."

Trying to absorb this odd revelation silenced Jem for a moment. "All right," he said finally. "I don't care if you take these things . . . weapons. Go ahead."

The young man nodded. "'Kay. That's smooth. We'll get 'em outa here." He glanced at the open drawer, then turned back to Jem, his brow furrowed. "So where's the Shonan 'Z'? The one you saw?"

Jem mentally cursed himself for speaking of the thing, but he'd had no way of anticipating the Sanndai's reaction. "I can't tell you where it is. Forget I told you about it."

The boy laughed, again showing off his white, strong teeth. "Forget? I can't forget—you told me, hossti, it's too late. I've gotta get it. Come on, you agree the Torviks shouldn't have it, don't you?"

"Probably not." Jem shrugged, letting himself step behind his familiar wall of apathy—what did he really know or care about such things? "Does it really matter? It's been here a long time. Leaving it now can't make any difference."

The stranger looked amazed. "But of course it does! Just think about everything that means, and . . . Maybe you don't know. But even if you don't, it's—it's obvious, aynit? Come on! Even these ordinary ones are . . . well, sacred! Torviks gotta have things they think are sacred, right? Everybody does. So it's like that. You know, partly 'cause of Zennix, partly 'cause of everything they represent. And of course the Shonan 'Z'—the one with the gold and the engraving and all—that one's really important. You gotta know what I mean."

Jem frowned. "I don't. But it doesn't matter—I won't tell you where it is."

"Why not?"

"I live here—I told you. And it's not my place—not my business . . . that weapon. Anything that doesn't belong to me."

"I don't understand."

"Look." Jem's anger resurfaced; he felt violated and trapped by this alien person who'd forced his way into his life as well as into his private sanctuary, and who acted so unnaturally confident and unafraid. "I'm nobody here. I have nothing. I'm—a servant. Do you understand that?"

"What?" The young man was clearly incredulous.

"And if almost anyone else saw you, they'd just kill you. They wouldn't ask what you wanted first. So you'd better get out." He stepped backwards again. "That's all I'm going to say."

"Wait, wait, wait—this isn't smooth here. It's just not right."

Jem put on one of his well-practiced sullen stares. "I'm sure it isn't 'right'. But it's the way things are. I can't do anything to change it. Neither can you."

"But maybe I can!" the boy protested.

He followed each time Jem stepped back, reaching out as if he wanted to touch Jem to express the urgency of what he was trying to convey. It was making Jem's skin prickle—he was being cornered by this freak from another world.

"How old are you?" Jem demanded.

The Sanndai sighed and rolled his eyes, as if he'd expected this question. "I'm seventeen. 'Kay? I'm seventeen, and I'm not really supposed to be here. But I am here, so can we just get past that?"

"Seventeen," Jem repeated. "And you're not supposed to be here. So you have no power—you have no authority with your own people."

"Well, no, but my father—"

Jem cut him off. "You're father's a sho-something, you said. Some kind of Sanndai leader with a 'sacred' weapon he can't use. It doesn't matter. You'll still be just as dead when someone stabs you with a knife."

The alarming dark eyes grew round with surprise and a touch of what might have been fear. "Easy, easy, hossti! Cool down, will you? I'm not looking for trouble, 'kay? I mean, the plan was to stay out of sight as much as possible. I'm not stupid—I know the history and all that stuff." He paused and took a deep breath, then regarded Jem with an exasperated smile, shaking his head and fluffing his hair with one broad hand again. "I still don't understand what you're doing here, though. I mean, you say you live here, so obviously nobody's going to kill you just for being a Sanndai. But I suppose that's cause they know you and you've got the same clothes and everything? It's like you've become one of them, aynit?"

"Hardly." Jem smiled bitterly at the Sanndai boy. Now he wanted to drive him away—to make him feel afraid. "I wish I could say no one's going to kill me for being a Sanndai. But someone might. Don't go thinking you have everything figured out. I'm not safe here either, boy." Years of being called 'boy' in a derisive tone made it too easy to do the same. "And if your 'plan' is to stay out of sight, you didn't plan very well, because you forgot about your clothes. That color would stand out a kilometer away."

"What?" The young man looked down at his clothing, as if to see what Jem was looking at. "Black?"

Jem scoffed at him in an acid tone. "In case you hadn't noticed, the ground here is covered with snow. And snow is mostly white."

The boy seemed unsure whether he should be amused or offended. He gave a reticent laugh. "Enough—'kay? I'll be careful getting outa here. But you're not dodging the issue. Where's that Shonan Zendi? I've gotta take it with me."

"I can't tell you!" Jem retorted. "And even if I could, maybe I wouldn't."

The boy rolled his eyes. "You're stubborn, you are."

Jem felt the heat of the anger rising inside him. He just wanted this horrid, bratty alien to go away—to get out of his space, out of his world. "Maybe that's why I'm still alive," he growled.

The stranger pursed his lips and stared back at him. "All right, then—if you're not safe here, why don't you come with me? I'll take you back with me. There's room for a passenger in the cruiser I borrowed."

"Take me back where?"

"To the System. You said yourself that Sanndai don't belong on this planet."

"Maybe you didn't notice this either, but I'm not exactly a normal Sanndai."

The boy shrugged. "Change your clothes and you'll be normal enough. Except for the accent, and that's no hugie. And you can cut your hair," he added. Since his own hair was cut with unnatural precision—just as Avakab had described—it seemed likely he disapproved of the long strands trailing over the shoulders of Jem's parka.

It struck Jem that it was even truer than he'd imagined that the Sanndai people existed in an entirely different world— this strange boy clearly had no concept of how things were in Kruvak, much less of Jem's position. And who would just up and leave the place where they were born and raised to fly off with a total stranger to an alien world, even if their life were far more horrid than Jem's? Not unless it was that or die. Even then, Jem was sure that some in that situation would choose death.

The boy pushed on. "Come on, hossti—it's smooth. I can take you. If you mean that about not being safe here, you need to leave quick; that's the only thing that would make sense, aynit? Besides, what do you do here, anyway?"

"I can't see why you care," Jem answered, his voice hard and sullen. "I work at the fort. I help the two old men who live there."

Wrinkling his brow, the Sanndai squinted at Jem. "Are they important or something?"

Jem rolled his eyes much as the boy had moments before. "They're elders. They can't hunt or work any more, so someone brings them food and supplies. Because I help them I get my share." He added with a hostile grin, "They used to be 'important'. They were rebels."

"Rebels!" the young man exclaimed. For a moment Jem was pleased at his reaction—it seemed this fact had actually impressed him. But then the Sanndai spoiled it by laughing. "Oh, that's wild. But I did read about the Torvik rebellions again before I came here, and there were some that they never found. One of the leaders who was really savage got away. Aba-something—I read about him."

"Avakab, you mean," Jem said, and couldn't help smirking.

"Yeah—that was him! You know anything about him?"

"Yes. I'm rather fond of him. He tells good stories."

The boy's strange eyes flew open wide. "So he's still alive? Is he one of the two old men you work for?"

Jem nodded. "The other one gets on my nerves, but the work isn't hard."

"Wow! This just gets weirder and weirder! And I still don't understand how you got to be living here. It doesn't make any sense."

Annoyed even more by his prying, Jem glowered at him and answered grudgingly, "I was adopted by a midwife. When I was a baby. She lost all her own children, and she raised me."

"I see." A pause. "Well, that sort of makes sense, except for one thing. How in the cosmos did some Torvik midwife get a Sanndai baby? That's just too weird. I mean, if some colonial girl got pregnant by accident and wanted to give the baby away where no one would find out about it, you still wouldn't think anyone would figure on a Torvik woman taking a Sanndai baby!" He added, "But even if you grew up with a nice Torvik hama, you really oughta come back to the System with me. I mean, what are you going to do here for the rest of your life?

Help take care of old people? I guess some people do that for a living, but shesh, hossti—you could do that at home and sure have a lot better life. Besides, are you gonna marry a Torvik woman?"

"No," Jem answered, wondering why that wasn't obvious to this absurd boy. "Hardly anyone talks to me but the old people. A lot of people are afraid of me. Most of the time, I stay in the fort. Except when I come here to be alone—have some peace and quiet. Which you've put an end to," he added bitterly.

"You stay in the fort all the time, huh? With the two old apes?"

"Mostly."

"And you said the someone who showed you that Zendi was an elder. I remember, you said that. So one of them has it—is that it? That Aka-what's-his-name—that would be just his tune, wouldn't it? I bet he has it. I bet he has it in the fort."

"I didn't say that," Jem growled, alarmed at how readily the boy had come to this conclusion.

"But you're not going to deny it, either." The boy grinned, looking smug and defiant.

"I'm not telling you anything."

"Yeah, yeah—you still didn't say he doesn't have it. So he does."

Jem stared at the strange black eyes—deep as night, but bright and alive in the warm tan of the young face. He started to speak, but found himself stammering. He was practiced at lying: lying to the midwives, like Nadka, and lying to Waltak—although he'd never lied to Avakab. So he was surprised to find it difficult now—difficult to get the words out as he looked into the alien eyes in the alien face before him.

Just make something up, he told himself. Make something up and send him off after someone who doesn't exist . . . Say something, anything. But all he could spit out was, "No! Avakab doesn't have it!" And it was partially true, since he'd only seen the object in Waltak's possession.

But the boy grinned again and shook his head. "Liar. I can tell you're lying." Then his eyes went to the ring of brass keys on Jem's belt. "So what are all those keys for—the fort? Gotta be, huh?"

Jem could see no point in denying it. "Yes—they're the keys to the fort. Most of the doors have locks, so there's a lot of them. Why do you care?" His simmering anger was rising again, threatening to boil over.

"Because if that old man is hiding a Shonan 'Z', it's gotta be in that fort somewhere, donit? And you've got all the keys. Come on, hossti—it's the right thing to do; I promise you it is. You've gotta help me find it."

"I don't know you," Jem retorted. "And I don't have to help you do anything." He'd had all he could take, and the only thing stopping him from trying to physically throw the alien boy out of the station was that he didn't trust him any more than he understood him—and the weapons in the drawer were still only a few paces behind the boy, easily within his reach. "You said you had to get out of here, so go."

"Look." The young Sanndai plastered another grin across his face and stepped right up to Jem, causing him to step back again. "My name's Dorion. I'm seventeen—I told you that. I'm from Laishani, and my Hada's on the High Council—means he's called a Shonan. I'm from a very respectable family, and I'm actually a good kid—most of the time." He laughed. "When I'm not, it's usually 'cause I'm bored with my readings 'cause I'm a stinking genius." He paused, raising his eyebrows and looking as if he expected Jem to be skeptical of that declaration. "Don't laugh. I really am a genius, and I've got the recs to prove it, in case anybody cares. Most people don't." His grin widened. "'Kay, what else do you wanna know?"

Then Jem realized it had taken until this point in their lengthy conversation for the boy to finish answering his first question. He was furious, and his anger was aggravated by the fact that the impudent stranger was standing very close to him again, always moving forward as if he were trying to crawl into Jem's skin.

"Nothing!" he shouted. "I want you to get out!" He waved his arms, fending the boy off without actually touching him—but he hadn't put his knife back into the sheath on his belt and it was still in his hand.

Dorion stepped back quickly. "Easy, hossti . . . Look, tell you what I'm going to do. I'm gonna hike out to my cruiser right now to get some lunch—I'm starving. I'm going to take these with me." He turned away from Jem as he spoke, returning to the open drawer and lifting one Zendi in each hand. "Since, from what you say, having some protection is probably a good idea here. Anyway, I'm gonna come back in a little while. If you're still here, I'll meet you then. If you're not, I'm gonna go find that fort. I've seen a picture of it in the Bakraga history I went over with the stuff about the Torvik rebellions. And hopefully I'll find you, too, and we can talk about this again. This way you can have some time to think it over, before you decide whether you're gonna help me find that Zendi or not. And then decide if you're coming with me."

Jem coughed incredulously. "You're mad. You can't just go jaunting over to the fort and look for me, especially dressed like that." He gestured at the young man's strange black clothing. "You'll be killed! Don't you understand anything?"

Dorion glared back at him. "Look, hossti—I know how to be sneaky; I've played all the stealth games in every virtual on Laishani, and quite a few in other places I've traveled to. Besides, I'd say I'm pretty well armed." With elbows bent, he brandished both Zendis at shoulder height—pointing them at the ceiling, to Jem's relief. "If anybody sees me," the boy went on, "and I see them watching me and acting even a little suspicious, I'll shoot first and call it self-defense. Nobody's ever going to question that—nobody. I could shoot ten Torviks in this ice pit and not be called out for a thing."

As the meaning emerged out of the strangely-accented speech, Jem felt a cold weight settle on him. He was startled as well as appalled by this callous proclamation. Nothing else in the boy's prattle had struck him as hostile or cruel—even if hostility and cruelty were what he'd expected from a Sanndai.

"That doesn't make it right!" he snarled. Ignoring the silver weapons that were so prominently displayed, he stepped toward the boy threateningly.

Dorion shrugged. "Of course not. But if I have to, I can. That's all I'm saying. So I'm not as foolish as you think, hossti." To further infuriate Jem, he grinned again.

Jem glowered and said nothing more.

The boy pushed the drawer closed with his back as he pulled open his tight-fitting black jacket and put one of the Zendis inside it. Holding the other weapon in one hand, he walked to the doorway. He shouldered the door open, turned to look back at Jem, and spoke with disarming ease and familiarity. "All right—I'll be back in a bit. And if you're not here, I'll find you. Just think about everything I said, 'kay? You think about it, you're gonna see I'm right about this. Take it easy, huh?"

Jem merely grunted. Though he was still just as angry, he was profoundly relieved that the alien intruder was going, and leaving him alone in his private space—even though it didn't seem so private now.

II

IT WAS SOME TIME after Dorion had gone before Jem felt truly alone, as if solitude had to slowly seep back into him. He felt violated by the experience—almost contaminated. Restless, he walked around the station, looking to see what had been disturbed, before finally lying down on the soft gray floor, right on top of the old bloodstain. He stared at the pattern of lights in the ceiling, and wished he could get the image of those eyes out of his head, the drawling voice out of his ears. Except for the damage to the door and the opened drawers, little had been touched. In that respect it was almost as if the boy had never been there—as if it had been a strange dream: a waking nightmare.

He was torn between the feeling that the encounter had confirmed that he hated all Sanndai, and an oddly opposing sense of redemption—some of Dorion's statements had so starkly contradicted the dark picture of his people painted by all the stories. And he was in no hurry to leave the station now. He needed to be alone more than ever. He felt as if he could lie motionless for hours, letting his thoughts chase each other in tortured circles. He wondered how long he'd been gone, and if Waltak had missed him yet. It seemed his sense of time had been jarred as well, and he didn't know how long he'd conversed with the intruder.

But Jem didn't care how long it had been—he wasn't going home yet. If Waltak were angry when he returned, he would just tell the old man to piss on himself. It didn't matter. As he alternately stared at the oval white lights and then closed his eyes to see the pulsing darkness behind his eyelids, he wondered if he really knew what mattered any more. He was still lying there when Dorion returned.

At the sound of footsteps crunching on the snow outside, Jem sat up. He'd deliberately left the door ajar so he could hear anyone approaching, but he'd also discovered that although the latch on the inside still worked, the damaged edge no longer fit smoothly and it took a firm push to get it closed. As he listened, he found there was even something in the rhythm and pitch of those footsteps that was unmistakably alien. He didn't move as the young Sanndai came through the door.

Dorion smiled, looking down with an expression that seemed to mix genuine pleasure and mild surprise. "Ay, hossti. You're still here. Super." He sat down on the floor next to Jem without hesitation, and crossed his legs. "So, what's your name?" he asked in a companionable tone, as if they'd parted on friendly terms—which hadn't exactly been Jem's view of the situation. "So I don't have to keep calling you hossti."

Jem refrained from asking what 'hossti' meant. He felt numb, now that he was back in the presence of this strange young man who was sitting quite close to him—although not touching the bloodstain—and looking at him out of those unbelievable black eyes. Jem saw now that they were actually a very dark brown, but the pupil was hard to see, and the dark color made the whites look very white. The eyelashes were long and black and thick, forming a fringe that was visible at a glance, like a reindeer's lashes.

Jem noted these things quickly before looking away, remembering the way he'd felt when he found the picture of the Sanndai faces in one of the station's small rooms. Now there was a live Sanndai right next to him, so close Jem could smell the strange materials and other odors foreign to his senses.

"Jem," he answered absently, thinking how odd it was that this boy didn't even smell human.

"Jem?" Dorion repeated. "Really? Well, that's a good name." He was smiling again when Jem looked back at him. "And it sure isn't a Torvik name."

"No. It was the one thing my mother gave me."

"I see." After a pause Dorion said, "Ay, you want some cookies?" There was a rustling sound as the boy pulled something out of his jacket—the strange black garment had a number of pockets—and set a small package in his lap, balancing it on his leg. The package was made of colorless, translucent stuff that made a soft rattling sound at the movement of the contents—a row of perfectly round, brown wafers that didn't look edible.

A large hand was stretched out to offer one, and Jem shook his head.

"Aw, come on. Who doesn't like cookies?"

Jem closed the subject by shaking his head again and looking away.

"Fine. I'll just have to eat them all myself then," Dorion announced, not sounding disappointed.

Jem found himself staring at the long black-clad legs, and the sheer size of the young man's knees and feet. If it weren't for the fact that his own were the same, he wouldn't have thought anyone had limbs of such a proportion. It was very odd to look at them and then glance down at his own legs—and admit that if he looked past the way they were clothed, there was little difference.

Dorion was quiet for a while, munching contentedly on the strange food. Finally he said, "So, Jem—are you gonna help me get that Shonan Zendi? I really need to take it with me. I know it's all strange stuff to you, but it's important. Trust me."

"Why should I trust you?" Jem had to repress an impulse

to laugh at his earnest expression. "In every story about the Sanndai, the fact that they can't be trusted is the one thing that never changes."

Dorion looked bewildered. "But that's the Torviks! I mean, that's just what they say about us, of course! They're prejudiced against us. Sure, they may have pretty good reason to be, considering the stuff that happened, but it's still prejudice! You don't really believe everything they say about us, do you? I mean, how can you when you're a Sanndai yourself?"

Meeting the boy's dark gaze was disconcerting, but Jem regarded him steadily. "I know we've done terrible things to them—it's not something anyone would lie about, and I've seen proof of it." He surprised himself by using the term 'we'.

"Well, yeah—some Sanndai did. But that's . . . that's like war, I guess. There isn't any human race who hasn't done something terrible to somebody at some time. By Zennix, it doesn't mean we're all evil and can't be trusted! Members of the Order—people like me—we're trying to fix those things, you know? We're trying to make good where other people went too far. Ay, I don't appreciate being lumped in with a bunch of greedy miners and power-craving monkeys who'll do anything to get what they want!" Resentment showed in his uncanny black eyes. "I really don't appreciate that."

Jem shrugged dispassionately. "I only know what I've heard—and what I've seen."

The boy shook his head. "Like this colony—and this station here—this wasn't supposed to happen. Zennix was very clear about it. I mean, some people argue about how far he meant some of his creeds to go, but I think it's obvious he was totally anti-imperialist." He laughed softly. "I actually won a debate using that as my topic." Glancing at Jem with a cocky grin, he added, "Of course, I could win a debate arguing that the cosmos exists inside a wad of vanilla taffy stuck on the sole of my boot—it's all a matter of how you present it."

When Jem answered with a blank stare, Dorion looked

away, shaking his head but still grinning. "Well," he said, "Zennix wouldn't have approved of what happened on this planet—nobody could deny that."

"Who is Zennix?"

Dorion's head snapped around and he stared at Jem, wide-eyed. "Zennix . . ." He gestured broadly with both hands, as if nothing should need to be said. Then he repeated, "*Zennix*," drawing the word out into two emphatic syllables. "The Fourth Messiah?" When Jem showed no sign of recognition, he made his lopsided incredulous face and gasped, "You really don't know who Zennix is?!"

"No," Jem answered, lapsing into apathy again and regarding the young Sanndai with a listless 'why should I know that?' expression.

Dorion looked stunned. "Wow! I don't believe it."

They sat for a moment in silence, both staring into space—Jem waiting for the boy to speak, Dorion seeming unable to get beyond this revelation.

Finally the boy said, "Kay, I guess I'm the idiot here." He spoke softly, almost as if he were talking to himself. "Stupid thing is, I've never talked to anybody who wasn't a Sanndai before—well, I did talk to a Melnian guy once, who was at Mainport, but we just talked about his cruiser and stuff, and he didn't seem very sharp. We certainly didn't talk about religion or history or anything! I mean, you're a Sanndai, of course, but you're in this other culture. I just didn't think other people wouldn't even know about Zennix. So weird."

Jem endured this patiently. "So who is he?" he asked again.

"Oh." The boy looked quickly back to Jem. "Well, he was— he was a really awesome guy. He was a scientist and a philosopher, a spiritual leader, an inventor. People started calling him the Fourth Messiah even during his lifetime. And he invented the Zendi. Well, he didn't actually invent it, because they had something like it before the Expansion, but he refined it and improved it. Kind of ironic, because he was against violence of any kind—basically against the use of all weapons.

"But he had complex reasons for doing what he did. And we identify Zendis with him. The whole thing about Shonan Zendis has to do with him, when you come down to it. It's about having power—like super tech weapons—but choosing not to use it. Like, you can have all the power in the universe, but when you make the choice not to use it, it means you're even stronger. That's how you reach the next level of society—get to True Harmony. If you keep using force to stay in power, you never get out of the war cycle, and eventually the people in power get taken down, and it starts over again. That's the theory of it, and even if no one's totally gotten there yet, we're pretty close in some ways. See, if you're in a position of power and you have the perfect weapon, and everyone knows you have this weapon—like when you're a Shonan wearing a pair of Zendis—but you never use it, that's showing that you, personally, are at True Harmony. Which is no small thing, that's for certs.

"Members of the Order—that's the Order of the Fourth Messiah—usually wear little . . ." He started digging under the collar of his black jacket with one hand. "Here, I'll show you mine." He fished out a thin silver chain and held it out toward Jem. Suspended from it was a tiny lump the same color as the chain. After a moment's puzzled scrutiny, Jem realized it was a piece of metal cut in the miniaturized shape of the Sanndai weapon.

"I see," he said dully, recalling that the boy had used the term 'sacred' in his attempt to explain the significance of the object he coveted. The idea that these people wore charms in the shape of a weapon gave him that cold, queasy feeling again, and he had to tell himself it wasn't too different from wearing a necklace of wolf teeth, like ongalaks did. And that was an ancient tradition going all the way back to the Motherworld. So perhaps it wasn't really that odd. But he looked past the swinging charm to the dark face and said, "Isn't that kind of . . . morbid? Wearing a thing in the shape of a weapon?"

Dorion laughed. "Well, yeah—it's ironic in a way. But it's the thing it represents: the same idea about True Harmony that's represented by a Shonan having the real thing." He swung the silver charm back and forth, watching it thoughtfully. "I like my little 'Z'." Then he glanced down at the weapon he'd hooked to his belt and declared happily, "And now I've got two real ones! Of course, that won't be for long. I won't get to keep them, that's for certs. Don't want to anyway—way too much responsibility." Then he looked at Jem and smiled slyly. "So did you think it over, Jem? You're gonna help me get the one you saw, aren't you?"

Jem snorted, got to his feet, and took several long strides away from the boy. "Nothing's changed. You may think you have good reasons for taking it—" he spun back around to face Dorion, who'd gotten up onto his knees, the charm on the silver chain still swinging from his fingers, "and that it's not stealing from your point of view. But the person who has it would call it stealing. I won't be part of it."

As Jem moved—standing, walking, turning—he felt strangely light and agile. For the first time in his life he was with someone as large and tall as he was—and someone who was even less graceful, with the lanky awkwardness Jem recalled being afflicted with only too well. Since Jem had filled out in the last few years, all the parts of his body, even his large hands and feet, were in balanced proportion to his height. But until today his awareness of being so large had still made him feel clunky. This revelation—this shift in perspective—was like rediscovering his own body.

Dorion groaned and rolled his eyes. Then he stood up and stuffed the necklace back into his jacket. Putting both hands on his hips, he gave Jem a hard look. "You just don't get it, do you?"

"No, you just don't get it," Jem retorted, mimicking the boy's accent on the last words. Then he dropped into a hushed, angry tone. "These people may not be my blood family, but they're the people I know, the people I've lived with all my life. You can talk all you want about your beliefs and your leaders and anything else—it changes nothing."

The torrent he'd been holding back broke through, and he recklessly let it run. "What kind of a selfish bastard would I have to be to steal something from an elder—whether he's a bad person himself or not, and that's not for me to judge—just to give it to some crazy alien who's only a boy who thinks too much of himself?"

Insulting a well-armed stranger was foolish at the very least, and Jem was braced for a reaction. But Dorion didn't seem angered at all—he didn't even flinch. Instead he frowned and cleared his throat. "Ay . . . Hossti Jem, if I'm an 'alien', so are you."

"Sure—I've been called that often enough. I'm used to it." Jem was reminded of his words to Rulskar shortly before Fenak had pulled out the knife—which seemed ages ago, though it had only been a few days. He may not have been afraid for his life now—since it didn't seem the Sanndai boy meant to harm him—but the turn of the conversation was like a twisted echo. And once again the words they exchanged were like icy beads of snow they flung at each other in frustration, cold and small and meaningless.

The young Sanndai sighed. "And I thought I was good," he muttered, then gave a half-hearted laugh.

As if freed from a trance, Jem strode past Dorion and straight to the door.

"Where are you going?" Dorion turned to follow him.

"Home. I'm late—and I'm going to have to deal with a very annoyed, very annoying old man!" He shot the boy a resentful glare as he pulled the door open. Dorion was immediately on his heels.

"Wait!" Dorion yelped, stepping in front of him and grabbing his arm. Jem pulled back, but the boy clasped his wide, tan hand firmly on Jem's sleeve.

"What?" Jem growled, his back brushing against the open door behind him.

"Shesh!" the boy hissed, standing so near that Jem could smell his breath, his clothes, his hair. His face was unbearably close—a startling visage of smooth, coppery skin framing the deep dark eyes, the large perfect teeth visible behind the red-brown lips that framed his wide mouth. "Why don't you want to come with me? Then you won't have to deal with any cranky old . . ." He stopped at the look on Jem's face. "Never mind—stupid question. But I'd think you'd want something better than how you live here, even if you . . . well, know this culture and everything. I mean, if nobody here really cares about you except some of the old people, and then they'll die of old age, and . . . All right, I'm digging myself into a hole here. Sorry. It just doesn't seem smooth, you know—you staying here."

Dorion babbled on, talking more and more rapidly, as if frantic to get the words out. "Man, it's so weird that you look just like somebody I've seen—maybe somebody I know—but for the life of me I can't think who. Your eyes, your eyebrows—your whole face really. You just look so familiar. Blast! Why can't I remember who? It's like when you have a word stuck in your mind and you can't quite remember it, but you know it's right there. Yeah, it happens to geniuses, too, I'm afraid."

"I'm sure it does," Jem muttered, leaning back stiffly as he tried to get away from the boy's smothering presence. "It doesn't matter! Let go of me."

"Why?" Dorion grinned impishly, now so close that Jem could feel the moisture of his warm breath. "Come on, Jem, I'm not gonna hurt you. How come you act like you're afraid of me standing next to you? Shesh! I don't think I've got any dangerous germs or anything. You're not very friendly, are you?"

Jem's back was pressed firmly against the door, his chin drawn in as he tried to pull his face away from the boy's. Dorion had leaned even closer, the front of his jacket actually touching Jem's parka; he was still clinging to Jem's arm. "Friendly?" Jem repeated breathlessly, so amazed at this absurd behavior that he would have found it laughable if it hadn't been so uncomfortable to have someone—especially someone so strange-looking—so close to him. He was finding it difficult to think.

"Yeah. Come on, Jemmo—I can tell you're really a nice ape. I knew you wouldn't really stick me with that little knife." He laughed, his voice coming quick and breathless. "I've got a way better knife than that—I've got a spark knife. That's how I cut the lock. And opened the cabinets. In case you were wondering."

"Uh, yes—I had wondered," Jem murmured. He felt almost paralyzed by the sense of invasion, and wondered if that had been a threat—if the boy really meant to harm him now. Perhaps he would be stabbed at any moment, or shot with one of the Zendis—which he couldn't see in this position, with the young Sanndai holding his left arm in a firm grip and standing pressed up against him as he jabbered on like a lunatic.

"I guess what's bothering me is, I've just gotta wonder: what do you really want, anyway? I mean, everybody wants something, right?" Still talking very rapidly, Dorion flashed a cloyingly sweet smile, and Jem had the feeling he was stalling for time.

"What do I want?" he echoed. He felt dizzy. Then he found his voice again and spat out, "I want you to go away and leave me alone! I want to never see you again. Why is that so hard for you to understand?"

"Aw, you don't mean that!" Dorion grimaced, and the expression melted back into the absurd boyish smile. He gave a strange laugh. "You really should come with me—you should."

The moment Jem felt the strong hand lighten its grip, he

wrenched his arm away and stepped sideways, giving the boy a shove at the same time. He'd pushed harder than he'd intended to, and Dorion staggered back, almost losing his balance as he stumbled into the snow banked up beside the doorway.

"Easy there, ape! All right, all right—I won't ask you again. Listen, I'm going back out to my cruiser. I'm gonna fly outa here for the night, go down to Northlite. Then I'll come back up tomorrow, 'cause I'm going to look for that 'Z'—with or without your help. So like it or not, you'll probably see me again. And maybe you'll change your mind after you sleep on it. Is that smooth with you?"

"Fine," Jem retorted; he was past arguing. "You do that. I won't be looking for you, but I won't give you away either. That's all you're going to get from me."

Dorion grinned, with an inappropriate look of self-satisfaction. "That'll do," he said. "Take care of yourself, Hossti Jem," he called over his shoulder as he ducked out of the entranceway. He took off at a surprisingly fast long-legged run over the snow, heading straight toward the open tundra.

Jem stood at the top of the slope above the door, staring after him. There was no one in sight, but it was late afternoon, and there could be herders or trappers skiing up the southeast track at any moment. It would be hard for them to miss a tall black-clad figure running across the white landscape, and from where the station sat, at the southernmost edge of the village, there was nothing between it and the East Ridge for some distance. Jem found himself willing that no one would appear, though he couldn't say why he cared what happened to this mad, foolish intruder from another world. Still, it was with relief that he watched the dark figure swiftly ascend the rise that formed an unbroken north-south line east of the village, then disappear over the crest.

After closing the door—swearing under his breath as he was reminded of the irreparable damage to the lock—Jem trudged gloomily back to the fort. Not until he reached the gray walls and came around to the side entrance he always used did he discover the tangible reason for the sense of emptiness he'd felt since leaving the station. Dazed and overwhelmed by everything spinning in his head, he hadn't realized anything was missing. But something was missing.

His hand went to his waist instinctively when he stopped. With his shoulder pressed against the weathered wooden gate, he groped for the ring of keys that was fastened to his belt with a sturdy loop of stiff felt lashed on with a leather strap. But it wasn't there. The keys were gone.

He swore and slammed his mitten-padded fist against the wood. Dorion! The little bastard! That was why the Sanndai had detained him—and that was why the boy had held his arm and pressed against him and rambled on for so long! How stupid he was! Stupid, stupid, stupid! What had he thought the horrid alien brat was doing all that time? What was the matter with him?

Shaking with anger, Jem scanned the gate and the stone walls on either side of it. It would be impossible to get any purchase on the wood, but the stone was rough, with many chinks and cracks. He would climb over. At least he could get back to the illus, and the old men now stayed there most of the time. Waltak made occasional forays to the pantry—but usually sent Jem, since he kept the keys—and the old man rarely ventured into any other part of the fort.

Jem took off both mittens and stuffed them in his pockets. He stretched up and felt for a knob to grasp, a crack to wedge his fingers into. Finding footholds was more difficult; the soles of his boots, smooth and well-worn, kept slipping down the wall. The pressure of his toes would hold momentarily, allowing his straining shoulders, arms and fingers to pull him upward—his face was centimeters from the icy gray stone, and he saw every grain, every pore, every vein of darker color in the rock in minute detail—then his feet would slip again so that he jerked downward. Though he kept moving, his progress seemed torturously slow.

Halfway up, he lost his hold altogether and dropped all the way to the snowy ground, landing hard on his back. Winded, for a moment he could do nothing but struggle for air. Then he cursed and got to his feet. To his relief, a quick look around confirmed that no one had seen him. He began again. Holding every muscle taut, he felt his warm gasping breaths on the stone in front of his face, his fingertips burning from the cold and abrasion, his toes aching. Finally he could see the top of the wall.

Making certain the other hand and both feet were secure, he freed one hand, stretched his long arm up, and got his fingers, then the palm of his hand, hooked over the top. He pulled, his feet slipping again, his shoulder protesting at the strain, the edge of the rock digging painfully into his palm. But he managed to get his elbow over the top, then draw himself up until he was bellied over the wall. He straddled it, righted himself, then swung the other leg over and jumped.

His feet stung as they struck the packed snow. He stood for a moment, his chest heaving. He'd come down in the shadowy space beside the gate, next to the sod wall on his right. Before stepping out into the open, he waited for his breathing to slow, staring at the cluster of illus in the courtyard. There was only a thin thread of smoke coming from the top of the large dome, and no sounds to be heard.

Neither of the old men were there when Jem entered the big illu, but the smell rising from the pot told him that in his absence Waltak had added a mixture of dried meat and herbs, which Jem had prepared and left in one of the clay jars, to the potato soup. Sinking down by the fire, he felt tingly and light, and oddly grateful just to be there. The place—with its bluish shadowy walls and dark doorways, the flickering firelight, the reindeer skins piled on the platform he sat on—had never seemed more like home, more comfortable, more right. He pondered this feeling as he rubbed his arm where Dorion had gripped it, wincing when he closed his eyes and saw the face floating in front of him, too close and too real.

His relief faded after Waltak shuffled in—not because the old man asked where he'd been, or asked for the keys, or berated him for anything, but because he paid no attention to Jem at all. He was muttering to himself and appeared both preoccupied and distressed.

Jem started to ask what was wrong—it wasn't the kind of thing he'd usually say to Waltak, but, to his own surprise, he felt concerned.

Just as he began to speak, Avakab called from the entrance to the illu the old men slept in. "Waltak? Did you hear me?" His voice sounded the same as always, but was followed by a long string of dry coughs.

Waltak straightened and turned to call out, "Yes. I'm making you some tea—I'll bring it in a moment." He sat down slowly by the fire and took some herbs out of one of the smaller jars in the kitchen box. He picked up an empty pot, then dropped it and swore, his voice quavering as he rubbed his swollen knuckles.

"May I help?" Jem asked.

Waltak looked up at him blankly, as if he hadn't even realized he was there. The old man's reddened and watery blue eyes looked more teary than usual, his puckered little face woebegone. He gave Jem one of his expressionless stares, but there was something different—a ghost of sadness showing through the wizened mask.

Then Waltak sighed heavily, looking at his hands. "I wanted to do it myself," he said, sounding a little more like his whiny old self. "I can't do anything." He picked up the herbs and turned them awkwardly in his distorted fingers.

"I'll do it," Jem offered. "If you want me to," he added quickly. He found himself actually wanting to be nice to Waltak, and he couldn't think of many times he'd felt that way before.

Waltak was silent for a long moment. Then he said, "You'd better do it, boy—or there just won't be any tea."

In making that pronouncement, the old man again seemed more like himself, but Jem still felt strangely concerned. As he hung the pot over the fire and put the herbs into the water, he heard himself say, "It's all right. That's what I'm here for."

There was a hoarse chuckle behind him, and a voice murmured, "That's right. It is what you're here for, isn't it?"

Jem looked up, startled. He'd been aware of hearing Avakab cough several times during his exchange with Waltak, but hadn't heard the old man's quiet steps as he'd shuffled out into the big dome.

Waltak turned around. "You didn't have to get up, Avak. I was going to bring it."

Avakab silenced him with a wave of his hand. "No, no—it's all right. I wanted to get up. Besides," he added as he approached the fire, walking as if being careful not to move anything too suddenly, "it's been some time since I've had a proper visit with our young Sanndai friend." He looked fondly at Jem and said, "And how are you, young man? I don't believe I asked you this morning."

"Fine," Jem said softly, a little taken aback. "I'm fine."

"Good," the old man answered. "Good, good." He had reached the platform, and now lowered himself slowly, clenching his lips tight as he did so. Waltak reached an awkward hand toward him, clearly wanting to help but unable to do much. Avakab managed unaided, and absently reached out to pat Waltak's arm, acknowledging and dismissing the gesture at the same time.

When Jem noticed that the bowstring the old man had been winding around his fingers was still on the platform beside him, he cleared his throat and pointed at it. "Could I have that—the bowstring?"

Avakab smiled faintly. He picked up the small coil of

string and held it out toward Jem. "Of course. I don't imagine I have any use for it." He coughed and added, "I haven't much use for anything now, have I?" The smile grew wider, as if he'd made a private joke.

Jem thanked him quietly and took the string.

Then the old rebel's expression became thoughtful—perhaps even wistful—and he murmured, "I am sorry about the bow, young man. And I'm glad to think that someone else enjoyed it for a time." He paused, then said, "It gave me pleasure once, a long time ago. I wasn't too bad of a shot with it. Though the knife was always my favorite. My special talent, I suppose." His gaze went to the pale string Jem held almost tenderly in his fingers, the color of the little skein contrasting with the brown skin. "That would work well for string figures; I imagine you could cut at least a couple of lengths out of it."

Cutting it hadn't occurred to Jem—right then the sentimental value of the bowstring seemed more important than any practical use for a length of string. But he was as touched as he was surprised when Avakab said, "I know you're good at those."

Jem hadn't thought that the old man paid much attention to what he did, although he often toyed with his loop of yarn when he sat by the fire, going through all the figures Enkara had taught him over the years, one by one.

The shadow of a smile touched Avakab's wrinkled face again. "Walt used to try to teach me how to do them—I'd always get them wrong, forget a step. But he was very good at them. Before his hands got stiff." The faintest hint of sadness crept into his voice, as if the reminiscence had awoken a sense of loss. Then he looked over at his companion and added in a stronger voice, "You knew quite a lot of them, didn't you?"

Waltak answered with a soft grunt and the barest nod, his woeful blue eyes now staring vacantly into the fire.

Avakab's gaze shifted back to Jem. "I'm sure they were the same ones Enkara teaches you."

Again, though it was logical, the idea that Avakab knew that Enkara was the one who'd taught Jem all the figures tugged at him in a curious way. "Yes," he said. "She knows a lot of them, too."

The old man was silent, but it was a silence that felt right for the moment.

Jem stirred up the fire and rehung the pot of stew, which he'd set aside to boil the tea. When it began to steam he filled his bowl. Pulling one of the skins off the platform, he settled on the floor, leaning against the edge of the snow table as he ate. In spite of the loss of the bow, in spite of the stolen keys and the entire mess he'd blundered into—which didn't quite seem real now—he felt the echo of comfort and contentment. Now if Avakab would tell a story, even just a short one, he could pretend everything was all right. Just for a while. Yes, he'd have to tell Waltak about the keys—he would tell him, tell him something. But later. Not now, not this afternoon.

But there was to be no story. Avakab only spoke a few soft words to Waltak, smiled at Jem, drank his tea, and nodded off to sleep. He'd had a brief fit of coughing, after which he'd looked over at Jem and said, "Well, it's good one of us is doing fine. I seem to be working on coughing my lungs out of my body." Chuckling dryly at this, he'd sighed and murmured, "Ah well, there are worse things."

When Jem crawled into his own illu that evening, Waltak still knew nothing of the lost keys; Waltak hadn't asked for them, and Jem had put it off. Tomorrow, Jem told himself—he would do it tomorrow. Today had been too much already. Now he wanted nothing but sameness—he didn't want anything else to change.

The old men had retreated to their illu much earlier, and were probably sound asleep. Jem almost envied them as he sank down onto his furs, angry tears stinging his eyes. The day couldn't be undone. The bow would never be resurrected from the fire, he wouldn't wake to find the keys back on his belt.

Perhaps the demise of the bow wasn't his own fault, but the keys—he was certainly to blame for the theft of the keys. Why had he even let the little monster near him? What had he been thinking?

From what he could remember now, he'd hardly been thinking at all. He rolled over and pushed his face into his folded arms. Here he'd met his first Sanndai ever, and right away the freakish boy had betrayed him, tricked him, and stolen from him. He shouldn't have been the least bit surprised. Why hadn't he just expected it?

Yet there'd been so much more to the young stranger than that—so much about him that Jem could never have imagined. Dorion. Dorion. The face still loomed in front of him, the voice still sounded in his ears, filling up his brain as he closed his eyes and the night closed in around him. I hate you, he thought. I hate you, I hate you, I hate you.

He groaned and rolled over again, staring at the flame in the lamp burning low at his feet. He didn't know what would be harder to face when he woke up tomorrow—the loss of the keys, or the knowledge he'd have to face each morning for the rest of his life: that he was a member of a race of people who truly were as deceiving and heartless as he'd always been told.

One night as a child, after hearing some disturbing tale of Sanndai cruelty, he'd lain awake thinking about his mother. Over and over again, he'd told himself that she must have been different—there had to be some Sanndais that weren't bad. Surely she had been a kind and gentle person. And he'd tried hard to imagine her, although in the end, as always, she looked like a taller and younger Enkara with black hair. Or—he thought now—like a grown-up version of the blue-eyed, black-haired girl who lived only in his fantasies.

He hadn't even thought of the dark eyes. Never had he tried to imagine eyes like that. So unfathomable. So dark. As if they held pieces of the night.

III

WHEN THE MORNING began everything was deceptively normal. There were enough provisions in the kitchen box next to the fire pit in the big illu that Jem, who was usually up before the old men, was able to add fuel to the fire and make a fresh pot of soup before he even saw Waltak—and, more importantly, without needing to get anything out of the pantry; the pantry was locked.

From the day Waltak had first given him the keys, Jem had followed the old man's instructions without much thought, and each and every door that had a key had been kept locked. Only now did it occur to Jem that, since he and the old men were the only people inside the fort, it could be argued that when they secured the inner doors they were only locking themselves out. Anyone else would first have to break through one of the outer doors—unless they also climbed over the wall—and there were only three entrances in that daunting stone barrier.

The smallest one, on the east side in a gap in the circle of sod walls, was the gate Jem used to come and go from the fort. The much wider door opening into the pantry could only be unlocked—and unbarred—from the inside. And the third door hadn't been opened for years. Made of thick wooden planks, it led into a long narrow room beside the old kitchen, and it had originally been the main entrance. The largest key fit that lock, but Jem had never tried it. Waltak had mentioned once that the rusted hinges had probably rendered the door unusable some time ago.

But that didn't matter now. What mattered was that he'd have to tell Waltak that the keys he'd been entrusted with were gone—there was no way around it. Perhaps he could tell Waltak about Rulskar grabbing him and threatening him, chasing him; that was all true, even if it had happened several days ago. Would the old man know that? Then he could tell him that he'd gone to hide in the station, and when he got back home, found that the keys were missing.

In reality Jem had no proof that the Sanndai boy had taken the keys, although there was no doubt in his mind. And there seemed no way to tell the old rebels about the Sanndai intruder without condemning himself—it would sound too improbable, too absurd. They might think he'd given the keys to the stranger. But what motivation could he have had for doing that? Unless the boy had offered him something in return?

But this was all crazy conjecture—and if Jem couldn't even fabricate a lie that wasn't in his favor, he didn't know how he would come up with a believable excuse for his carelessness. There was still no solution, no path leading out of this maze. He thought about going to the Birthing House to see Enkara. But what could she do? He could tell her the truth and she would believe him, but what difference would it make?

In the end he simply sat by the fire, swirling the tea in his bowl and staring into the whispering flames, waiting for Waltak to show himself, waiting for the moment when he'd have to confess that the keys were lost.

When the old man finally appeared he seemed distracted, as he had the night before, and scarcely spoke to Jem. Jem was distracted himself, trying repeatedly to think of how to start but unable to force himself to break the illusory peace of the silence between them. So when Waltak shuffled out again, returning to Avakab, nothing had been exchanged beyond a couple of murmurs from the old man and a wordless grunt of assent from Jem.

Jem stayed at the fire, wondering what he could do in the way of work. Without the keys his access was restricted to the courtyard and a few of the smaller rooms in the inner wall that didn't have locking doors. Not that the old men would notice if he didn't do anything. For many moons now he'd undertaken most of his chores on his own accord, making the decisions about what needed to be done.

After a time he heard the men's voices coming from the illu where they slept, and where Avakab now stayed most of the time. They were louder than usual, and it became apparent that they were arguing.

"No." It was Waltak's thin nasal voice that he heard first. "You should stay in. You'll get chilled."

Avakab's voice—normally very soft—rose just loud enough for Jem to make out the words. "It doesn't matter," he said. "I need some air. I want to go outside. Just to sit—just for a while." He coughed several times, then added, with a hint of the fierce intensity that made him so intimidating, "So don't argue with me."

"But it's going to snow! Please, Avak," Waltak implored, "you need to take care. You need to . . ." His voice trailed off despairingly.

Avakab spoke slowly but forcefully. "No, I don't need to do anything. Let me do as I wish. It will make no difference. Believe me. It's my own body, I should know."

Their voices dropped again and Jem didn't hear the end of the argument. But he gathered that Avakab, having dismissed Waltak's smothering concern, would be going to sit outside. As far as Jem knew, he hadn't done that in a long time. Jem felt even more remorseful then, wishing things were normal; he would have liked to find something to work on outside so he could stay near the old rebel—and perhaps ask him to tell a story, or just to talk.

When Waltak reappeared, Jem was still seated at the fire. He'd finished sewing a tear in one of his mittens that he ordinarily might have ignored, as it was only on the edge of the cuff, and was watching the flickering play of colors in the flames.

"You left the pantry door open," the old man whined, glaring in Jem's direction without really looking at him, as he so often did.

"I did?" Jem said, blinking at him stupidly.

"I don't mind much if you leave it unlocked—don't mind if I can get something without always having to fetch you for the keys—but don't just leave the door open."

Jem continued to stare at him. "Waltak . . ." he began.

Waltak carried on absently, as if he were talking to himself. "One of the other doors wasn't all the way shut either. If they won't shut tight, you should fix them. As you say, it's what you're here for."

This surprised Jem. He hadn't expected Waltak to fully grasp—much less remember—yesterday's comment, or for that matter, anything Jem had ever said to him. He often just seemed to be rambling, oblivious to anything outside of his own little world. But he was evidently more aware than he appeared—just as Avakab had clearly paid more attention to Jem and his activities than Jem had imagined he did.

The old man went on. "And I thought you were locking all the doors anyway—they've always been locked before when I've checked. Not that I've been checking lately, but I thought I'd told you to keep them locked, just in case, you know."

But Jem was scarcely listening. He was staring past Waltak toward the opening that led to the second largest illu, which was closest to the outer circle of the fort. He'd heard a sound—the sound of a door creaking on its hinges, then banging shut. He glanced hastily at Waltak, but the old man hadn't looked up. Perhaps he hadn't heard the noise.

Jem stood up. He said nothing, but put a hand almost protectively on the old man's shoulder as he brushed past him; he'd never touched Waltak before, and if he'd thought about it instead of doing it instinctively he wouldn't have dared. He rushed out of the illu into the courtyard, and then into the nearest sod room—the wooden door was wide open. As he ran, he glimpsed another of the doors that opened into the courtyard hanging open.

He passed through the first room and into the corridor circling the sod rooms, with the outer wall of stone on his left. His legs moving so rapidly with each long stride that he was nearly running, Jem tore down the passageway, opening every door and looking inside. The doors were all unlocked, and several not even closed.

He abandoned all discretion. "Dorion!" he yelled at the top of his lungs, "I know you're in here! Show yourself, you thieving little bastard!" As he had when he fled from Rulskar, he shouted every curse, every horrid word he knew. Continuing through the corridor, he jerked each door open violently and slammed it shut when the dark and musty interior didn't disclose the intruder. One did disclose two chests that had been opened and ransacked, and a room left in disarray, and he saw in another that things had been moved—carelessly. Many of the other rooms were empty, so there was nothing to show that they'd been disturbed.

Jem had gone more than halfway around the fort when he finally glimpsed a figure ahead of him. A tall, black figure.

"Dorion!" he bellowed again. The lean form darted into another doorway up ahead, like a shadow without substance in the dim light. By the time Jem reached that door, the one on the other side of the room it led into was open as well, and the Sanndai was nowhere to be seen.

Jem followed the boy's footprints out into the courtyard. They were clear and distinct in the snow—not only had they been made by uncommonly large boots, but they showed the imprint of a strange zigzag pattern and distorted letters. The Sanndai had left the doorway and angled across the courtyard, away from the illus. Then the prints partly overlapped another set made by the same boots, but coming the other direction, away from the only break in the sod wall. The gate was hanging open, and the tracks led out into the snowy street beyond. Jem was about to follow—but the shrill, nasal voice he'd heard shouting for some time was now loud and close.

He turned. Waltak was standing outside the nearest of the white domes. "Boy! Boy!" he was shrieking over and over. "Come here!"

Jem stopped, gasping from exertion. For a moment he stood where he was, wondering what he should do next. He chose to start toward Waltak, crossing the path of the alien boot prints as he trudged through the snow. Had the old man seen Dorion?

As Jem approached, Waltak stopped his repetitive cries and began to rattle off angry questions. "What are you doing? We heard you—shouting and slamming doors. Have you gone mad, boy? What do you think you're doing?" The old man was trembling and gripping the front of his bulky parka with his distorted fingers.

Stopping a short distance from him, Jem fell into one of his habitual postures when facing Waltak—an insolent sideways slouch with one hand on his hip—and pushed his long hair back with the other hand. "Waltak . . . Look, I'm afraid I lost the keys." His words were punctuated by each panting breath. "And it looks like someone found them. Because we have an intruder. I just saw him."

"You lost the keys?" Waltak repeated, his pallid face showing more color than usual.

"Yes. I don't know how it happened. I ran into Rulskar and his friends in the street—and then they came after me. One of them had a knife. So I took off running. Then I went to the station. But I don't know—" Jem cut himself off, seeing that Avakab had emerged from the big illu, holding a bundle of dark furs in his arms.

Waltak turned, following Jem's gaze. When he saw Avakab he announced spitefully, "He's lost the keys!" Shifting his small, glittering eyes back toward Jem, he added in a mutter, "Or so he says."

But Jem was looking at Avakab instead. As always, he found that he couldn't bring himself to tell even a half-lie in front of him, and he fell silent.

"And someone has gotten in?" Avakab asked in his controlled, soft voice. In spite of his frail appearance and the way his wrinkled round face and even his white-haired skull seemed to have shrunk in size, Jem was struck once again by his presence, and by the sense that this man was as strong-willed as ever—and no less skilled at choosing his words and concealing his feelings.

Jem nodded.

"Rulskar!" Waltak hissed. He had stopped clutching at the front of his parka and opened it—to pull out what was hidden there. Now his gnarled, awkward hands held the gold and silver Zendi gun. "He must have stolen the keys off you, and now he has—"

"No." Jem interrupted. "It isn't Rulskar. It's a Sanndai. Dressed in black. I just saw him."

"A Sanndai?" Avakab repeated.

"Yes." No matter the consequences of telling the true story, there was no way Jem could stand there and say nothing to Avakab. "I met him—yesterday. This Sanndai. I talked to him—I didn't want to. I went to the station and he was there. He was—he was looking for something." Jem paused, then quickly added, "He was rude and acted very strange—I didn't like him at all," feeling it was important for the old man to know this. "Now he has the keys."

"You gave him the keys!" Waltak turned the Zendi in his

trembling hands.

"No!" Jem shouted, infuriated by how readily the crazy old fool had jumped to that conclusion, just as he'd feared they might. "I didn't give him the keys!" Even though the Sanndai weapon was now aimed at him, he glared at Waltak. "I'm not on his side, if that's what you think! Why would I be? I know nothing about him—and I hated him! He was the most irritating and most . . ." for half a second he struggled to grasp the right word, then spat out, ". . . *offensive* person I ever met!" Biting his lip, Jem pushed aside the small voice in his head that wanted to add, 'With the possible exception of you, old man!'

Avakab regarded Jem with a thoughtful expression. "Offensive, was he?" Then he added, speaking slowly and carefully, "You said he was looking for something. What was he looking for? Do you know?"

Jem looked away, scuffing one foot back and forth in the snow. There was little wind and the air had grown warmer. The sky hung low above the fort, the grayish-white clouds veiling the winter sun. Although none had fallen yet, Jem could taste snow in the air. He looked back to the two old men standing before him—Waltak trembling and holding the large Zendi gun in his crippled little hands, Avakab calm and unmoved, his arms cradling the reindeer skins he'd brought outside to sit upon. From Avakab's clear blue eyes, Jem's gaze returned to the Zendi, whose metal shape shone in the pale light.

"He was looking for . . ." He paused for a second, then gestured wildly at the object Waltak held. "That! He's looking for that!"

Avakab's eyes narrowed, boring hard into Jem, and Jem was relieved that he'd told the truth. But when the old man spoke as if he were musing to himself, he was clearly asking the question of Jem. "How did he know we had it, I wonder?"

Jem gulped—he couldn't admit he'd been so stupid as to tell a strange Sanndai about the weapon's existence.

Waltak saved him. Spluttering, he proclaimed, "The

Sanndai could have caught Rulskar—then tortured it out of him!"

Jem shook his head in disgust. "No—this Sanndai couldn't have done that. He's just a boy. Well, he's as tall as me, but very young. And he was alone. Or he said he was."

"That could have been a bluff," Avakab said, still looking intently at Jem, his eyes holding him.

Jem agreed wholeheartedly. "Yes—he could have been lying." He turned and looked back toward the gate. "I was going to go after him—he can't have gotten far, and I can track him easily."

"Yes, you could," Avakab said. "But what good would that do?"

"I want to get the keys." Jem spun back to face him. "He's got my keys!"

"And is he unarmed?" The old man's white brows arched skeptically.

"No—he's got . . ." Jem stopped himself. "But maybe I could . . ." He abandoned that effort as well, and for a moment he stood there, silently regarding the two familiar figures.

"You're not leaving!" Waltak snapped, lifting the Zendi again. "Especially not to go looking for another Sanndai. How do we know you didn't do this on purpose?" he added in a hiss.

"Waltak!" Jem scowled down at the little man, struggling to hold onto his composure but aware that the hurt he felt was no longer deeply hidden. "Why would I do that? Why don't you trust me? What have I ever done?"

"You lie to me, you call me names behind my back. You think I don't know!" the old man retorted, shaking harder than ever, and Jem wondered if Waltak weren't simply terrified of him, even after living beside him for seven years.

"All right! I've been disrespectful," Jem admitted, too rattled now to keep anything back. "But that was all. And it was only because you hardly ever treat me like a person!"

Avakab cut in. "Never mind that, young man. It can't be

undone. At present, we are in something of a predicament."
There was a moment of silence, after which Avakab
announced, "I am going to sit down—as I came out here
intending to do. Then we shall talk about our options."

As Avakab tottered forward, unfolding the skins in his
arms, Jem saw the first snowflake fall, sticking to the ruff of
Waltak's hood. Jem held out his mittened hands and looked
up, watching the flurry begin in earnest, gray spots falling out
of the sky to become white when they reached him. Still gazing
up into the sky, Jem heard Waltak say, in little more than a
whimper, "See, Avak? I told you it would start soon. Please,
why don't we go in?"

Avakab sighed, but when he spoke there was fondness and
a touch of amusement in his voice. "No, no, Walt. Enough. I
told you I'm sitting out here, and I'm going to do it. A little
snow never hurt anyone."

Jem looked at the old men in time to see Waltak,
burdened by the Zendi held in the crook of his arm, awkwardly
reaching his other hand out to help Avakab.

Avakab waved him away. "I can do it," he said, dropping
the furs on the ground beside the wall of one of the illus, in the
spot where he used to sit to watch Jem work. "Mind that evil
thing you're holding, my dear fellow—you'll have it going off."
There was definitely humor in his voice as he said this, and
Waltak straightened up, returning his attention to the Sanndai
weapon and carefully positioning it in both hands.

Slowly Avakab lowered himself to the ground, wincing as
he did so. Jem watched him, chewing his lip and grimacing as
if he felt the old rebel's pain. The exertion of the movement
caused a long session of coughing, during which Waltak stared
miserably at the weapon he held, and Jem stood where he was.
It seemed he was only an observer now, disconnected from this
scene.

Avakab's coughs subsided and he settled himself into the
furs, sitting cross-legged. The fat white flakes of snow were

falling steadily upon him.

Waltak faced Jem, again raising the Zendi. "Don't go anywhere, boy," he ordered.

"Do I look like I'm going anywhere?" Jem asked in exasperation. But he felt as sorry for Waltak as he felt annoyed with him.

Then Avakab spoke to his companion in his slow, musing voice. "If you shoot our Sanndai friend, Walt, you and I will be in a rather awkward position. I shouldn't want to ask the midwives to take care of us—even if it weren't for long. You know how most of them feel about us." He surprised Jem by chuckling at this.

Turning his head but still pointing the barrel of the Zendi at Jem, Waltak looked mournfully at Avakab. "I don't trust him, Avak. And now anyone can get in. We gave him a responsibility, and he failed."

"Perhaps. Perhaps it wasn't his fault. In either case, we do need him—more than we've ever needed him, as you well know." There was a silent moment. Then Avakab smiled. "On the other hand, you might just as well do it. I won't go asking the old women to care of us, but I can surely get one of them— Enkara, probably—to give us enough sleep tonic, or something stronger. She might be glad to do that."

Waltak grunted in acknowledgment, not clearly agreeing or disagreeing, and looked back to Jem, his brow furrowed and his face forlorn.

"Or," Avakab added, his voice a little louder, "we could just use that." He gestured at the Zendi.

Looking down first at the weapon, and then at Avakab, Waltak swallowed visibly. "Yes . . . But I don't know if I could, Avak."

"Well, perhaps it doesn't still work," Avakab murmured, sounding faintly amused. "Perhaps you could give it a try?"

Waltak looked sharply at his companion, swallowed again, and lifted the Zendi gun in hands that trembled still more. "I don't know," he mumbled. "Maybe it doesn't."

Jem thought of how Waltak had so recently bragged that he knew how to use it. Relieved, he imagined that in those crippled old hands the weapon was surely harmless after all.

But Waltak was staring at Avakab, who nodded and gestured toward the small square room jutting out into the courtyard, where Jem had found the mute's body seven years ago, and where—on the opposite side—he'd hung his target.

Jem barely caught the soft words, "Aim it over there and see what happens."

As if to prove himself—as he might have done many years ago when Rulskar's grandfather had belittled him—Waltak turned abruptly, looking where Avakab had pointed, and raised the alien weapon in clenched hands. Jem saw the frail little man grimace and shut his eyes.

Without any sound, and without seeming to have any specific source—as if it came out of the snow-filled air around them—there was a burst of intense white light. Jem flinched, and it was a moment before he understood what had happened. When his eyes followed the gazes of both old men, he saw a dark mark high in the leaning sod wall. Above it, a thin trail of steam and smoke wavered up into the falling snow.

Waltak had lowered the heavy, shining thing in his hands, and was shaking visibly. A crust of ice sparkled on the fur trim shielding the lower part of his wizened face, as puffs of steam betrayed his rapid breathing.

"Ah," Avakab said, with little emotion. "It does work, then."

Still looking down at the weapon, Waltak said nothing. After a moment, Jem heard Waltak's thin voice speak with a quaver. "I don't know, Avak."

"Then give it to me, and I'll do it," Avakab answered gently. "But what about our young friend? Could you do that?" He chuckled again. "You've been threatening to for the last half hour. Perhaps you could actually make good on it?"

Jem took a step back, staring at Avakab. He couldn't really mean it. Was this some kind of joke?

"In any case," Avakab added in the same quiet voice, still gazing at Waltak's miserable face, "we should take him with us, for his sake also."

"Take me with you?" Jem echoed, comprehension blurring under the haze of disbelief. "Where? What do you mean?"

Avakab turned his narrow blue eyes to Jem—eyes that were almost hidden in the pale wrinkles that surrounded them, but still glimmered intently, as if they belonged to a different being hidden behind this mask. He smiled fondly at Jem and gave a deep sigh. "Where we all go in the end, my boy. I like you, you know. I think you're really a good-hearted man. But you just said that this Sanndai thief—the only Sanndai you've ever seen, I'm certain—was the most offensive person you've ever met. You would find all of your own kind offensive, I'm afraid. Part of you believes you are a Torvik. That was inevitable. I can't blame Enkara for what she did, but it doesn't change the fact that it was wrong."

Although he was speaking, Avakab was sitting so still he might not have been a living thing, an illusion aided by the falling snow covering the shapes of his parka and the furs under him with an even layer of white. "You have no future here—I think you know that. So you belong nowhere. You've been a great help to Waltak and me." With another sad smile he added, "For the most part, you've behaved remarkably well. It's only right we should take you with us; it's the only kindness I can offer you now. Lately I've been wondering a great deal about where we will go—where it ends. I don't know, and I believe no one else does either. But perhaps we'll meet there, and I shall tell you some more stories."

Jem had started to back farther away. Entranced by the soft rhythm of the storyteller's voice, he froze again. He was touched by the tenderness in the old man's words. But now the full realization of what the two old men were speaking of, and what they intended to do, came down like a heavy blow. His chest tightened and his heartbeat thudded in his ears.

"No!" His voice came out in a hoarse whisper. "I don't want . . ." He stopped, instinct telling him that he should just run.

As Jem turned, aware that the open gate was a fair distance behind him, in his mind's eye he saw the old man shooting him as he ran. But the feeling of terror ebbed swiftly when it occurred to him that it would mean shooting him in the back. Surely not even Waltak would do that.

Yet instead of giving him the assurance to go, that thought made him pause and look again at Avakab and Waltak, torn. He still didn't want to believe that these two elders, so frail and so familiar, who had come to seem gentle and innocuous in spite of their violent pasts and in spite of Avakab's intimidating presence, could—or would—really do such a thing.

He heard a scraping sound behind him, and his head snapped around. Crouched on the top of the stone wall behind him was the black-clad Sanndai. As Jem's mouth opened but no sound came out, Dorion jumped down. The lanky figure bent his knees to absorb the shock as he hit the snowy ground, then rose to his full height, holding a silver rectangle in his outstretched hand.

"Never mind, Walt," Jem heard Avakab murmur, undisguised tenderness in his voice. "Never mind. Give me a hand up and give me the horrible thing. I'll take care of everything."

When Jem looked back, Waltak was bending over to help Avakab to his feet, and he knew they hadn't seen the intruder.

Jem quickly looked again at Dorion. The Sanndai was standing against the wall, his head bowed over his weapon. He was holding it flat in his hands, apparently trying to do something to it. Then he heard the boy hiss, "Blast! Open—you stupid thing!"

The snowfall was growing heavier, and both old men's hoods and shoulders were thickly coated. Avakab was now on his feet. The silver and gold weapon was still in Waltak's hands when Waltak gave a furtive glance over his shoulder at Jem. It was then that the old man saw the Sanndai boy—who at that very moment looked up, aiming the silver Zendi at the two old Torviks.

Jem heard Waltak's wheezing gasp of alarm and saw him stumble forward with the Zendi held awkwardly in front of him. Avakab was reaching out to take the weapon from Waltak's hands.

There was a flash of the eerie white light. Waltak jerked and leaned back. He made a whispered sound, then dropped to the ground, the Zendi still in his hands. Very slowly, Avakab looked up.

This time Jem saw Dorion's thumb press down on the weapon in his hand, saw that the blinding flash emanated from the weapon. He watched with horror as the old man winced and put his hand to a small dark hole burned into the front of his parka. Avakab pulled the hand away and looked at it, his face calm. Then he crumpled, slumping onto the snow-frosted furs.

A long-legged black figure rushed past Jem, slipping in the snow and lurching sideways to brush against him at the moment of passing. Though the contact was light, Jem staggered, losing his balance and nearly falling himself.

The Sanndai slid to his knees beside the two bodies and tugged the Zendi from Waltak's hands. Then he jumped to his feet, waved the weapon in the air over his head, and let out a boyish whoop of delight.

Aghast, Jem could hardly believe what he was seeing.

Dorion turned and seemed to notice him for the first time. "Ay, Jem! You all right?"

Jem was aware that his mouth was dry, and that snowflakes were brushing his face. It seemed a long a time before he managed to say, "What did you do that for?"

Dorion made his incredulous face. "What do you mean 'what did I do that for'? I was spying over the wall—freezing my fingers and barely hanging on—and I heard everything! I almost choked and fell off when they fired this and it worked! But I heard everything they said—these old fossils were gonna kill you! And then they were gonna kill themselves. That's the truth, aynit? They weren't talking metaphors! Besides, from the way you were acting, I know they meant it! I just saved your butt, hossti—don't I get any thanks?"

Clenching his hands into fists, Jem drew his lips together. "You just shot a man in the back. An old man. And he didn't know you were there until the second before you did it. And then you shot another old man—who didn't even have a weapon!"

"But they were gonna kill you!" Dorion protested, staring at Jem as if he were astonished by his response. "And they'd decided to kill themselves too! They wanted to die!"

"It doesn't matter!" Jem retorted furiously. "That was up to them—it wasn't for you to do! You had no right."

"But they were gonna kill you *first*!" Dorion yelled, his voice rising even higher. He paused, gasping, and looked down at the weapon he held. "And by all the stars, I don't know how they got this to work."

"Look under that rag!" Jem snarled. "If you thought the evil things couldn't be fooled, it shows how much of a genius you really are!"

"What?" Dorion tugged at the stained strip of cloth. When he lifted it off the silver and gold Zendi, he held it away from him. His eyes grew wide as he stared at the matted lock of dark hair against the surface of the pale rag. "Oh, Zennix!" he whispered, holding it even farther away. "I don't believe it!" He gulped visibly. "This is sick . . . really sick." He continued to stare at the hair as flecks of white appeared on it. Then he slowly opened his hand and let both hair and rag drop into the snow at his feet.

The Sanndai boy cradled the ornate weapon in both hands for a moment, as if he wished to soothe away the shame of what had been done to it. Then he opened the front of his black jacket and placed the Zendi gun inside. He let out a shaky breath, then bent down to pick up the Zendi he'd used. He'd apparently dropped it before pulling the other weapon out of the old man's grasp.

Rubbing ice crystals off the silver barrel with a bare hand, he walked toward Jem. "Look. I tried to dial this thing down to stun, but I couldn't get it open; I think someone coded a lock on it. But I really did try—honest. And it might not have been better that way, anyhow. I've heard some apes come out of a stun in a real rage, so it's best if you're close enough to grab them quickly, and sometimes it can even make a person's heart stop—especially an old person." He hooked the weapon onto his belt and looked imploringly at Jem. "Besides, they said they wanted to die. And they wanted you dead, too! I mean, isn't that what you understood?"

Jem stared at him silently. The boy had no hood, and the thick white flakes were stark on his black hair and shoulders. Jem was especially aware of the warm color of his dark skin and the eerie depth of those unnerving black eyes, glaringly real in the white scene around them.

"Just tell me I'm not crazy, and that's what you understood!" Dorion pleaded. He seemed both dismayed and exasperated by Jem's reaction—but not remorseful, or stricken at the thought of having committed murder.

Jem didn't want to answer; he spoke only in an effort to end the encounter. "Yes—that's what I understood. They were going to kill me first. All right?" His tone was even more bitter when he said, "And now you have the horrid weapon. Are you satisfied? Will you leave?"

But the boy lunged forward and grabbed Jem's arm. "You're coming with me, aren't you?"

Shaking his head, Jem pulled back.

"Come on, Jem—you've gotta come with me. Something terrible could happen to you here. You said it yourself—it's not safe."

As Jem tried to free his arm from Dorion's grasp, he continued to shake his head. "You tricked me." Anger brought a tremor to his voice. "You tricked me to steal the keys, then shot the old men in cold blood. Maybe the real reason was just to get the weapon—not to save me. How do I know different? You tricked me."

"Jem!" the boy wailed. "I had to! I didn't mean to get you in trouble, but you wouldn't listen." He gave a groan of frustration. "Come *on*! You're gonna be killed!"

Dorion was pulling hard, but Jem reached up under his parka with his free hand and drew out his knife. Stupid, again, since Dorion had two Zendis on his belt. But it was a gesture that showed he was serious.

Dorion let go of Jem's arm and held his hand out in a conciliatory manner. "All right, all right! I can't force you to come with me. But I think you're doing the wrong thing. And I just want to help—really!" He shook his head as he retreated, heading toward the gate.

Jem watched as Dorion stood in the entrance for a while, looking out. Finally the boy ducked through—and transformed back into a lanky black shadow that slipped away into the snowfall.

Walking in the prints of the strange-soled boots, Jem followed their path to the gate. Just as Dorion had done, he stopped at the opening and looked out. The young Sanndai had already gone behind one of the other buildings; Jem could clearly see the tracks in the fresh white surface, but the dark figure was out of sight.

As he turned to go back into the courtyard, Jem saw the glitter of something metallic in the snow, right at his feet. He bent down.

It was a ring of brass keys trailing a leather strap, dropped so that the keys fanned out, each one making an imprint in the powdery new snow.

IV

THE STILL FORMS of the old men were blanketed in white. Lying close to each other, they looked peaceful. Jem watched the snow fall on the shapes, a growing numbness pushing all emotion out of him. There was nothing they needed him to do. The thought that he had no purpose here any longer left him with a hollow feeling he could never have anticipated. Perhaps Avakab had—and perhaps that was one reason he'd felt that taking Jem with them would have been a kindness.

As the emptiness settled through him, like the soft white flakes accumulating on the brown sleeve of his parka, a small voice from inside Jem spoke into the void. If the rest of him were numb and silent, the child he'd once been still knew where to turn—where to seek protection and warmth when the world seemed as harsh and cruel as the east wind cutting across the tundra like an icy blade.

Enkara. He hadn't wanted to burden her again, but without the thought of her there was only the hollowness. His memories of Enkara and his feelings about her, held close behind those walls within him, always had life and substance.

And as he thought of what he must tell her, Jem realized there was another reason to go to Enkara—the Ongalak would have to tend to the bodies of the old men, and someone would have to bear the news to him. Jem had never been intimidated by old Neskeb, a gentle man who'd often squatted down beside the children to speak to them, but he'd never met Boskur, the current Ongalak, face to face—he'd only seen him in a crowded room during festivals. Since Jem was a stranger to him as well as an outcast, it seemed wrong to approach him now only to bring news of death.

When Jem turned away from the snow-covered bodies, a fleck of color on the ground caught his eye. He'd forgotten about Dorion dropping the rag that had been tied around the alien weapon. Almost obscured under the snow, one end of the stained strip of cloth was still visible. Jem gently picked it up and brushed off the snow. The hank of dark hair was still pressed into the band of cloth.

He held it in the palm of his mitten, watching the snow speckle the dark strands and the stained and tattered cloth. Then he went back to the snow domes. Inside the large illu, he knelt beside the fire pit. It seemed only right to bring a kind of closure by disposing of this strange and gruesome trophy, and not only was it easiest to burn it, it seemed more final. And after all, the person it came from was not of this world, so perhaps rather than placing it in the earth it was better if it became smoke that would rise into the sky.

Jem folded the strip of cloth around the hair, rolled it up, and dropped the little bundle into the coals. He wrinkled his nose at the sour odor as it smoked and then crackled in the flames.

The moment when he'd recognized the shapes of the bow and arrows being consumed in the fire suddenly came back to him. He was startled by the deep, aching sense of loss that surged over him. It left him breathless. The strength of the emotion seemed disproportionate, as if it had arisen from nowhere, inexplicably summoned by the burning hair and cloth.

He closed his eyes and breathed slowly. Opening his eyes again, he sat very still, gazing into the whispering flames.

When nothing remained but the embers, he broke a chunk of snow off the platform beside him and dropped it into the fire pit. He squatted there for a moment longer, watching the steam released from the dying fire.

In his own illu, Jem collected his meager belongings and bundled them up inside a small reindeer skin. He crawled back out into the steady snowfall and trudged across the courtyard, again crossing the path of the alien boot prints still faintly discernible in the snow. When he went through the narrow gate in the east wall, he took care that it was latched behind him, but didn't lock it, although the keys were back on his belt. The bodies of the old men would be all right until the Ongalak came.

Jem turned and walked away from the fort without a backward glance, the hood of his parka pulled snug about his face, the bundle slung over his shoulder.

When he got to the Birthing House he stood in the street for a moment, staring at the familiar building behind the veil of snowflakes. It had been a couple of moons since he'd last been there, but it looked the same as always. It seemed strange that it didn't change, no matter what else occurred. And everything had changed now.

He knocked at the big wooden door, as he always did when coming to visit Enkara; although he'd lived here for fifteen years, he was only a visitor now. It was Enkara herself who answered, and for that brief moment—seeing her form and face in the shadowy space of the entryway—he was flooded with relief.

The old woman ushered him inside without a word. He followed her as she passed through the big room and into the smaller one where low sleeping platforms covered in skins and blankets encircled a fire pit. The fire burned over a bed of smoky orange coals, making Jem's eyes water; he'd been spoiled by the fresher air inside the illus he'd built.

Enkara turned to face him, her sharp eyes missing

nothing. And the meaning of the bundle, hanging awkwardly in his left hand, could only be obvious. "What happened, Jemren? What's wrong?"

Jem shook his head and looked away from her, lifting his gaze to the ceiling and the dim spot of light coming through the smoke hole. "Before I tell you, have someone go to the Ongalak and send him to the fort."

When he glanced at her he saw that her eyes widened, but she only murmured, "All right," and left the room. After a brief moment she returned. She coaxed him to sit beside her, near the fire, and said, "Now tell me."

"I'm sorry. I didn't mean to come here like this. But . . ." He swallowed, looking toward the ceiling again. "There was a Sanndai here. He was just a boy—seventeen, he said. He was at the station. I still go there sometimes to be alone, and he . . . well, what matters is he stole the keys off my belt. So he got into the fort, and went through everything—looking for the Sanndai weapon Waltak was keeping."

"Waltak?" Enkara echoed, her voice barely above a whisper. "I'd heard that Avakab had one, but none of us knew if it was just a rumor."

"I don't know how they got it, but I think they'd had it a long time. And the Sanndai boy, he wanted it badly—he said it was a special kind." Jem went on, the words tumbling out. He felt as if he were describing a nightmare he'd had, for even as he heard himself telling the story, it was hard to believe it had been real.

Enkara gasped when he told of how the old men had died, how the alien boy had shot Waltak in the back. Jem saw the horror in her eyes and had to look away again.

He was breathing hard by the time he'd finished, as if it had taken a great effort to push his way through the story. He ended by confessing, "I don't know what I'm going to do now."

Enkara took a deep breath and drew her small form up to its full height. Jem knew she must be feeling the cold, for she was wearing a fur robe over her familiar red and blue shawl, and she pulled it closer around her shoulders. "What you're to do now, young man, is to take off your parka and your boots and warm yourself, while I get you a bowl of tea."

He obeyed, sitting on one of the beds and staring down at the haze of smoke rising from the glowing coals as he tugged his boots off.

When Enkara came back, she shushed him, telling him not to speak any more of what had happened. She sat beside him, sharing the everyday news of the village just as she usually did, as if nothing had happened, nothing had changed. But the pain in her eyes had deepened, and he imagined regret in her expression as well.

That evening she made up a bed for him in the little storeroom opposite the pantry. He couldn't stretch out, but he was grateful for a quiet spot to sleep where he could pretend to be hidden from the world. He pulled his feet up under the furs Enkara had given him, drawing his knees almost to his chest, and put his head on the reindeer skin bundle he'd brought with him. It wasn't long before he fell asleep, but that sleep was marred by strange dreams.

Jem stood amid the ruins of a stone building. The ruins were filled with snow, with drifts banked against the broken walls and fallen stones. He was wearing black, looking down and seeing his arms and legs all in black against the white around him. Standing not far from him was another figure clad in black—tall and dark-haired. The face wasn't distinct, but the person was familiar. The dreamer responded to that familiarity, and along with that recognition was the sense that they were much the same. Jem knew also that he was with that person, and yet not with him; they hadn't come from the same place. All of these things were dream facts that needed no explanation.

Then there was an old man, sitting in the snow on a pile of furs, a dark fur over his shoulders. It was Goplak, the old poultry keeper. But no, it was Avakab, though he looked different—his eyes vacant instead of intense, as if the mind behind them were feeble, empty. The other man wearing black tried to help the old man get to his feet, then started to drag him over the surface of the snow, using the furs like a sled.

Jem started shouting at him, arguing with him, but in the way one might quarrel with someone they knew very well—were even fond of perhaps—and were merely annoyed with. It seemed they were trying to do something together, something that had to do with the old man, and were held together by some bond.

Then his twin figure in black, still faceless but familiar, was waving to him from a distance and hurrying away across the snowfield. Jem knew the man would be back, but a long while later, after Jem had done something—something very important he had to do. He walked a long distance, struggling through deep snow. Then he saw a dark shape not far ahead of him, and knew he'd found what he was searching for. Yes, it was the old man sitting on the furs.

Relieved, he started to call a greeting, then noticed something strange about the figure slumped on the brown and gray furs in the middle of the empty white landscape. He walked up to it, gripped by the suffocating horror only a nightmare can bring. He looked down at a frozen, desiccated carcass, twisted awkwardly onto one side, dusted with snow and ice, the grimacing round face looking upwards. And the eye sockets were empty.

It was his fault. He hadn't come quickly enough. He had failed. And he would have to tell the other black-clothed man he'd been too late. But the dream setting shifted, and he was inside a long corridor, dimly lit and smoky, with walls of gray stone. And when he reached the end of the corridor there was a doorway, with the door hanging open. He went inside, and there was the man dressed in black. But he was different—shorter and younger.

And when the figure turned to face Jem, it had Dorion's face, and the boy was laughing. Laughing and laughing, as if taunting Jem, jeering at his failure, his fear. Unable to turn away, Jem could see nothing but the too-vivid images before him—the unfathomable black eyes, the bronze-colored skin and broad white smile, and the strange boyish features.

Jem began to shout and curse, saying the boy was to blame because he'd left and hadn't even tried to help. But Dorion only kept smiling, oblivious, as Jem yelled until he could scarcely breathe. His head and his chest hurt, and it felt as if his heart would burst. Still he kept on yelling and yelling, desperate to convey his outrage.

He awoke, quivering, lying in the complete darkness of the tiny room. The vision of Dorion's cocky young face still loomed in his mind, and he hated it as he'd never hated anything or anyone. He tried again and again to drive the image away, but could not. Now even his mind had been invaded, contaminated.

He was going mad, he thought, listening to the pounding of his heart as he stared up into the darkness and felt the rough edge of the pelt he clutched in his hands. The evil Sanndai was in his head. In his head, where he couldn't get him out and couldn't touch him. He could do nothing but futilely imagine over and over again that he was striking the boy down, stabbing him with a knife, or clubbing him over the head and beating him into the ground. But then the Sanndai would be there again, with the same heedless smile, the same uncanny eyes—and the same laughter.

Finally the torture ended and Jem fell back to sleep. Again he dreamed, but all he could remember after waking was the image of a wolf. A single wolf following a trail. He remembered the dream he'd had the night after he first entered the abandoned Sanndai station, so long ago—the dream he'd never spoken of to anyone, about the old wolf searching for her shadow. It seemed this had been an echo of that one, in the way that dreams sometimes repeated themselves.

And he woke to the sound of children's voices, much to his surprise. But it gave him a sense of relief and comfort, too. He felt a quietness settling inside of him, as if he'd gone through the worst and something meaningful still remained.

As Jem lay still, surrounded by familiar smells and sensations, the hatred and anger in his dream about the Sanndai boy now seemed childish, like the anguish felt in a nightmare that isn't frightening at all when the dreamer wakes. Though he still despised him—and wished the image of his face had never entered his mind—he knew it was too simplistic to say the boy was evil. Was anyone truly evil?

That was a hard question when he considered Rulskar. But even Rulskar had the love of the dog, Trika—what did that signify? Perhaps nothing.

He recalled the Sanndai boy's expression when he'd pleaded with Jem to leave with him, and the anguish in his voice when he'd claimed he was acting to save Jem's life. Clearly Dorion had thought he was doing right—he wasn't trying to be cruel. As much as Jem hated to admit that, he knew it was true.

It was wiser to say the boy was ignorant, and that he did wrong out of ignorance. Though Jem cared nothing for his claims of being a genius, he didn't seem stupid. If he weren't stupid, but merely unknowing, perhaps he—and other Sanndai—could learn to act differently. They could come to understand why what they did was so unjust and heartless.

Besides, he was a Sanndai himself, and he was sure he wasn't evil either. As Avakab and Vechnor had both said, he wasn't 'dangerous'. But if he, a Sanndai, could be decent and honest and kind to others, as Enkara had taught him to be, there was no fundamental reason any Sanndai couldn't be a decent person. And if he didn't believe that, Jem realized, he couldn't believe in himself.

For a while he listened to the high chatter of children and

the occasional murmur of one of the women's voices on the other side of the wall. Later it was quiet again, and still he waited, only sitting up to stretch, and to fumble in the dark for his boots. But he made no move to put them on or to get up. He would wait. Rest while he could.

He had a long journey ahead of him, and he had no idea where it led. But he understood what old Avak had meant when he said Jem had no future—not in Kruvak, anyway. There were too many risks, too many things that would make it go wrong. Even if Vechnor really wanted to invite Jem into his home, and take him hunting and fishing on the coast, those old reasons—the ones that had made Enkara let him go with Waltak that day—were unchanged. Vechnor knew it as well; it had showed in his eyes when he'd acknowledged his companion's words and looked back at Jem.

But there had never seemed to be an option before. That was curious, because it wasn't as if Jem had ever doubted that the Sanndai existed. And yet they were shadow people, living only in dreams. Now that he had met this horrid boy, and experienced the jarring reality of him, there was certainty—proof of their existence on another level. There truly were other people who looked like him. And there was another place, a real place, where they lived. Where Jem might live.

Though the idea of leaving still brought a queasy dread and the familiar weight in his stomach, he knew his only chance was to find his way to that shadow world where his own kind lived—and to try to believe that many of them really weren't bad people.

It seemed a long time later that the door opened, letting in the dim light from the room beyond and the smell of fish and oily smoke. Enkara's silver head came around the edge of the door. "Jem?" she whispered. "Are you awake?"

"Yes," he answered.

"Come quickly. Get dressed and bring your things. Hurry."

"What is it?"

"Shhh! I'll tell you everything. But you must be quick."

He came out of the room, pulling his parka over his head as he ducked through the doorway and switching his bundle from one hand to the other as he put each arm into the sleeve, then shoving his disheveled hair out of his face and down his back. He followed Enkara into the room she'd led him to yesterday, smoky and colored with orange light.

Again Jem sat on the foot of the low fur-covered platform she gestured to, looking up at her as she stood beside him. Her little hands were clenched in fists at her sides, her face flushed and her eyes bright with emotion.

"What is it?" he said again, concerned more for her concern than for himself.

"Rulskar is telling everyone you did it—that you killed the old men—because . . ." She stopped, shaking her head and pressing her lips together, then went on. "Because you went bad, and became like one of your people, as he knew you would. That's what he's saying. I don't know who believes him, but of course everyone wants to find out what really happened."

"Of course."

"But now he's looking for you—he and his men. And Karya just heard that someone may have told them you're here. I don't want them to find you—I don't trust them. I don't know what they might do."

"Oh, I have a pretty good idea," Jem growled.

Enkara reached out to take hold of his hand, which swallowed up hers. "Oh, Jem—how I wish I knew a way to hide you! You'll just have to leave, and we'll try to detain them, but I don't know for how long . . ."

He cut her off, rising to his feet. "It's all right. I'm going anyway. You tried—and I'm grateful. I can't even say . . . But it doesn't matter. It'll be all right," he assured her, gently squeezing her hand.

"But I must tell you something before you go—and give

you something you must take with you."

Jem knew his face darkened at this, and he felt torn. She wouldn't risk detaining him long enough to endanger him, he was certain of that, but now the desire to get far away from the House as quickly as possible loomed above everything else. "Now?" he said.

"Yes," she pleaded, her eyes sparkling with tears. "I must tell you. I never told you everything, Jem—everything about your mother."

He pulled his hand from her grasp. "It doesn't matter, Enkara. Don't worry about it."

"No!"

The urgency in her voice stopped him. "All right. Tell me." He didn't sit down again.

There had been a time, he recalled, when he'd incessantly asked her for details about his mother, wanting to know more of the reason he was different, as each day made him more painfully aware of those differences. So he had asked and asked, and she'd never given him more than the original story: when his mother had come to the Birthing House, she was clearly a Sanndai—tall, with dark skin and eyes and long black hair and strange clothing—but she didn't say where she'd come from, and she died shortly after he was born. That was all— never anything more.

Now Enkara sat in the place where he'd been, clenching her hands on her lap as she spoke. "Your mother . . . Telana, Neskeb's wife, found her in the street. She'd been beaten badly—bruises on her face, and her mouth bloody, and her head bleeding where some of her hair had been torn out. She wasn't conscious at first, but they were able to wake her. Telana was with a friend, and they helped her up and brought her here as quickly as they could. We knew she couldn't have walked all the way from a Sanndai village—they are far from here, and there is the border fence. But she'd walked from somewhere, looking for shelter and help, and when she reached the village someone attacked her and left her in the street. We never found out who—no one confessed to having seen her before Telana found her.

"When they got her here she was talking, but strangely, and seemed confused. We asked her what had happened to her, and who had beaten her, but she couldn't tell us anything that we could understand—only that somebody was dead. The others were all dead, she said several times, and she said that she'd walked, walked alone. I remember that, but little else. But she was very gentle, and she smiled at us, and thanked us, and seemed so grateful. We were surprised, and afterward Telana said she'd never seen a Sanndai woman up close before, and perhaps the women were not like the men, and they knew how to be kind.

"But in a little while her labor started, and I knew she wouldn't live; she was too weak to bear the strain—she was so deep into cold shock when she was found, on top of the injuries. Even if she hadn't been with child, I don't think we could have saved her. And if I hadn't felt you moving when I first put my hands on her belly, I would have thought it likely her baby was already dead.

"She surprised us still more—she was very strong, I think—and she was awake most of the night, while you were born. We couldn't make sense of everything she said, but we knew she understood we were trying to help her. She kept grabbing our hands, and asking if the baby was all right. Then, after you were born—and you were big and healthy, the healthiest baby I'd ever seen, so strong and heavy, with a swirl of black hair—I put you in her arms. She did nurse you a little, but she was so weak I had to help her to hold you.

"But she'd started saying a word, 'Jemren, Jemren,' over and over again—at least, it sounded like that to me. And when I asked her what she wanted to name you, she stopped and looked at me, as if she'd heard and understood, and she said again, 'Jemren.' I decided it must be a name, so I called you that. It didn't seem right to give you one of our names."

"Tell me again what she looked like." The question had been part of Jem for as long as he could remember.

"Like you." Enkara gazed at him steadily, a faint smile touching her lips and pride in her eyes. "She was the tallest women I've ever seen, and her hair was black and so long it reached to her waist. Her eyes were strange, and yet there was something about her face—I don't know what it was, but I thought she was beautiful from the first moment I saw her, even with the bruises and swelling, the blood in her hair . . . And when she smiled, she smiled like a child, so full of hope. She smiled at you when I put you in her arms, even though she was barely conscious by then."

"And then?" Jem asked, glancing over his shoulder at the door.

"She died shortly after that. Neskeb came with Cherskel and some other men, and they took her body out. When old Cherskel saw her, he said her face was beautiful, too. And Neskeb said she shouldn't be judged by anything her people had done, because whatever had brought her here, we had no knowledge that she'd ever been unkind to anyone. He said we needed to remember that Sanndai were people too, so it wasn't possible that they were all bad any more than all of us were good, although we might wish it were simple that way. And he told me he would do a prayer ceremony for her, the same as if she were one of us. I cried then, and held you close in my arms and swore I would protect you. I wouldn't listen to anyone who said I shouldn't keep you, and Telana sided with me."

Jem remembered Avakab's words about Enkara. "It's all right," he told her. "I think I understand why you didn't tell me more when I was small—when I was always asking you. But it's all right," he repeated. "I have to go now."

"Wait!" she pleaded again. She knelt beside a very old wooden chest next to the bed, unlocking the padlock and opening the lid. After lifting several items out and placing them on the bed, she pulled out a voluminous piece of dark cloth. The strange material was soft and thick, and the color was odd; it was burgundy—which reminded Jem of a vat of red dye, though even darker—and it was trimmed with black embroidery. "This was her cloak—I saved it. You must take it with you."

Trying to think only of leaving quickly, Jem shrugged as if it were unimportant to him, but he was deeply touched. And it would surely be wrong not to accept such a gift. The emotion rose into his throat, making it hard to feign apathy. "All right," he said gruffly. "I'll take it—it does look warm."

Enkara gestured for him to come closer. He walked around the bed to take the cloak from her arms. As he did so, he saw her glance furtively in the direction of the doorway, then lay a finger to her lips. "There is something else," she whispered, so quietly the words were barely audible. "The other thing she had which I saved for you. Telana knew about it—no one else saw it, because we took it off her and hid it."

"What?" he hissed, squatting awkwardly in the tight space beside her, and feeling both suspense and frustration at the delay.

Bending down so she was shielded by Jem's back and shoulders as he leaned over her, Enkara lifted something out of the bottom of the chest and pushed it into his open hands.

It was a very heavy and very familiar looking object. A Zendi gun. Gold and silver, with detailed engraving on the rectangular barrel, the shining weapon was identical to the one Dorion had coveted and taken—and which the old rebels must have had for many years before Jem first saw Waltak holding it.

"Oh," Jem gasped. He got to his feet, clumsily shifting the weapon to one hand as he helped Enkara up with the other. She sat back down on the bed and began to caress the white ermine blanket that lay on top of it, as if to soothe something away.

Placing the weapon down, Jem removed his belt, his hands shaking. Strung from the belt was a sealskin bag containing his flint, tools for sewing and leatherwork, and a few laces and scraps of leather and cloth. He pulled everything out and pushed the weapon down inside the satchel, replacing the original contents on top of it. It was a tight fit, and not easy to pull the drawstring closed again. Then he put the belt on underneath his parka, so the bag was hidden.

When he looked up, Enkara was gazing at a small object she held in her hand, which she'd apparently taken out of the open chest. It was a crude bone carving, the size and shape of an egg with a small knob on one end.

A breathless laugh escaped him. "You still have that. I made it—I remember."

She looked up from the lumpy little figurine and smiled. "Of course."

He was able to smile back. "It doesn't even look like a seal."

"I think it does," she replied with conviction.

He swallowed and pushed back his hair. "Only because I told you it was supposed to be one." He'd been only seven when he'd decided he wanted to make her a gift for the Autumn Festival, and for many nights he'd worked hard by the light of a small oil lamp, carving his meager present.

Enkara shook her head, the tender smile lingering on her lips, and then bent over to nestle the little bone seal into a fold of cloth inside the chest.

Jem swallowed again and blurted, "I wish I had something better to give you."

"Never you mind," she said. "You've given me many things."

"But something to keep," he mumbled, torn between the urgency and a sudden feeling of inadequacy that made him wish to prolong this moment until he could find a way to compensate for it.

The old woman lifted up a large basket from the floor beside the trunk. The handle of it was wrapped with a long woven band, and she unwound one end of it and held it out toward him. "You know, this is a gift from you, too."

Enkara was one of the best weavers in the village. She taught her craft to many of the young people, and she'd tried to teach Jem. She'd shown him how to weave using cards of stiff leather with holes punched in them, creating endless patterns by changing the way the cards were turned. He'd never had the patience to become good at it, often losing count of the turns and breaking the pattern, but he'd enjoyed watching how she did it, her hands and fingers moving so deftly and rhythmically it was as if they had a will of their own and needed no conscious direction from her.

The intricately patterned belt she showed him now was certainly not one of the few he'd woven; it was perfect. But it was the one he'd contributed to making in another way; diamonds of black in the middle of the pattern were made from trimmings of Jem's hair twisted together and woven in among the blue and white yarn. He recalled that Enkara had asked his permission before collecting the pieces when she cut his hair. She often commented on how strong and thick the strands were—and how she thought it was beautiful—and she'd said it would be a shame not to try to use them in her weaving.

And Jem, as always only wishing his hair wasn't different from everyone else's, had shrugged and consented without much thought. Only later had he come to understand that something from a person's body, like their hair, could be seen as a kind of charm that carries a strong connection to them. But even after he knew that, he'd felt that Enkara had every right to that bond and never objected to the idea.

Now he was reminded of the much more substantial lock of hair he'd put into the fire back at the fort. The way it had been used took the concept of a potent charm to a different level, giving credence to the superstitions in a disconcerting way. Jem shuddered inwardly and pushed it from his mind, trying also not to think of the hidden object whose weight he could now feel pulling down on his belt.

But Enkara was right that the hair in her weaving was a part of himself he'd willingly gifted to her. "I suppose it is," he told her. "Though you did all the work."

"But you made this one special," she insisted. "I've had more compliments on this weaving than any other I've done."

"Maybe the black attracts attention to it, then people have to notice how good your craft is."

She laughed softly. "That might be true."

As Jem added the cloak to his bundle, Enkara watched, her eyes never leaving him. When he straightened up and pulled up his hood, she asked, "Where will you go?" and he saw the renewed shine of tears in her eyes.

He shrugged. "South. Out of Kruvak. Look for Sanndai settlements. It's the only thing I can do." Putting it into such simple words gave him a sense of purpose, sharpening his focus.

Enkara nodded. "Yes. That's probably best. There must be some way through the border fence. Perhaps there are guards who patrol it; because you're Sanndai, they will let you through." Then she said, "I'm sorry I didn't give you these things sooner. I think perhaps I should have sent you away to find other Sanndais as soon as you were old enough to travel on your own—maybe I could have gotten you skis, or even a little sled. Now we have no time to try to find you anything, and I don't even have my snowshoes to give you—I traded them long ago. Well, if I still had them they probably wouldn't help much; they'd be too small for your feet."

Jem shook his head, biting his lip. No words would come. As he stepped toward her, tugging his second mitten on, she rose and gave him a warm smile. Reaching up as far as she could on tiptoe, she put one thin arm around his neck. He bent over and felt her cool lips brush his cheek.

"Go now," she whispered.

He could only nod. She followed him to the doorway, ushering him through the big room and then into the narrow passage that led to the pantry. In the pantry they stood below the entrance he'd so often snuck in and out of as a boy. As he stepped up, pushing open the door, he turned to look back at the old woman standing behind him, her tear-streaked face illuminated by the outdoor light.

"Thank you, Enkara," he murmured around the thickness in his throat. He managed to show her one of the woeful boyish smiles that only she was ever privy to. "For everything," he added, and it came out in no more than a whisper.

"Take care, my little big one," she whispered back. She added in a stronger voice, "And remember, Jemren, you must look out for the wolves—they are bolder away from the village."

"I will," he assured her. Then he gestured at the front of his parka and attempted a teasing grin. "And I'm armed now."

She nodded, wiping tears with the back of her hand and pushing a stray wisp of silver hair from her reddened cheek. "Yes," she said firmly. "Just be careful."

Pausing on the steps, he squinted into the white glare. The street was empty. He clambered out, then closed the door behind him. He began to run, though it was difficult—the top layer of the snow was soft, being from yesterday's storm, but the deeper layers were grainy and hard, sometimes holding his weight, sometimes allowing him to break through. He went around the corner of the building, darting into an alley that wasn't visible from the front of the Birthing House.

When he reached the next broad street he heard voices and laughter—and he recognized a manic laugh he knew all too well. Backing away from the corner, Jem held his breath and waited. He wanted to see which way they were going.

Half a dozen men came into sight. The tallest, who wore a white fur hat, walked at the head of the group. His voice carried clearly. "It would be easier if you'd all just believe me in the first place. Because I'm always right, aren't I?" the tall man gloated. "So just listen to me from now on. That's easy enough, isn't it?"

As some of the men laughed while some groaned loudly and protested, Jem pressed his shoulders and the back of his head against the sod wall behind him. He was safe unless one of them looked between the walls at just the right angle, but for half a second he closed his eyes, willing the shadows to conceal him. He heard the voices growing louder, the feet crunching in the snow.

The men drew closer and closer. Though they were moving purposefully, time seemed to slow as they passed him, no more than five meters away. And then they were out of sight—all but the last member of the party: the white and orange dog who trotted behind, tail curled over her back.

Jem breathed out slowly.

The dog stopped, cocking her head. She was looking straight at Jem.

A drum beat inside his head as he looked down to avoid challenging the dog's curious gaze and encouraging her interest. The colors in the scene around him—brown walls, white snow, the gray and tan of his trousers and boots—seemed to grow more vivid.

"Come, Trika!" the hard voice called, just as it had on the day when Jem had first seen the little dog. And as she had on that distant day, Trika responded without hesitation and trotted away.

Jem leaned against the wall, aware that he'd begun to sweat inside the bulky skin of his parka. He felt jangly and light, as if his bones had no weight. And he felt the shadow of a smile touch his lips. Karya's source had been correct, for they were headed toward the Birthing House. They would search very thoroughly there; he could be sure of that. And by the time they headed out to look elsewhere, Jem would be gone.

Keeping close to walls and cutting through alleyways, he

moved from shadow to shadow. His plan was to skirt the village by heading out to the East Ridge before turning south. Then he would use the ridge—the long, low swell on the eastern tundra that ran north-south and was the only landmark visible from the village—as his guide. Although he didn't know how far it went, he knew that it would at least direct him south for some distance. And if he were leaving Kruvak, the only way to go was south.

Unless he wanted to be certain of finding his own death. If that were his intent, he could go north onto glaciers and plunge into a crevasse, go east across trackless tundra and be frozen by nightfall, or go west toward the ocean and survive a little longer, only to perish in the coastal mountains or fall through ice in some snow-covered inlet. But the thought of seeking death was foreign to his mind—it was a conjecture that never would have occurred to him if Avakab hadn't presented it.

In a purely abstract sense, he understood how circumstances could make someone feel that life had little more to offer them—that it was no longer worthwhile to continue the struggle. He'd heard of old people sitting outside without shelter when they felt their time had come, and he recalled Avakab's story of how his rebel partner, Rastok, had given up his life.

Once he'd heard one of the old women say that a man who took his own life was one who saw his shadow and found he couldn't bear to look at it. There was probably a tale in which this happened, but Jem couldn't remember the rest. And the midwives might have spoken of Rastok when the subject arose, as most of the older women had known him. Being only a small boy at the time, Jem had been puzzled by the idea—why would anyone be afraid of their shadow?

Even now Jem couldn't say he truly grasped the meaning of the old woman's words. Surely an illness or injury coupled with ceaseless pain might lead anyone to that point, but in metaphors or reality, it was difficult to imagine making that choice for himself. Perhaps if he were very old—like Avakab and Waltak—and felt his life had been fully lived out, it would seem right. But at twenty-two he felt as he always had, for as long as he could remember—he felt that everything was just beginning.

It wasn't too hard to see why some—again, like old Avak—believed that a life lived as an outcast could have little value. But Jem knew no other life. It was one thing to be bitter and resentful because he was treated unfairly and unkindly through no fault of his own. It was one thing to wish he'd been born a different person, to wish he could change. It was something else altogether to wish not to exist.

He paused at a corner to wait for a couple of children to pass in the white street. Perhaps because seeing them reminded him of his own childhood, it struck him that no one would ever tell him what to do again. He was free.

Being alone in the station, and spending all those secret hours with the forbidden bow, had been the beginning of that feeling—a kind of rebellious independence. But this was no longer a fantasy. The independence—the freedom—was real now.

When he slipped into the courtyard at the fort, he went straight to the nearest door in the outer circle of rooms. Inside, he found a lamp that had a little oil in it and ignited it with a spark from his flint. With the flickering light held before him, Jem went through the corridor that ran along the stone wall, closing and locking the doors he passed, for no reason other than it seemed it ought to be done.

He made his way to the pantry, his real purpose for coming here, and added a few items—dried fish, smoked cheese, and a loaf of moss bread—to his reindeer skin bundle. He could have finally taken all he wanted—for the first time in his life—but he didn't, telling himself it would be better not to carry too much; and he already carried the uncanny weight of his mother's weapon.

In spite of that weight, Jem felt light again. It seemed the whole world had opened up, becoming larger. Leaving all that was known, seeking only what was unknown, should have been frightening. He wasn't afraid now. A tingle of excitement and eagerness was spreading through him. He felt empowered, strong. It had nothing to do with the weapon he'd inherited. Enkara had given him something more important.

Enkara's story had given him proof. The proof that some of the Sanndai—like his mother—were good and kind. That meant there had to be others like her. Just as old Neskeb had said, they were people too.

But Jem was glad he hadn't gone with the boy. He would never change his mind about that. He was leaving, but he would go on his own, find his own way.

When he stepped back out into the courtyard, he momentarily closed his eyes against the light. Then he crossed for the last time to the gate in the outer wall, turning his head away from the impressive cluster of illus he'd built.

A few flakes had begun sprinkling down out of the white sky. Jem locked the gate behind him. Pausing only briefly to consider, he left the key in the lock, the ring of heavy brass keys hanging from it, tapping and rattling against the wood as they moved in the icy wind.

# # #

## About the Author

**Lara Campbell McGehee** is a native of Flagstaff, Arizona and attended Northern Arizona University, where she earned a BA in Anthropology and an MBA. She grew up in a house full of books and began writing at an early age. Raised with a passion for the outdoors, she especially loves the wide open landscapes of the Southwest, and her favorite places often find their way into the otherworldly settings of her stories.

An avid equestrian, she has dabbled in other sports such as archery, rock-climbing, and cross-country skiing, and enjoys using those experiences to add realism to her writing. She is also an amateur folk singer with a large repertoire of Scottish and Irish ballads, including songs in Gaelic. She blogs about the writing craft and about speculative fiction on her website, *www.lcmcgehee.com*.